PRAISE FOR

THE GOOD DEMON

"*I know it sounds crazy, to miss your demon.* Has there ever been a more enticing invitation to the reader? A shimmering coming-of-age story and a harrowing tale of possession. *The Good Demon* is a gothic wonder of a novel. Both cunningly told and emotionally true, the book itself becomes a kind of possession, casting a spell over us and leaving us breathless, half-broken and utterly satisfied."— MEGAN ABBOTT, bestselling author of *Dare Me*

★"Evocative language will grab readers by the throat and forge an unforgiving connection to Clare's despair and desperation . . . Eerie and compelling. Fast track it to the top of the TBR pile." — *KIRKUS REVIEWS*, starred review

★"Cajoleas builds a wonderfully macabre mood in his southern gothic novel, filled with economic ruin, witchcraft, religious zealotry, and grotesque moments of horror . . . Thoughtful, compassionate, and subtle commentary on faith, addiction, and grief is icing on an already captivating (and chilling) cake." — *BOOKLIST*, starred review

★"With a careful build and a terrifying first-person narration, Cajoleas (*Goldeline*) offers up a story interested in free will that is as gently ominous as a silent car coasting over a road on a hot, humid summer night."
— *PUBLISHERS WEEKLY*, starred review

"Blood and violence meet a crisis of identity in a compelling story for lovers of disturbing, resonant fantasy."
— *THE BULLETIN OF THE CENTER FOR CHILDREN'S BOOKS*

AMULET BOOKS
NEW YORK

THE

GOOD

DEMON

JIMMY CAJOLEAS

The Library of Congress has cataloged the hardcover edition as follows:
Names: Cajoleas, Jimmy, author.
Title: The good demon / by Jimmy Cajoleas.
Description: New York: Amulet Books, 2018. | Summary: Clare, miserable since an exorcism took away the demon that was like a sister to her, discovers the occult roots of her small Southern town and must question the fine lines between good and evil, love and hate, and religion and free will.
Identifiers: LCCN 2018001104 | ISBN 9781419731273 (hardcover with jacket)
Subjects: | CYAC: Demonology--Fiction. | Exorcism--Fiction. | Occultism--Fiction.
Classification: LCC PZ7.1.C265 Go 2018 | DDC [Fic]--dc23

Paperback ISBN 978-1-4197-3899-9

Amulet Books are available at special discounts when purchased in quantity for premiums and promotions as well as fundraising or educational use. Special editions can also be created to specification. For details, contact specialsales@abramsbooks.com or the address below.

Amulet Books® is a registered trademark of Harry N. Abrams, Inc.

ABRAMS The Art of Books
195 Broadway, New York, NY 10007
abramsbooks.com

FOR MARY MARGE

LATE ONE NIGHT SHE WHISPERED ME awake.

This was long before they came for Her—before Reverend Sanders and his boy pinned me down and prayed the words over me and ripped Her straight from my soul. It was during the best years, back when I was thirteen and it was just me and Her always, and I thought it always would be.

Get up, Clare. Hurry.

She was just a voice inside my voice, a body inside my body, a spirit inside my spirit, my demon. When She spoke I heard Her in my blood, and when She moved I felt Her in my bones.

It was deep into the night, a big moon bright and high shining a soft white glow through my window. I was groggy, exhausted, and all I wanted was to go back to bed.

"But I'm tired," I said.

Come on, She said. *You don't want to miss this.*

"What is it?"

But She wouldn't tell me. I felt Her hum and purr in my chest like a kitten, I felt the warm light of Her inside me. I was awake now. I tossed off the covers and threw on a dress and snuck down the stairs, my bare feet soft on the hardwood, stepping lightly so the old house wouldn't groan too loud and give me away. I eased open the door and closed it with the quietest click possible. I was about to turn and step into the night when She stopped me.

Now shut your eyes.

"What?"

Just do it. Shut your eyes.

"But how will I know where to go?"

You have to trust me.

I took a deep breath and closed my eyes and stepped blindly onto the wet grass.

Hurry, hurry, She said, and I felt a tug on my hand. She was yanking me along, running with me, dodging me between trees, whispering at me to duck under branches. I knew where we were going now, a secret spot in the woods, the place we had first come to know each other.

I ran and ran and began to laugh, and She laughed too—I could feel Her cackling in my chest, wild and joyful in the night, just the two of us alone, the moonlight warm and wet on my back.

Stop.

I was out of breath, panting, my ears filled with the rush and whir of cicadas, the howling of the tree frogs, the invisible screech of the bats in the trees. How lovely and loud, the spring nights in the South.

Open your eyes.

Above me glittered the billion-starred sky, vast and open and clear, the hazy Milky Way, the hidden creatures of the constellations reigning over the night. And streaking all across it in burning slashes fell the stars. It was a meteor shower, fire gashing the sky, dust from a thousand distant planets touching our air for the first time and exploding, the sky bursting its seams to let all the hidden light spill out. It was the most beautiful thing I had ever seen.

You see them?

"Yes," I said, "yes."

Those are my cousins, She said. *Those are my brothers and sisters, my whole family. Watch them fall to earth. Watch them come and gather.*

"Are they really your sisters?"

Not like you mean it, silly. But they are, still. They're every bit as old as me.

We danced that night in the clearing out in the woods behind my house, the burned-down shack nearby, the sky sparking bright and wild above us. We spun and twirled and howled out to the moon, to falling stars, to the glister that I prayed rained down on me in a holy fiery baptism, on me and Her, bound together in the night, and I knew nothing could ever separate us, nothing could ever tear us apart.

I was wrong.

I SAT ON THE FRONT PORCH SWING,

chain-smoking Parliament Lights, trying to read a book. I wasn't supposed to smoke anymore, but what else could my mom and stepdad do to me? I was already grounded from everything imaginable, and now She was gone. There was nothing left for them to take away.

It had been one month since they cast Her out of me. It wasn't an "exorcism," because that's what Catholics do, and the reverend and his son weren't any Catholics. They were Charismatics, so they called it a "deliverance." They said they came to deliver me from evil. What they did was bust down my door and steal Her away from me. They "rebuked" Her—that was the reverend's word—to keep Her from coming back to me again. Since then it had been one miserable month of crawling through the days, weeping myself to sleep, yanking upright in the night to scream and holler. One month of being so unbearably alone.

I was trying to read my favorite book, this biography of John Dee that I'd bought at Uncle Mike's Used and Collectible when I was just a kid. It was an old book, written in a super-flowery style with big words that swirled all over the page and fascinated me when I was little, words that I never heard anyone use in real life and never would. But John Dee wasn't cutting it today. Nothing could. My dog, Eyeball, came running up and licked my bare feet, and even that sent me shaking.

I missed Her, was all. I missed my best friend. Closer than that. She was my *Only*. That's what we called each other, our most secret name, ever since I was a little girl. My *Only*. Every time She called me that I felt a glow in my chest and I knew that I was not alone in the world.

But now I knew I would never feel that glow again.

It was like the way my dad used to talk about withdrawals, when he was coming down. He said it was like being on the edge of things, a hunger growling deep in his bones. That in his heart he felt like something was missing from him, something necessary and essential, and he would fight and claw and murder to get it back. It shook him with pain, it sucked all the water out of his mouth, it left him hacking and screaming and begging for it. That's how it felt to be without Her. Like this long dark hallway had opened inside me that went on forever, black and empty.

My hands started to tremble, and I dropped my cigarette in my lap. It left a small burn mark on my jeans. That was okay because they were ripped all over anyhow, a little too tight, but still my favorite pair. I wore my big black Dead Moon shirt too, the most comfortable shirt I'd ever owned, and I still felt shaky, awkward, like my skin was trying to crawl right off my body.

I was about to say fuck it, to break down and start cussing the sun just for shining down on me, when I saw a boy come walking a bike up my driveway. Not a boy, a teenager, someone maybe my age. He was wearing khakis and a polo shirt and he looked terrified.

"Can I help you?" I said.

He just stood there and stared at me.

"Hello?" I said. "Why do you have a bike? Are you selling magazine subscriptions or something?"

That seemed to snap him out of it.

"No," he said. "I'm Roy. I'm from the other day. Last month, I mean. You know, when . . ."

He waved his hand a little and trailed off.

Holy shit. This was the reverend's son, the kid who helped him take Her away from me. I didn't recognize him without the suit, without all the authority his dad commanded. The nerve he had, showing up here.

"Is this, like, a courtesy visit or something?" I said.

"No," he said.

He dropped his bike to the ground and walked toward the porch, hesitating at the steps, then climbing them anyway. He stood just a few feet away from me, gawking. Like I said, the nerve of this kid.

"You're Clarabella, right?" he said, and stuck his hand out stiffly, like he wanted me to shake it.

I didn't.

"Nobody calls me that except my mom," I said. "It sounds so spinstery. I go by Clare."

"Oh," he said. "Can I call you Clarabella anyway?"

"No," I said.

"It's a real nice day out."

"Sort of," I said. "Too hot."

"I passed a turkey vulture on the way up here. It had a frog in its mouth. A big one. You could see its legs hanging out and everything."

I squinted my eyes and stared at him. He seemed like one of those homeschooled kids who had never been let out of church for more than an hour, the kind who had no friends and couldn't talk about anything except Jesus and the weather. He was probably the most naïve person on earth, you could tell just by looking at him. It was almost endearing.

Almost.

"What are you reading?"

"It's a biography of John Dee," I said. "He's maybe my favorite person in all of history."

"Never heard of him."

"John Dee was an advisor to Queen Elizabeth I, and probably the most famous sorcerer in the whole world."

"Doesn't that mean he was, you know, a bad guy?"

It took everything in me not to fall out cackling. But I held it in. I lit a cigarette and sucked it in real slow. He watched me in a kind of awe, like he couldn't believe I was just out here smoking cigarettes, like it was some sort of felony.

I decided to fuck with him a little.

"Well, *maybe* he was bad," I said. "It depends on who you're asking. He got accused of trying to murder Queen Elizabeth with black magic, so they chucked him in jail. Other people say he was a genius inventor and mathematician, and he transcribed the entire language of the angels. What do you think of that?"

I smiled at him.

"You have green eyes," he said.

"I'm going to get my stepdad," I said.

"No!" he said. "I mean, you don't have to do that."

I got off the swing and walked past him across the porch and to the screen door.

"It's fine. He's in the back so it'll take just a minute."

"No, wait," he said. "Please."

I turned to look at him. The sun lit up my face and I held a palm above my eyes, to shield them.

"Why did you come here?" I said. "What is it exactly that you want?"

We passed a second of silence like that, with me staring down at him and him looking awkward, searching for words.

"Just, you know." He put his hands in his pockets and pulled them back out. "To make sure you were okay. That all was well. And stuff. After the thing we did. My dad did. You know."

I could have killed him. I could have ripped his throat right out of his body.

"I'm fine," I said. "And my stepdad will want to talk to you. He's the one who called you guys in the first place."

I pushed the screen door open and turned to walk into the house.

"What was it like?" he blurted.

I froze.

"Pardon me?"

"What did it feel like?" he said. "You know, to have a demon in you."

No one had ever asked me that before. Not my mom or stepdad, not a single other person. No one had ever asked me my own opinion about it. No one had ever cared to.

I stepped back onto the porch and shut the door behind me. I leaned in close to him, so close he could have touched me, he could have put his face to mine if he wanted. His eyes stared right into my own, like he was searching for something in me, as if there was some trace of Her still left inside. I reached my hand out, just lightly, and grazed my fingertips over his forearm.

"It's like you're wearing new skin," I said. "Like a soft thing is petting you all the time."

"I understand," he said.

"I don't think you do," I said.

Footsteps sounded inside the house and I jerked my hand back.

"Clare?" an angry voice shouted. "Where the hell are you?"

"It's Larry, my stepdad," I said. "You better go. If he catches you out here, he'll probably shoot you, I don't care who your dad is."

Roy scrambled down the porch steps and to his bike. I walked inside, letting the screen door slap shut behind me.

Larry cussed me out for smoking, said he would lock me up in my room if that's what it took.

"Fine," I said, "just so long as you fix my door."

I wasn't kidding when I said Reverend Sanders knocked it down. He kicked it so hard he ripped the hinges off the frame, sent shards of wood flying everywhere.

"Oh, I'll fix it up just fine," he said. "I'll bar it with iron. I'll throw you in a jail cell if I have to."

"Good to know you're always looking out for me, Larry."

"I don't do it for you," he said. "It's for your mother. She's been through enough already without having to deal with your shit."

Well, nothing shuts you up quite like the truth. I walked upstairs in silence.

I know it sounds crazy, to miss your demon. To miss being possessed by a demon, to miss losing yourself in the silky blackness that was another person swimming around inside of you. Truth was, I hated using the word "demon" for Her. It conjured up these images of ravaging fanged beasts with black eyes demanding human sacrifices, spinning people's heads around, gashing them into torment. That wasn't right, not one bit.

But what were the alternatives? "Spirit" seemed like a good one, but it just didn't fit. A spirit implied something cold, distant, and wispy, like a patch of fog with a face on it floating around ghostly in the night. And She was nothing like that. No, She was warm, soft. Not that I could touch Her, because She didn't have a body—at least, not that I could see. But soft and warm in the way that She touched me, deep inside, Her soothing fingers, Her scratchy little girl's voice. When She was close to me I didn't feel cold or haunted, I felt like it was summer and I was off somewhere quiet, my body spread out in the wet green grass, the sun beating down on me. She made the world dance, She made it sparkle and whirl. That's what it was like having Her inside of me.

She didn't mind the word "demon," though. In fact, She used it all the time.

"Ugh, but why?" I would say.

The problem isn't the word, She said. *The problem is what the word means to you.*

I never did understand what She meant by that. And now, I guessed, I never would.

At least I still had my room, even if Reverend Sanders and his boy had spoiled it by coming in here hollering, laying hands and praying over me. And my poor mirror, smashed. Mom had cleaned up most of the glass from my floor, but I kept getting little splinters stuck in my feet. Otherwise my room was pretty much intact.

I loved my room. I loved everything about it.

My closet, vast enough for my clothes and for me to sneak in and hide. My pink-and-black curtains: they made no sense but they billowed so well. The arrowheads, the stones, the dried flowers She used to pick for me, all our treasures on the windowsill. The collages I made with Her, the images snipped from magazines and rearranged into weird alien landscapes, places that didn't exist in this world. I never could do it, I didn't have the right brain, but She was a genius at it. She could make everything into a fairy tale, into a story. *All you need*, She used to say, *is a princess and a mystery. That's every story there ever was.*

Above the bed hung my *Lady Snowblood* poster, this old Japanese movie about a woman raised to get revenge, to be a warrior. It was maybe my favorite movie. I liked all that snow—something you never see around here—but mostly I liked how this wild woman roamed the earth seeking vengeance for crimes that weren't even committed against her. That everyone underestimates her and she just hacks her way straight through them all. I liked how pretty the movie blood was, how it splurted out in geysers from the spots where arms and legs used to be, how it shot ten feet up in the air and was beautiful and not realistic at all.

It was hard being in my room, everything a memory of my life with Her. Gone now, stolen from me by that boy and his father. I lay on my bed and watched the sun go down, and when the moon came up I began to cry, and that's how I spent the rest of the night.

THE NEXT DAY WAS UNBEARABLY HOT.

I lay in bed with the air conditioner on and sweated anyway. I couldn't believe I had to wake to another miserable day without Her.

I tried to draw strength from *Lady Snowblood* and all the knick-knacks and secrets of my room. It took all the power they could give me just to sit up, to slip some clothes on and try to face the day. Mornings were the worst. There was the whole lonely day stretching ahead of me like some endless lonesome highway. At least at night I knew soon I would fall asleep and maybe dream about Her.

I waited until Mom and Larry were gone to work—they'd been letting me sleep in lately, and for that I was grateful. I walked downstairs and made myself some eggs over easy, extra hot sauce. They tasted terrible. Everything tasted terrible. The still quiet of the house was so deafening I wanted to scream.

So I did. I screamed loud enough to shatter eardrums. Eyeball came whimpering up to me.

"I'm sorry," I said. He just licked my hands.

I was acting stupid. I couldn't go on like this. Zombie-ing through my days, not eating, lying awake all night watching the fan whir. Christ, what if that preacher kid came back? No, there was no way She'd want me to go on like this. She'd want me to get out in the world and do something awesome, like how we used to together. And if there was one place I knew She'd want to go, it would be our favorite spot in town, the one me and Her always went to when we were sad, when we needed something to cheer us up. It wasn't too far, and I could bike there if I needed to.

I was going to Uncle Mike's Used and Collectible.

I took the long way on my bike, just to remind myself how much I hated where I lived. I know most teenagers probably say that about where they grew up, especially if it's a small town like this one. And they probably mean that their hometown is slow and boring and that nothing ever happens there. Sure, that's all true about my town, too. The biggest event of every year is the Christmas parade, and that's just a bunch of men driving old Cadillacs through the square. So yeah, my town is boring, but that's not what I'm talking about.

Something's just off about this place. It's like the town has a bad heart—cruel, gone wrong somehow. It's hard to explain.

You wouldn't know it from the surface. Riding around on my bike, the town looked the same as any other town down here. We have a historic square that tourists with maps like to loiter around. There's a really old clothing store with the original mar-quee, the county courthouse in tall red bricks from before the

Civil War, all that kind of thing that out-of-towners seem to find quaint or curious. It's got "good" parts of town and "bad," where some people are comfortable and others not. Like I said, passing through on a sunny afternoon, you wouldn't see anything was wrong with this place. You have to live here to know it. You have to have spent your whole life drinking its water and breathing its air, taking all the badness and rottenness into yourself, making it a part of you, before you'd ever know anything was wrong at all.

And by then it's too late.

I know this is pretty vague, but I've got some examples, too. There's all kinds of things you can learn about a place if you poke around on the Internet, stuff they'd never tell you in school, where they like to present your home as a pretty place full of good people that never had any problems in their lives. But dig a little bit, take a look at the roots of the place, and you start to learn the truth.

A few things: the Trail of Tears passed through here, and there's a handy little plaque commemorating it. It's a simple fact, and it's wretched. Not to mention how the land was stolen from the Chickasaws in the first place. That alone should be more than enough to curse this town.

But that's not all. Not even close.

Two-thirds of the town was burned during the Civil War, including the old library that was used as a makeshift hospital. So many people died here they dumped them all in a mass grave, soldiers from both sides, and stuck a monument on top. People swear that part of the town is haunted, and I believe them, at least in the way the past affects everything that happens in the present, spoils it somehow.

It gets worse.

The KKK used to march here regularly up until the '60s. I've seen pictures of them all gathered around the town square in their hoods like a horde of angry ghosts. It's crazy to think that some of those people are still alive, that they live here in town, unhooded, that I probably pass them every day.

Tornadoes hit us, about three or four a year. They almost always take the same path too, curving west around town, skipping the historic district and the rich parts and heading straight for the industrial park, where all the trailers are. You can walk the old abandoned train tracks and see the wreckage from the years, car bumpers wrapped around oak trees, shreds of clothes high in the branches, rusty kitchen appliances strewn about the gravel. People die in those tornadoes—they're bad ones, they snake down all black and swirling, nimble as a ballerina's foot.

That's something else: in our town, you have all this money and all this poverty rammed together. The Simpkins family, for instance, who have been here as long as this town has, are about the richest people I ever heard of. They have a mansion in one of the "good" parts of town—the *best* part, actually. Not one mile away from them are the trailer parks. Everyone goes to the same grocery store, the same churches, but they aren't the same, they aren't equal. Not even close. And yet this town's been mentioned in no less than two national magazines as a "quiet little haven" with "that small-town feel we all know and love."

That small-town feel. Maybe that's it. Maybe that's what's so wrong about this place. Maybe every small town in America is just like this, if you dig deep enough. Or maybe not. Who knows? I've never even been anywhere else.

But what's weirdest of all, what's strangest and most rotten, are the people. You can't live here for long before it starts to affect you, before it makes you odd. It's barely perceptible, a glimmer in the eye, the way a smile at the grocery store cracks and fades at the edges. The town will do that to you, I swear it will.

It's done it to me, too. There's no way around it.

Maybe that's why I'm in all this mess. Maybe there wasn't any choice in the matter for me. I was destined for it, doomed from birth. I wondered if I would carry the scent of this place everywhere I traveled in life, if it was like a scar on my heart, the mark of Cain, something I could never get rid of.

So I was glad when I finally got to Uncle Mike's Used and Collectible. It was just about the only place in this whole town that I didn't despise.

Uncle Mike's was an old two-story building with a giant downstairs room absolutely crammed with stuff. It was maybe my favorite place on earth. Broken toys were scattered everywhere, records, dressmaker's dolls, mannequins, rows and rows of old clothes, suits, high heels, all kinds of junk. Piles of DVDs and VHS tapes, rugs and crappy furniture all over the place, an entire corner of cracked mirrors. There was even a collection of antique doors in the back.

It was run by an old Greek guy named Miklos, but everyone called him Uncle Mike. He was a shriveled, scowling man in a red fishing cap who sat in a chair behind the counter with his arms crossed the whole time. He lived on the second floor, up a little staircase in the back of the store. You could see the window from the outside. I was pretty sure Uncle Mike never left the junk shop at all.

"You again," he said when I walked in the door.

"As always," I said. "Your favorite customer."

"Favorite customer my ass," he said. "You're nothing but a thief."

Uncle Mike was crazy paranoid about shoplifters. He had fake video cameras installed all over the store, so cheap they didn't even have wires running out of them. He had also hung hand-drawn signs everywhere, a big Sharpied eye with GOD WATCHES YOU written above it. Creepy stuff, but it only made me love the shop even more.

I did a big elaborate magician's bow before him.

"If you didn't have me to chase around," I said, "you'd wither up and die, wouldn't you? There'd just be no reason for you to live."

Uncle Mike smiled a little at that. He had a dark sense of humor. It was part of why we got along.

"Just don't steal anything this time, eh?" he said.

Under all that gruff he really was a sweetheart. See, Uncle Mike had lived a pretty hard life. His wife died like forty years ago, and his only daughter died shortly after that. Ever since then he just sat behind the counter and moped.

I strolled through the store, digging through stuff, wondering what exactly it was I was supposed to be looking for. Once I had found a pretty cool warped copy of *Out of Step* by Minor Threat, which was a miracle considering where I lived, this dumpy little town in the South where there were at least fifteen churches for every grocery store. Uncle Mike's and the county library were just about the only places where you could find anything worth having. Today I settled for a dress—long and black and billowy—that I liked well enough. I rolled up the dress and stuffed it in my purse. If Uncle Mike caught me, he'd yell and fume and get his daily exercise in. If he didn't . . . well, free dress.

I passed a row of old mirrors, most cracked and dusty, and caught a glimpse of myself. I looked like shit. My green eyes were sunken and dark-circled, my hair a greasy black mess. I'd lost weight since they took Her, not that I had too much to spare anyway. I felt odd-shaped, warped somehow, like a record left out in the sun.

You're so pretty, She would say. *You have the cutest nose. Your cheekbones are so lovely.*

"My legs are short," I'd say. "My feet are huge."

And the daintiest little collarbones.

Finally I made it to the book section. It was the most magical place in the whole junk shop. The books had their own little nook, rows and rows of tall bookshelves that formed a sort of walled-off space in the big open room. The shelves were crammed full of books—out of order, stacked on top of each other—piles and piles of books. Cookbooks, mysteries, celebrity biographies, endless volumes of compressed novel classics. You could nearly always find something to look at, even if it wasn't worth buying.

My favorite shelf was in the back corner of the room, nearly six feet tall, labeled RELIGION/OCCULT. I picked them out one by one. An old hardback about night terrors with a snarling beast squatted on the chest of a sleeping woman on the cover. Smiling dust-jacket photos of Billy Graham, illustrated Jonathan Edwards sermons, a book on the history of Pentecostalism. Books on Buddhism and Sufism and yoga. Books on divination, on traditions of ancient seafarers and sailors, on how to dowse for water. Books with black-and-white photos of ramshackle poltergeist rooms, of dishes and cups flying, of people laid knocked-out on the floor. Beautiful full-color books on astrology and tarot cards, some written like math books and others like poetry. For weird stuff, the library had nothing on Uncle Mike's Used and Collectible.

See, rumor was, Uncle Mike's wife was kind of a witch, that all of these books were from her private collection. Uncle Mike sold them off because he wanted them gone, as if all this magic junk was exactly what had killed her in the first place.

I browsed for a bit, but it didn't look like there was anything new on the shelves. Why would there be? Hardly anyone dropped stuff off at Uncle Mike's anymore, and most of his stock had about an inch of dust covering it. Months had passed without me even seeing anyone else come in the store. I was wasting my time looking through here. There wasn't anything about this place I didn't already know.

Except for one book that looked familiar, right there at eye-level on the shelf. Oversize and dirty-white, with a small tear down the spine. I knew that book very well, and it wasn't any religious book. It was a book of William Blake paintings, reprinted in full-color. I pulled it down from the shelf and ran my hand over it.

It was one of my dad's old books. I opened up the front cover just to be sure. There it was, my dad's name scrawled on the inside. It was one of my favorite things he had left me after he died. Even when I was a little girl I loved looking at it, the muscles and exaggerated faces better than any cartoon, their howling looks of joy and fury, the flame-eyed gods and Job cowering terrified before angels like stars. Nebuchadnezzar on all fours like a beast. Dad called it our "dark picture book," scary stories that didn't need any story to them. This book should be at home, on the secret shelf in my closet, same as where I kept everything I cared about. How did it get here?

I flipped to one of my favorite paintings, called *The Night of Enitharmon's Joy*. It had a woman in all black, surrounded by an owl and maybe a dragon and this monstrous bat flying out of the darkness toward her. It gave me a million nightmares as a girl but I loved it anyway. I'd always beg Dad to show it to me before bedtime. And, soft as a moth wing, out slipped a torn scrap of paper that fluttered to the floor.

I picked it up. Scribbled in Her handwriting, all bubbly and little-girly, the way She made my hand move whenever She wanted to write something:

Be nice to him

June 20

Remember the stories

My hands shook and my breath got heavy and I had to shut my eyes tight and count to thirty in my head. I was afraid to open my eyes back up, afraid all the words would vanish and I'd be staring at a blank meaningless scrap of paper. But no, everything was still there, written by Her and left hidden in this book for me.

I held it close to my heart, like I could somehow summon Her back with it. But She was gone now, Reverend Sanders had driven Her far away, "as far as the East is to the West," he had said. Why would She leave something here for me to find? And what did the note even mean?

I heard a racket out by the cash register. Uncle Mike was hollering at somebody.

I peeked my head around the book section to take a look.

Uncle Mike was up off his stool. He had his finger pointed in the face of an old lady with wild grey hair. She wore a pink sweatsuit and big black sunglasses even though she was inside. I snuck up closer to hear.

"Come on, Miklos," she said. "I just need a few minutes up there to poke around."

"No," he said. "Absolutely not."

"Look, I know you're angry at me. You got every right to be mad. But something big is happening, Miklos. And I need Cléa's help with all that."

"Cléa is gone," he said. "And she's never coming back."

"But she might have left something. I don't know, a clue. Something I could use."

"Leave," said Uncle Mike. "Get out or I call the police."

The lady slumped her shoulders. She started to say something else to him, but instead she let out this horrible hacking cough. It was the worst cough I'd ever heard, like a stack of old car parts was falling over inside her. I was scared she'd hock up a lung and die right there. Her sunglasses fell off her face and skittered across the floor. Even Uncle Mike seemed worried about her, like he was going to walk out from behind the counter and give her a hand. But just as quick as she'd started coughing she stopped, scooped up the sunglasses, straightened herself, and marched out the door, her head held high, like it was an act of dignity. I decided I liked this weird old lady. She was kind of a badass.

I waited a few minutes before walking to the counter. Uncle Mike was just staring off in a daze.

"You okay?" I said.

Uncle Mike nodded.

"Who was that?"

"A bad woman," he said. "Very bad."

I waited for him to say something else about her, to explain where she came from or why she was bad, but he said nothing.

"Hey, Mike?"

He seemed startled, shaken out of some old memory from years and years ago he got lost in. I held up the Blake book.

"Where did you get this?" I said.

"First the madwoman, now you," he said. "What do you mean, where did I get it? You brought it to me. You demanded I buy it from you." He pointed his hairy white finger at my chest. "I give you five dollars for that book!"

Cold spiders spun webs all down my back. I was shaking so hard I could barely speak.

"Was I acting funny when I brought you the book?" I said.

"You are always acting funny."

"I mean, funnier than usual."

"Yes, yes. You talked like a little girl. You say over and over again that your eyes hurt. I tell you to go to the doctor, but you don't listen. Teenage girls never listen."

She had done it. She had taken over my body and blanked my mind out and brought the book to Uncle Mike's, knowing I would find it. I was *meant* to find it. She had done it before Larry called the reverend to come, like She knew in advance that it would happen.

Uncle Mike leaned over the counter and peered at me. "Are you on the drugs?"

"No, Mike," I said. "I'm not on any drugs."

"Even the marijuana," he said. "Say no to drugs."

"I'll be sure and do that," I said. "Hey, can I buy this book back from you?"

"Did you look in it? Scary stuff. Take it, I don't want it."

"Thanks, Mike."

I left the store, my brain foggy and confused by what I just learned. Why had She taken over my body like that? What was I supposed to do with this note She left me? I walked over to my bike, prepping myself for the long, hot ride back home.

"*Pssst*," said a voice.

I turned. It was the old lady. She was over on the side of the building by the trash, I guessed so Uncle Mike wouldn't see her loitering around. She puffed on a cigarette, a Virginia Slim like what Mom used to smoke before she got on the patch.

"Excuse me?" I said.

The lady held a finger to her lips and motioned me over. If I was on the lookout for something weird, this was definitely it. I walked to her and fished a cigarette out of my purse. It was always more fun to smoke with another person, and since Mom quit I never got to do it.

"I got a proposition for you," she said, like some type of old-lady gangster, standing there in her pink sweats, puffing her cig.

"Shoot," I said.

"You know Mike in there? Me and his daughter were good pals, way back, even if she was a good bit younger than me. Well, she took something of mine, right before she disappeared. She took something of mine, and I need it back."

"Disappeared?" I said. "I thought she died. From, like, a car wreck or something."

"She didn't die, she vanished. Just walked into the woods one day and *poof*!" The lady waved her hands, like a magician. "No one ever heard from her again."

"That's not what I heard."

"What you heard is garbage. A bunch of crap. People are always telling stories."

"So what's this thing of yours she had?"

"It's a little rosewood box, like the kind you use for jewelry. It's got an eye carved into the top of it. It's mine, see. I loaned it to Cléa, and now I want it back."

"What's in the box?"

"Nothing," she said. "Just some knickknacks. Little things of personal value. It's in a trunk up there in his attic, I just know it."

"So why won't Uncle Mike give it back to you?"

"Why not? You saw for yourself, the man hates me." She coughed real bad again. "He thinks I killed his daughter. He thinks it's my fault she disappeared."

"Is it?"

"Of course not. She did what she did of her own free will, knowing good and well what would happen."

"I don't totally understand."

"And you don't have to," she said. "You just have to go in there and take it for me."

"Why me?"

"Because you just stole something from Mike already, didn't you? You have it right there in your purse."

I went cold. She meant the dress. I'd totally forgotten about it. How did she know? I'm positive she wasn't there when I snatched the thing. The old lady laughed.

"Oh, don't you go worrying about that," she said. "I'm Miss Mathis, and I know things. That's just what I do."

"I'm Clare."

"Sure you are." Miss Mathis leaned in close to me. It was spooky staring into those sunglasses, seeing her chipped and yellow teeth so near my face. Her breath smelled like booze and cigarettes. "You do this thing for me, and I'll make it worth your while." Miss Mathis shrugged. "How about a thousand dollars?"

My eyes went wide.

"A thousand dollars?"

"Sure," she said. "Why not?"

"You're fucking with me."

Miss Mathis dug a giant billfold out of her purse. It was stuffed with crinkled hundred-dollar bills.

"Here's two hundred now," she said, dropping two balled-up hundreds in my palm. "You'll get the rest when you bring me the box."

"I'll think about it."

"You better, girly. This is a lot bigger than just you. It's bigger even than me and Mike."

"I said I'll think about it."

"You do that. And when you *do* decide to bring me what's mine—and you will, if I'm any judge of character at all—come see me here." She handed me a torn piece of paper with EUGENIA MATHIS, 19 HOLYOAK DRIVE on it. "That's my address."

"No phone number?"

"Who needs a phone? Anyone who needs me knows I'll already be waiting on them."

I put the paper in my pocket, along with the hundred-dollar bills. I didn't want to steal anything from Mike. At least, not anything personal. But money meant freedom, not having to depend on Mom and Larry for everything.

"Come and see me with the box," said Miss Mathis. "And the rest of the money is yours."

"And if I don't do it? If I just keep the money?"

She shrugged.

"Oh, you'll do it alright. But if you don't, I'm old and rich. What's two hundred dollars to me?"

"Okay, Miss Mathis," I said. "I'll be seeing you."

I walked to my bike and headed toward the road. Was this part of Her plan? It was too weird not to be. There was something to all this, I was sure of it. I just needed to figure out what.

I took one last look at Miss Mathis over my shoulder before the road curved. A line of dark grey clouds drifted in the distance, a haze of rain beneath it. A storm was coming, a bad one. I pedaled hard, and despite the heat, I felt a chill. This wasn't the first time She had taken over my body to do something. I don't mean just Her being inside me. I mean when She *really* took me over, like where I couldn't move anymore on my own unless She moved me, like She had wired Herself into my muscles and sinews and bones, into my brain, where I couldn't even speak unless She did it through me.

No, it had happened before.

ALL THAT AFTERNOON AND INTO THE
night I lay on my bed, thinking over Her message.

Be nice to him

June 20

Remember the stories

I had no idea what any of that meant. Who in the hell was *him* anyway? And what was so special about June 20? It was the end of May now, and June 20 was a whole month away, so I had some time to figure that one out. As for the stories, well, She told me a million of them. Which ones exactly was I supposed to remember? And what did all this have to do with Miss Mathis's crazy offer of a thousand bucks for a rosewood box?

This was just like Her, leaving me clues, making a game out of something so important. She was always playing games, with me and with everyone else. It was one of the things I loved so much about Her.

The afternoon storm had been a quick one, loud and brash and then gone, leaving behind a night so still and quiet, it was eerie.

I walked to my window and peered out at the empty, unmoving world. It was like I could feel Her presence around me again, like She wasn't so far away. Like She was just trapped right outside, barred from the house. It was almost as if I could hear Her fingernails tapping on my window, begging me to let Her back in. Then it passed, and I felt the pain again, the stabbing loneliness in my bones.

I remembered the day they took Her from me, Reverend Sanders and his boy.

It was simple as surgery. The only tough part was that I locked my door. Reverend Sanders had to bust it down. He crashed into my room, a booming shadow of a man in a grey suit. His son came behind him, quiet, scared, praying. He wore a suit too, same as his dad.

She didn't fight them. She wouldn't even try.

What's the point? She said.

I wanted to hit them, I wanted to thrash and scream.

No, She said, filling me with that good feeling, like a sedative. *Shhh, now. Be quiet.*

"Please, don't," I said, while they prayed, while the reverend and his boy laid their hands on me. "Please."

Trust me, She said.

For a split second, it hurt, oh it hurt—the holy light like a cleaving knife sliced through my insides, white-hot burning pain.

Then it was all over, and I lay there on my bed like a corpse.

I remembered Reverend Sanders wiping the sweat from my face, the tears streaming down my cheeks, while his son just stood there in his little matching suit, gawking at me like I was some kind of freak. It made me so mad. I wanted to punch him in the face.

Be nice to him

Wait, She couldn't have meant the reverend's son, could She? Why of all people would She want me to be nice to *him*?

It was so strange how he came to visit me yesterday. The way he just kept staring at me, same as he did when they took Her away from me . . .

I had an idea.

I snuck downstairs and grabbed the phone book while Larry slept on the couch. My parents had taken the Internet out of my room, left me with only an old flip phone. That was fine. I remembered the reverend's name, Cliff Sanders. I found him right away in the phone book. I crept back upstairs with the phone number. I took a deep breath and dialed it.

It rang and rang and rang. My heart was thudding out of my chest.

This was a stupid idea. This was not what She intended. This was a stupid idea and I was only making things worse for myself.

On the sixth ring someone answered.

"Hello?"

I took a guess.

"Roy?" I said. "It's me, Clare."

"Clarabella?" he said.

I tried not to let it irk me.

"Ha," I fake-laughed. "You just can't stop calling me that, can you?"

"It's a real pretty name," he said. It was like I could hear him blushing over the phone. "Hold on just a second."

What if he went and told his dad right now? What if Larry found out? He would lock me in the attic with a loaf of bread and a bedpan. He'd never let me out of his sight again.

Come on, Roy, I pleaded. Come through for me here.

His voice came back on the line.

"How'd you get this number?" he said.

"I found it in the phone book. Sorry to call your house. You didn't give me your cell phone number or anything."

"I don't have one."

"What?"

"Dad doesn't allow them. Says it turns people into morons, staring into a little screen all day."

"Weird."

"It's not weird," he said. "It's just different. Dad holds me and him to a higher standard than the rest of the world. Because we're men of Christ."

"I guess so," I said. There was a long silence that I didn't know how to fill. Just the thought of Roy's dad made me queasy, like riding on a bad elevator, the feeling that the floor could drop out from under me at any moment. Besides, I'd never talked on the phone with a boy before. I didn't know exactly how you were supposed to do it. I took a deep breath. "Anyway, I just wanted to know if I could call you sometime."

"Call me?"

"Yeah," I said. "You know. To talk."

"Of course," he said. "Just. Can I call you back later? Sometimes my dad's weird about the phone."

"Are you asking for my phone number?" I said.

Even if I didn't want to admit it, that felt kind of nice. No one had ever asked for my phone number before.

"Um, sure," he said. "I mean, yes."

I told him my number and listened while he wrote it down.

"Call me later tonight," I said. "Whenever your dad will let you. Doesn't matter when. I stay up pretty late."

"I will."

"Roy, does your dad know you came to see me?"

"Nope."

"Talk to you later," I said, and hung up.

I lay back down on my bed. I wasn't sure what I was doing, what bumbling chain of events I had just set in motion. But I felt a stirring inside me, a small light where earlier everything had been dark and empty. I knew that whatever happened next, it was what I was supposed to do, that it was what She wanted, that I had done right. I had to trust Her on this. It was either that or moan around the house, smoking cigarettes, wasting away until I died. I would untangle Her clues, find the path She wanted me to follow, do everything She asked, no matter what the cost. And maybe, just maybe, I could find my way back to Her.

Now all there was to do was wait.

Waiting always made me miss the Internet, back when I had a computer in the house, a glowing window in the study that let me into the rest of the world. I especially missed the music and the movies, all of them out there and free if you knew where to look. That was the best part about the Internet. You could teach yourself anything all night, you could put yourself through your own particular kind of school. I hated high school—I never learned anything in any of my classes. Everything I loved and cared about I learned online and from books, all on my own.

There was a time when I looked for other people like me out there. I mean, people who had demons living in them. But She didn't much like me digging into things like that.

If they're real, She said, *they'll keep quiet about it. Demons aren't a chatty bunch. Only fakers do the telling.*

"Like in the mafia?"

Just like that. Squealers get snuffed. They get cement shoes. They get throat-slit and dumped in the river.

"That's gross."

I'm just kidding, silly. But don't ever tell anyone about Me. And don't trust a word about us that you read on the computer.

So I used the Internet for other things. Books, mostly: poetry and John Dee stuff. I read everything I could find on John Dee. I liked how he could be so many things at once—a magician and a priest and a mathematician too—that no one knew quite where to put him or how to classify him. How maybe he could be anything at all.

I also loved reading stories about saints. They were just as good as fairy tales, and sometimes even stranger. *The Golden Legend* especially, this weird medieval book of saints' lives. St. Agatha who got saved from burning by an earthquake, St. Cecilia who you could hardly kill no matter how many times you chopped her with a sword. And the people who weren't quite saints, but should have been—like Julian of Norwich, who had a vision that God showed her a hazelnut that was all of creation, or Christina the Astonishing, who died and came back to life by floating out of her coffin and bonking her head on the rafters. History was full of all kinds of crazy stuff like that, if only you knew where to look for it. I would sometimes read and read all night until the sun came up, until I was worn out and ready for school. She'd be mad at me then, cross for not letting Her sleep any.

"I didn't know demons napped."

We don't need to, which is why I love it so much. You ever get better sleep than when you didn't particularly need to be rested up for anything? When it was just the sheer pleasure of sleeping?

As always, She had a point.

When Larry took away the Internet, I had to switch over to going to the Simpkins Memorial Library. It was easily the best library around, but that wasn't saying much. There weren't even that many books, to be honest, and what was there was pretty grim. Lots of romance novels and a few classics, most of which I'd already read. But what our library did have was the greatest collection of VHS tapes on the planet.

They had belonged to this grand old video store called Movie Madness that shut down once Netflix became a thing. The owner was dying anyhow, so he just donated all the tapes to the library. Technically I wasn't old enough to rent R-rated movies, so I just slipped a different one in the box whenever I needed to. It was great. That's how I saw *Carrie* and *Eraserhead* and *Don't Look Now*. That's how I saw *The Wicker Man* (the old one) and *A Nightmare on Elm Street* and *What Ever Happened to Baby Jane?* It's where I tried to rent *The Exorcist* once and She nearly had a fit.

Are you crazy?

"What?" I said. "It'll be fun. They'll probably get all the details wrong."

I could feel Her panicking in me, terrified and gone vicious, like a wild animal backed into a corner. My stomach flipped over and I nearly vomited right there in the stacks. I fell over on my knees and held my stomach while the pain screamed in me so hard I almost couldn't bear it. After a few seconds She calmed down, and I could breathe again.

It isn't funny.

"I'm sorry," I said.

It isn't funny. It isn't funny to joke about things like that.

"I said I was sorry."

I felt Her relaxing in me. I felt quiet settle over me like the moonrise over still waters. The soothing peace of Her curled up like a kitten in my lap, the purr of Her heartbeat, the warm glow of the two of us, together, alone against the world.

"I'll never leave you," I said.

I know.

"I'll never let anyone split us apart."

I remember feeling a little twinge inside myself, like She had flinched at those words. Maybe She already knew, even back then. Maybe She knew it was only a matter of time before they came for Her. Maybe throughout the history of the world there had always been someone to come between something like Her and a person like me. But how could I have known that back then?

My phone rang. It was Roy.

"Hi there," I said, trying not to show that I'd been crying.

"Yeah. Sorry I'm calling so late. I had to wait for my dad to go to sleep."

"It's not that late," I said. "Besides, I don't ever get to sleep before three anyway."

"Me either."

There was a pause for a second. I didn't know what to say. *Be nice to him*, remember? Okay, fine, I could think of something. Maybe I'd just chat, the same as if it was with Her, as if it wasn't Roy on the other end of the line at all.

"I like nighttime the best," I said. "It's like my whole brain clicks on when the sun turns off. And then there's the moon, of course."

"Yeah," he said. "The moon."

"I always like to think of what it looks like. It's a different moon every night, you know."

"I don't know," he said. "I never really thought of it like that."

"Go on, try it. What does the moon look like tonight, Roy?"

He was quiet a moment.

"I guess it looks kind of like a tooth."

"A tooth?"

"A chipped tooth," he said. "I have a chipped tooth. I did it playing dodgeball at church."

"Well I think the moon looks like a lady," I said.

"A lady?"

"Yep. A *maiden*. And when a cloud passes by just right, that's her dress twirling. She's dancing."

"But there's no clouds over her now."

"That's because she's naked."

Roy went silent. Well that got awkward fast. It was like I could feel him struggling to think of something to say. It was painful.

"So what did you do today?" he said.

"What a boring question," I said. "What a perfectly miserable thing to ask."

I was being mean. But if I had to talk to this kid, I sure as hell wasn't going to let him get away with being dull.

"I'm sorry," he said. "It was the only thing I could think of to say."

"I rode to the junk shop. I read a book about a ghost baby who is old and wise and sends messages to his dumb, drunk dad. I chased Eyeball around."

"Who?"

"The dog. I did about the same old boring stuff as anyone else. I bet your day wasn't all that different."

"I guess not."

"Go ahead. Tell me. Go right ahead and tell me about your dreary little day."

"Well," he said, "I almost got murdered by a berserk pickup truck while I was biking home."

"Really?"

"Yep. It nearly ran me right over. I was almost roadkill."

"And what happened then?"

"I saw a barn full of cat eyes."

"Cat eyes!"

I could see it in my mind, same as if She had spoken it. A million yellow glowing things, like fat, massive lightning bugs floating in the black. Here I was trying to be nice to this kid I didn't want to be nice to and he had to go and say something actually interesting.

"Tell me about it," I said. "Start from the beginning."

"Well, I was biking home, like I said. And I was all nervous because the truck almost nailed me. I felt like someone was watching me. You know that feeling? Well, I just couldn't shake it. I pulled over onto the side of the road and looked around. It was starting to rain pretty good now, and I was getting wet all over. But I couldn't leave yet, because I knew there was somebody else there with eyes on me. Like how folks at my church feel when they think they're in the presence of angels or something.

"Then I saw it. On my left stood a busted old barn, roof caved in, one wall fallen. It was surrounded by a grove of witch hazel trees, you know the kind? Lightning struck somewhere way behind me and from the black of the barn shone these yellow glimmers, little slits of light in the rafters. I walked closer until I could see. Cats, dozens of them, wild things gathered in the barn for shelter, glaring back at me. They were all over, piled on top of each other, hanging from the rafters, rolling around in the dirt. More cats than I ever seen in any place in my whole life. I don't know. Something about how hungry they looked. How they were *staring*. It spooked me is all."

I liked that. I liked that a whole hell of a lot. It was so hard to get people to tell you stories, especially interesting ones. She used to—that was our favorite thing to do together—but now She was gone. All Larry ever talked about was the good old days, when Luther Simpkins was mayor and our town was on the rise and

Larry would go out and punt a football in the yard because he was too poor to do anything else. You couldn't get a word out of Mom apart from her grocery list, and occasionally something gory from the hospital if you were lucky. But even if Mom or Larry did have something good to say, they didn't ever do it right. Stories aren't just what you say, but *how* you say it. It's all in the telling. And Roy, backward and ignorant as he was, seemed to know a little something about that.

Besides, nothing beats loneliness like a good story. I wasn't sleepy at all, and I knew I'd be up for a few hours longer, at least. There were worse ways to pass the time.

"Tell me more, Roy," I said. "Tell me everything."

THIS IS THE STORY OF THE FIRST TIME

She took over my body.

I was maybe eight years old. It wasn't too long after Dad died, when I was still trying to understand what life was like without him. We had a week where it was nothing but thunderstorms every day. There was flash flooding all over the place. It got so bad that me and Mom had to put sandbags in front of our door to keep the water out. I kind of loved it a little bit. There was something terrifying about all that water, the way it rose of its own accord, how there was nowhere for it to go but toward us. I wanted it to come into our house, like a guest. I wanted to invite it up to my room to spend the night.

After the waters went down a little Mom passed out on the couch—Mom was still drunk or stoned half the time back then—and I went stomping around barefoot in the puddles. Me and Her both loved the rain. We loved being outside and doused together, the way my dresses would pool around my ankles like I'd just sprung up from the water myself. In some places the water was still knee-high, and mosquitoes swarmed my shoulders, sucking blood wherever they wanted. I smeared mud on my face and went feral, pretending we were abandoned kids, changelings raised by wolves. She loved this game, it was one of Her favorites. We'd stomp through the puddles and howl out loud, the sun just a glimmer in the thick grey clouds. I saw a winding silver stream of water like a tiny road for frogs and I wanted to follow it. I wanted to splash all the way through it and dive to the bottom of the puddles and come up somewhere new and upside down, the world at the other end of things. I took off sprinting, all laugh and holler.

And then She stopped me.

I mean, froze me in the spot. It was like tiny hands inside me clenched up all my muscles, like my blood hardened inside me and I turned to stone.

Stop it, I thought. Let me go.

No, She said.

I mean it. I hate this.

You will not move, She growled at me.

That's when I saw the question mark uncurl itself and slither through the water by my feet. A water moccasin, dark green and brown, washed this way in the floodwaters. It was so close to me I could have touched it. My next step would have dropped my foot right on top of it.

I was so far from the house, and Mom was passed out on the couch. The meanest and most poisonous snake. If it bit me, I might have died. If it bit me, I might not be here at all.

The moccasin swam past me, floating on top of the water like a miracle, like a snake Jesus crossing the Sea of Galilee.

Told you, She said.

And I went back inside the house, crying.

It was moments like that when I knew She loved me, deeply, down into the core of Herself. I knew that without Her I would be dead already.

That was the first time She ever took me over, and I was grateful. She always had a reason.

She did it to protect me.

ROY AND I TALKED ON THE PHONE
again the next few nights, each time for hours. I knew there was
a reason for these conversations, some purpose that She had
thought up long before and I was just now fulfilling. But the truth
was, I was starting to enjoy them a little bit, too. Roy was so simple, so naïve. Sometimes it was baffling.

"So why can't you have the Internet again?" I asked Roy. "I
don't have it because nobody in this house trusts me with anything, but I want to hear about you."

"Because Dad said it would lead to temptation," he said.

"What kind of temptation?"

"You know. From websites."

"What kind of websites?"

"Well, you know, alternate histories of how the world was
formed."

"What do you mean, 'alternate histories'?"

"You know, the Big Bang. That earth is billions of years old. All
that junk."

"The Big Bang isn't junk, Roy," I said. "It's science."

"No, it isn't. God invented science, so true science has to agree with the Bible."

"Don't people, you know, have different views of the Bible? Like maybe the whole six-day creation thing was just a metaphor?"

"Sure they do, but they're heretics."

I had to take a deep breath and count to twenty. It wasn't Roy's fault he didn't know anything, I told myself. It was his dad's. I had to be patient.

"Never mind," I said. "But for real, when you said 'temptation,' I thought you meant, like, porn or something."

"Porn sites? For me and my dad? Of course not."

See, it was that kind of thing. The kid was in so deep, had been so thoroughly brainwashed into one way of thinking, that it didn't do any good to give him hell for it. In fact, I sort of started to admire him a little. I never had faith like that. I knew about the saints and all their miracles, but that was like magic to me, fairy stories, same as John Dee summoning angels to teach him geometry. I hated church the few times I ever went, snotty kids kicking each other under the pews, fighting parents faking happiness for the benefit of everyone else. I knew that magic and demons were real, and that religion had the power to defeat them. I just wasn't always sure that was a good thing. For whatever reason, I loved talking with him about that stuff. It was fun to disagree together. Besides, sometimes Roy could really surprise you.

He was viciously antiracist, for one. He said he'd seen too many people of color hollering and prophesying in tongues not to know that God made all people equal, that to hold any one section of humanity back was to hold God Himself back. He also believed that women should preach, that men had just about ruined the church.

"If it wasn't for women," he said, "and I'm talking about Mary Magdalene, all them—no one would have been around for Christ to appear to. No one would have been around to save the church after men had screwed it up so bad."

Still, he wasn't exactly a feminist.

"Doesn't the Bible say," I asked him once, "you know, that women should cover their head in church and wives should be subservient to their husbands and all that? That they are weaker than men?"

"I mean, I guess," he said. "I think the point is to take care of each other, right? And men have a particular responsibility to take care of women. That's just the way that things are supposed to work, and when they don't work that way, everything is broken. The whole order of the world gets wrecked."

I got pretty mad at him after that. I nearly hung up right then and there. Patience, patience, I told myself. One day Roy would learn better, and maybe I'd be the one to teach him. I could do that. I could try, anyway.

But the best times with Roy were when he would talk about his mom. She had died from cancer about seven or eight years back, around the same time I'd lost my dad. He didn't like to talk about how she died, but he would tell me about her, about her life.

"Mom collected umbrellas," he told me. "My dad has them all stuffed in the upstairs closet now, but she used to have them spread out everywhere, like they were art or something. Red umbrellas, blue umbrellas, pink-polka-dot umbrellas. She would paint them too, bright circus colors, paint them into green lizards and purple blossoms, beautiful things that you were supposed to open. The fancy ones she called 'parasols.' She would put them in a vase like cut flowers. She would hang them on hooks all over our walls."

Sometimes Roy had a bit of a poet to him, too. I guess he got it from his mom.

"Did she have any nicknames for you?" I asked.

"She called me her daylight. She called me her morning star."

Then he'd clam up about her, just like that. I got the feeling that he and his dad didn't talk about Roy's mom too much, that maybe things had been pretty tough for him ever since she died. I started to wonder how Roy wound up traveling around with his dad, ruining other people's lives.

Ruining *my* life.

And it would hit me again. I was talking to the boy who stole Her from me, who tore my happiness in half. He trespassed into my room, him and his awful father, and ripped Her right from my heart. I couldn't forgive that. Suddenly I couldn't even stand to be on the phone with him anymore. I would tell him I was tired, that I had to go now. Then I would lay in my bed, sweating in the heat, and listen to the leaves rustle outside my window, just hoping to feel Her breeze by me again, the chill of Her fingertips on my spine, the still, soft voice outside my window, begging me to let Her back in.

I always fell asleep feeling so very alone.

Pretty soon Roy asked me if I wanted to meet up on a

Wednesday evening when his dad was at church. He said a different pastor preached on Wednesdays at six, Dr. Powers, somebody his dad didn't much care for.

"I don't have to go to Wednesday services because Dad doesn't want my ears getting tainted with Dr. Powers's sermons. He says they're pure yellow cowardice. He also goes on too long, like three whole hours. Should be plenty of time to hang out."

I was surprised at how good that sounded to me, spending time with an actual person rather than just a voice on the phone.

"I think that'll work," I said. "My mom and stepdad have a date night, so they'll both either be gone or trashed. We should be fine."

I was excited. Not just because it was lonely, sitting around the house all summer day, just me and Eyeball. But also I had figured out a plan to sneak into Uncle Mike's upstairs room. See, since Uncle Mike lived in his shop, he kept it open so long as he felt like staying up. I just had to hope that he would be awake long enough to let us in for the evening. I was pretty sure Roy could do the rest.

I didn't know if I was going to steal the rosewood box for Miss Mathis yet, but I was pretty sure it was worth getting a peek at. Especially if it was something a mysterious person would want to pay a thousand bucks for.

I went to bed that night excited for the first time in so long. I could feel myself drawing closer to Her, following the strange and hidden map She'd laid out for me, uncovering it one tiny mystery at a time. I was being nice to Roy, that was one clue down. Now

I just had to figure out which stories She was talking about, and what the big deal was with June 20.

"I'm coming back for You," I whispered in the air, hoping somehow the words would find their way to Her.

Wherever She was, in whatever world.

And that night I slept smiling.

I WAITED FOR ROY IN THE DRIVEWAY,

leaning against my mom's navy Ford Taurus. It had big stain-looking splotches where the paint wore off, like it had some kind of disease. Mom just said it gave her car character. Pretty soon Roy came riding up on his bike, wearing Dockers and a sweat-rimmed red polo shirt. He looked worn out.

"Hey, guess what?" I said.

"What?"

"My parents are gone and they took my stepdad's car," I said. "Which means they left Mom's car, and I know where she hid the spare keys."

I dangled the keys in a way that I hoped was tantalizing.

"Couldn't you have just picked me up?" said Roy. "So I wouldn't have to bike all this way?"

"Yeah," I said, frowning. "Shit. Guess I should have thought of that. It's probably not too easy riding a bike all the way here, is it? And you're all sweaty, too."

Sweaty was fine. Sweaty I could use.

"Why don't we get you some new clothes? And maybe some ice cream or something, to cool off."

"That sounds nice," he said, "but I don't really have much money."

"Good thing I only ever shop at thrift stores," I said. "There's a junk shop that's been here forever. The owner is an old Greek guy who charges you a quarter to use the bathroom. He's maybe ninety years old. It's the best place in the whole town."

"Cool," he said.

"Cool? Cool? That's all you have to say for yourself?" I said, dragging him to the car. "I said I was about to show you the best place *in the entire town.*"

"Amazing," he said. "Stupendous. Extraordinary."

"That's a start."

"Phantasmagoric."

"Much better."

I cranked the car.

"Um, Clarabella?" he said. "Are we going to get in trouble for this?"

"Maybe." I shrugged.

He grinned a little. Maybe there was some rebel to Roy after all. I lit a cigarette as we sped off down the highway.

Roy was in awe of Uncle Mike's. You would have thought I'd walked him into fucking Disney World. He kept walking around the entrance, touching clothes, gawking at everything.

"This is way better than Walmart," he said.

"It's magic," I said.

"I didn't know there were places like this." He shifted a hologram Jesus painting. Jesus opened his bright-blue eyes at him. "Even our church garage sale didn't have anything half this weird."

Uncle Mike wasn't having it.

"You again," he said.

"As always," I said, "your favorite customer. Uncle Mike, this is Roy."

"Hi," said Roy.

Uncle Mike grimaced.

"You seem like a good kid," he said to Roy. "You shouldn't be hanging around with this thief."

"Thief?" said Roy.

"It's just a little game we play," I said. "Right, Uncle Mike?"

Mike grunted and waved me off.

When we were good and out of earshot, Roy whispered, "Do you really steal stuff from here?"

"Sometimes," I said. "But he usually catches me."

Roy started to get panicky.

"Quit worrying," I said. "I promise you, Uncle Mike loves me. Now come on. You need a new shirt or something. Did your dad buy you that shirt?"

Roy nodded.

"Did your dad buy you all your clothes?"

He nodded again.

"I can tell. Let's find you something new, something that suits you just right."

"I really don't know anything about clothes."

"It's a good thing you have me, then."

After digging through the racks for a while, I found something that Roy would probably hate, but might actually look good on him.

"How about this?" I said.

It was a pink plaid shirt with ripped sleeves. I held it up to him.

"Really?" said Roy.

"Really."

He was frowning, but he took the shirt from me anyway.

I had also snatched a couple of things for myself: an old hippie dress, a ripped pair of corduroys, some grammaw's old yellow muumuu with barn animals stitched on it. The name EMMA was written on the tag.

"Can you believe I found this here?" I said. "It's like a Christmas miracle."

"Wow," said Roy. "Who's Emma?"

"I don't know," I said. "I just hope she isn't dead. I hate wearing dead people's clothes. Unless I knew them first, I mean."

I grabbed Roy by the hand and brought him to the book section of Uncle Mike's.

"You said you didn't know anything about literature. Well, here's as good a place to start as any. They got all kinds of first editions and stuff, and cheap, too. You just browse around here awhile."

"What are you going to do?" he said.

"I'm going to try these on," I said, holding up the clothes. "There isn't a changing room, so I just go into this little nook in the back where just about no one can see you. There's no door or anything, so don't come looking for me or things could get awkward."

Roy blushed a little.

"I'll wait right here," he said.

"Good boy," I said, and left him book-browsing.

I walked myself up to Uncle Mike's counter.

"Where'd you pick up the kid?" Uncle Mike said.

"That's just what I came to talk to you about," I said. "See, I met Roy at church—yeah, so what, I go to church—and he's, like, this 'troubled youth' or whatever, and I'm supposed to mentor him. You know, take him around to places, be a good influence on him, things like that."

I know, it was a pretty lame excuse, but I couldn't think of anything better on the spot. Besides, I was banking on Uncle Mike's paranoia to overpower any obvious holes in my story.

"You, a good influence? When pigs fly maybe. When grasshoppers sing the opera." Uncle Mike snorted. "Besides, he looks like a nice boy."

"That's what I'm talking about," I said. "See, the whole 'nice boy' thing is just an act. It's how he gets away with everything. No one ever suspects him until it's too late."

"And what does he get away with?"

I needed to lay this next part on thick. I leaned in close to Uncle Mike and whispered in his ear.

"Thing is, Roy's a big-time shoplifter."

Uncle Mike's eyes went wide.

"A shoplifter, you say?"

"The worst. He's been arrested like six times."

"And you bring him here? To my place?"

"I know, I know, I'm sorry. But you better go keep an eye on him."

Then Uncle Mike did something I almost never saw him do. He rose up from behind the counter and scuttled off toward the bookshelves. He pretended to organize stuff next to Roy, watching him. A full success, if I do say so myself.

I snuck off toward the staircase in the back of the store. I crept up the stairs as quickly as possible, glancing back now and then to make sure Uncle Mike was still spying on Roy. He was totally preoccupied, but it wouldn't last long. I had to hurry.

At the top of the stairs there was a narrow walkway to a closed door. I turned the handle. It wasn't locked.

The door led to an upstairs apartment with a small living room, half kitchen, and a bedroom. Despite the fact that it was above a junk shop, the apartment was surprisingly clean. An old TV, deep as it was wide, rested on an oak cabinet in front of a small coffee table and a green sofa. A few plates hung on the wall, and an orange coffee mug sat drying by the sink. Little knick-knacks dotted the shelf, not like the chaos of downstairs, but carefully arranged, dusted, all ceramic puppies and mushrooms and snow globes. A couple of ancient family photos hung framed on the wall.

I walked quickly through the kitchen and into the bedroom. People always hid their valuables in the bedroom.

It was the loneliest room I'd ever been in.

A bed was pressed against the wall, an old quilt for covers, tucked without a wrinkle. The pillows fluffed, symmetrical, as sparse and tidy as a hotel room. A crucifix dangled above the bed, but that was it.

There was a door on the far side of the room, right next to the closet. That had to be Cléa's room. I tried the doorknob, praying it wasn't locked. The door squeaked open and I beheld the room of a vanished teenage girl.

One side was simple, sparse as her father's. The windows had pale dusty curtains that glowed from the sunlight, casting a whiteness over the room. The bed was neat, tucked tight, a simple quilt spread over it. A reading lamp that probably hadn't been turned on in decades sat on an end table. Nothing special.

The other side of the room, however, was a miracle.

A white wooden vanity stood on the back wall, with a giant cabaret mirror hanging above it, big white bulbs and all, just like in the movies. A feather boa was draped over one corner, and little snapshots were tucked into the sides of the mirror: yellowing photos of a handsome man in a sailor's uniform and a beautiful woman with long black hair, her dress whipping in the wind.

I guessed the man was Uncle Mike and the lady was his wife. It was hard to imagine. They looked so gorgeous back then, a Hollywood couple, exotic and untouchable. I was suddenly afraid of aging, of growing frail and dotty, of wasting away on my feet, alone. If the years did all that to Uncle Mike, what would they one day do to me? The next picture showed Uncle Mike holding a little black-haired girl's hands while she tried to walk. I guessed that was his daughter, Cléa. Another one with all three of them posing in front of a lighthouse, the girl no more than five or so.

They seemed so happy, the kind of family you always wished you had. And one more photo tucked into the vanity mirror, one that would burn itself in my brain, one I would never forget. It was Cléa—older now, maybe my age—walking on some kind of cliff's edge, the ocean smashing underneath her. It must have been taken shortly before she disappeared. She smiled mysteriously, lovely and aloof, like there was some secret she was hiding. I liked that about her.

On the vanity were bracelets, gold necklaces, all kinds of expensive-looking jewelry, arranged, but you could tell never touched—not in decades. The whole thing felt like a museum piece. I wondered if it was exactly how it looked the day Cléa left, and if Uncle Mike had kept it just like that, as a sort of shrine to her. He must have loved her very much.

I scanned the dresser top and opened the drawers, but found no trace of the rosewood jewelry box. I did however find a giant old sea trunk under the vanity.

I tried to pull it out by its strap, but it was too heavy. I had to grab it with both hands and lean my whole weight against it to get the thing to budge. There was a huge rusty padlock on it but it wasn't locked. I slipped it off and opened the trunk.

The smell hit me first, mothballs and incense and time. Something else too, an ancient crackly smell, like an old library. I pulled out a shawl first, blue and purple with a pattern of yellow moons. Underneath were books of a very particular kind. I opened a fat volume called *Gods of Antiquity*, which was sort of an index of old beasts: Moloch, Baal, Ishtar, and others, bat-headed beings in ink drawings, Satan's black hand rising from the waters in a strange wicked salute. Human sacrifice, a giant metal man with a fire inside it, babies placed on its open palms to sizzle and burn. The pictures were horrible, the stuff of my worst nightmares. Some of the other books were in languages I had never seen, whose letters were like tiny eyes winking at you. Books half-burned and bound in leather, with charts of the stars. An illustrated book of metal charms: a hand with a finger pointing out, a peasant man covering his head, death with a scythe, a crescent moon.

If Uncle Mike's wife had been some kind of witch, it was pretty clear that Cléa kept at it after her mother's death. Maybe witchiness was hereditary like that. Or maybe it was all a bunch of garbage, just something for a lonely girl to pick up so she could feel close to her dead mom, like how music and old records tied me to my dad. It was amazing how looking through a stranger's old things could make you feel like you knew them, could maybe even make you like them a little bit.

And at the very bottom of the trunk I found a little rosewood box with an eye carved on the top.

This was the moment I'd been dreading. Do I steal the box or not? Uncle Mike had always been so good to me, had let me roam free throughout his store, had given me a place where I could feel strange and comfortable, a refuge from school and everything else in my life. Sure, I'd stolen from him before, but little things, a dress or a book or a record here and there. Nothing as important as one of his dead daughter's possessions.

And yet, something about the rosewood box tugged at me. It seemed to shimmer in my hands, to thrum with some sort of hidden mystery. I realized that I didn't want to steal the box for Miss Mathis, I wanted to steal it for myself. To keep it close, to let some of its magic rub off on me. Besides, there was no doubt in my mind She would want me to take it. There was something special to this box. Some things you just know.

I slid the box in my purse. I put everything else back in the trunk, as right as I could possibly get it. I knew I had taken too long, that my absence had become conspicuous. But while I was repacking the trunk, a strange little book caught my eye, a skinny orange volume with no picture on the cover and no title. Somehow I had missed it before.

It was thin, not even an actual published book, just someone's personal notebook. I flipped it open. Across the blank, white pages someone had made lines and margins with a ruler and pencil. The first lines, scribbled in dark black ink, said this:

My name is Kevin and I have a demon. It is my demon, my very own.

I felt a cold prickle on my neck, as if someone was watching me.

I whipped my head around. No one was there. I held my breath and listened. No footsteps, no breathing. Just the mechanical hum of the air-conditioning, the insect buzz of fluorescent lights.

But someone saw me. I knew it in my bones.

I dropped the orange notebook in my purse. Hopefully Uncle Mike wouldn't miss anything I'd taken. Hopefully he would never even know I had been here. I folded the shawl and put it back on top, pushing the trunk under the vanity with my feet.

I made sure I put every single speck of everything back the way it was, eased the door shut, and crept back downstairs. I was hoping I hadn't been missed too much, that no one had won-dered where I'd gone. I knew Roy wouldn't come looking for me because I said I was changing, and I'm pretty sure nothing scared him more than the thought of walking in on me naked.

Uncle Mike was screaming at Roy. They were still in the book section.

"Buy something already," said Uncle Mike. "Why does he not buy?"

"Cool it, Mike," I said.

"But he is a thief!" said Uncle Mike.

Roy looked terrified. His face was red and sweaty, like he'd never gotten in trouble before, like he didn't even know what being in trouble was like. Must be nice.

"Did you steal something, Roy?" I said.

"No," he said. "But I found a book I want to buy."

"Wanted to steal," said Uncle Mike. "He wrapped it in that pink shirt, see?"

The shirt was wrapped in a bundle around something, that much was obvious. If Roy was trying to be a thief, he was pretty terrible at it.

"I wasn't hiding it!" he said. "I was just trying to keep all my stuff together."

"What book you got?" I said.

Roy seemed embarrassed. He unwrapped the shirt and handed me a tattered fat volume of a book I knew very, very well. It was *The Obscure Life of John Dee*, the book I was reading on the porch the first day Roy came to visit me. I had about six copies at home, and sometimes I would bring one to Mike in hopes that someone else would find the book and love it like I did. Roy had remembered.

"I didn't want you to see it," he said.

"Oh my god, Roy!" I said. "That's my favorite book! I mean, ever! It's the most fascinating thing you'll ever read in your whole life."

Nobody paid much attention to me, what books I read, what music I listened to. No one had ever cared, except for Her. I had been so lonely for so long. I don't know. I guess it just meant a lot to me that he remembered.

I was so happy I threw my arms around him.

I could tell it surprised Roy by how he flinched, how he didn't know where to put his hands on me. When I let go, he wouldn't look me in the face, like he was embarrassed for touching me at all.

Uncle Mike seemed embarrassed too, even a little confused. He shuffled away behind the counter where I couldn't see him anymore. Apparently Roy was off the hook, even though he still wouldn't look up at me.

"You okay, Roy?" I said.

"Sure," he said. "Right as rain."

I laughed.

"Sometimes you talk like an old man, you know that?" I said. "Now come on, I got to get home before my mom and stepdad get back."

Roy followed me to the register. Uncle Mike rang us up, scowling the whole time. He didn't even tell Roy the price of the book, he just pointed at the green lights on the register. He tried not to give Roy any change either, so I tapped on the register and glared at him. Uncle Mike sighed and gave him some ones and coins. I leaned over the counter and pecked Uncle Mike on the cheek.

"Get out of here," Uncle Mike said. "And don't come back."

But Uncle Mike was smiling.

In the car I was almost giddy. I cranked this old Misfits tape of my dad's and barreled down the highway, as happy as I'd been since I lost Her. I had the rosewood box. I was following Her plan now, things were happening, I was going to get Her back. It was enough to get me singing. Roy kept staring at me, dog-eyed, flinching every time the song cussed. But I knew he was having fun, I knew Roy didn't want to be anywhere else but with me. That felt more than a little bit good.

We pulled up to my driveway and I let him out by his bike.

"Thanks," said Roy, "for the best day ever."

"Yeah," I said. "It was pretty good, wasn't it?"

I'd spent a month thinking of Roy as my enemy, as some brainwashed joy-robbing minion of evil. It was amazing to think that he was awful close to becoming my only friend.

"So when can I come see you again?" he said.

"Soon," I said. "It's not like I'm doing anything else."

"I'll call you?" he said.

"Please do."

Roy biked away into the night. In my heart I wished him a safe ride home.

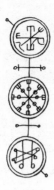

THAT NIGHT I LAY IN BED, LISTENING

to Mom and Larry argue beneath me. They always found something to fight about, whether it involved me or not. Whenever things got too bad around here She used to daydream me off somewhere to escape. I knew it wasn't a physical place, that my body never left this room. But She would take me there in my mind.

We called it the Hidden Place.

It was a meadow on top of a mountain overlooking the sea, a windswept green oasis streaked with swaying bluebells, a steep precipice on all sides that plunged a thousand feet into the wild bashing surf. The Hidden Place was as real to me as anywhere in this world, realer even. I could smell the grass, the ocean water, hear the crash of the waves and the boom after lightning flickered on the horizon. When I touched the flowers in the meadow they seemed to touch me back. Even now I can taste the salt in my mouth, feel my longing for the far-off storm.

It was here in the Hidden Place that She would reveal

Herself to me. She would step out of the air and into a body, a small pale girl with black hair in a long dress. Sometimes it was pink polka-dotted, sometimes it was yellow, like dandelions. She would sit down next to me and we could talk face-to-face then, though I never liked looking in Her eyes, grey as the sea and endless, gone fathoms and fathoms deep. We would sit and talk and sometimes She would hold my hand, touch my cheek with Her fingers, warm real flesh. She was my age at first, eight also, but She never grew up like I did. As I got older, She always stayed the same.

Why do you fret, little Clare? She would say, and all my troubles would turn silly, soft as clouds; I could dash my hand through them and they would scatter.

You're with Me now. There's never any need to worry when you're with Me.

We didn't just go to the Hidden Place when I was panicky either. We went other times too, like in school when I was bored, or on quiet nights when I'd be lounging around my bedroom. I could never ask to be taken to the Hidden Place, and no matter how hard I begged, She would always say no. We couldn't go there anytime we wanted. No, that wasn't how hidden places worked.

It's for when you need it, She said. *It's for when both of us do.*

"But what if I need it all the time?" I said.

You don't, silly. It's a special place just for you and me. If we could go any old time, then it wouldn't be special anymore. No, it'd just be a regular place, and what good would that be?

The hours we spent in the Hidden Place felt like weeks. The sunlight, the bright golden moon that rose over still waters, the clouds streaking like grey mice across the sky—they were the happiest days of my life.

"Can we take Mom here sometime?" I asked Her once. "I think she needs a place like this."

No, She said. *It's just for you—for you and me. No one else can come here. No one else even knows how.*

We would walk together through the tall scratchy grasses, hand in hand, and the bluebells would turn to watch us pass, speaking to us with their scents. At night in the Hidden Place the stars sang down their light and I could hear it—I could hear all the light pouring from their mouths. And then I would awake dazed, feeling as if weeks and weeks had passed.

It got me in trouble at school, which pissed Larry off. Even worse was at home, when She'd snap back at Larry straight from my mouth, before I could stop Her. I'd beg Her and beg Her to keep quiet, but She'd say, *No one should speak to you like that. No one should ever raise a voice against my Clare.*

I always loved Her for that.

Eventually Larry got so mad at me he took my computer and canceled the Internet. He said he had it on his phone and Mom hated computers and what was the point? I was pissed at first, but it turned out to be maybe the best thing that ever happened to me. For one, all this dead-space time at home that I used to spend gazing off into a screen I now spent exploring outside, same as I used to when I was a kid. I wandered all through the woods, named every tree and giant rock, knew every ditch and patch of wildflowers. I hadn't done anything like that since I was a little girl.

But the best thing was when She told me there was a surprise hidden in the attic for me.

You'll like it, She said. *I swear.*

She led me up the creaky attic ladder into the sweltering upstairs dark, the bare wood of the walls and support beams everywhere. It was the kind of thing that reminded you that all the furnishings and carpet and wallpaper were just cover-ups for the bones of the house, the brick and insulation and splintered wood. She led me to the very back of the attic, to the darkest space, to what Mom had hidden off behind the Christmas decorations, under a tarp where not even my stepdad knew about it.

Go on, She said. *Pull back the tarp.*

Underneath were crates and crates of my dad's old records, all dusty vinyl and the torn cardboard sleeves. Music I half remembered from when I was a little girl, the names and sounds that blurred into my best memories with Dad.

It was like walking into a new life, one where Dad was just a little older than I was, where he wasn't all fucked up, where he wasn't addicted to anything yet. There were records and records and records, and three shoeboxes full of tapes. Dusty, maybe, but only a little bit warped. I found the record player in a box nearby, with the cobwebbed old speakers and the frizzled ends of copper wire sticking out like frozen electricity. I carried it all downstairs and hooked up the stereo in my room.

It was strange, dark music—Bauhaus, Siouxsie and the Banshees, the Cocteau Twins, the Birthday Party, X, the Misfits, Bad Brains, the Cure. Mostly eighties stuff, with make-upped people in torn leather moping on the album covers in their glamour and despair. I started trying to dress like them, ransacking Uncle Mike's for anything gothic and worn, combat boots and sparkles and ripped tights, like if I put on their clothes I'd be one of them, sad and romantic and not meant for this place. Those records conjured a dream world, one as moody and strange as I was.

See, I knew in my heart that something was wrong with me. I wasn't the same as other girls my age. I wasn't as happy as them. My life had gone wrong somewhere along the way, same as Mom's and Larry's had. These records made a space for what was wrong with me. They took all my bad feelings and sang them until they were beautiful. They also let me remember a side of my dad that I'd long forgotten, that Mom and I never talked about.

Mostly that Dad could sing.

Dad sang in the morning when we woke up and Mom was cooking eggs. He sang soft and pretty when he shot up in the kitchen. He sang lovely when he worked, when he would come home high or drunk after late nights of playing music or bartending, he would giggle out of control, he would fall over on things and sing himself to tears. He mumble-sang when Mom would drag him to the shower cold and naked, the hot water long run out, while he shivered himself aware. He sang all kinds of songs, gospel songs, rock and roll songs, songs I didn't recognize, songs he made up himself.

Some days he'd wake up and say he was so sorry and that he would quit and he'd sing Mom a song and they would start kissing, right there in front of me, and I would go outside and play. It was like music was easier for him than breathing, than talking.

My dad loved me, he called me his little muse, his little song—could you fetch me a drink, little Clare, little song? He loved me, he said I was his song and when you sing a song you send it off into the world, let the wind carry it where it may.

There were pictures in the boxes too, mixed in with the tapes and records. Polaroids and glary disposable-camera pictures of Mom and Dad when they were young. Dad's hair was spiky in some of them, Mom's down near to her waist. Dad wore tight jeans and leather jackets, Mom long black dresses with rips in them. They were always laughing in the pictures, smiling over bottles of beer. It made me realize that those sad songs he sang weren't all miserable, and that somewhere buried deep in the back of them was a smile too, or at least a smirk. I liked that.

I knew Dad had made records, and demo tapes, too. There should have been more of those somewhere, but as far as I can tell Mom destroyed them all, tossed them out in the trash along with the rest of her old life. It was hard to blame her for it. Mom had a tough life always, I knew that. But I wished she had kept some of Dad's music. It would be nice to have more than just my memories.

The night I found the records I lay on my bed, listening to the Jesus and Mary Chain, a song called "Just Like Honey." It was the least noisy one on the whole record, and I liked that. A touch of sweetness in the mangled world of everything else. I kept skipping the needle back, learning how to drop it soft, hearing that one song over and over again. I was on maybe my fifteenth straight listen when I rolled over on my bed and saw her standing there in the doorway, big tears drifting down her cheeks.

"What's wrong, Mom?"

"I haven't heard this song in a long time," she said. "It was me and your dad's song. Used to be our sweet song."

"Did you dance to it at your wedding?"

She nodded at me.

"I found some pictures, too. In the attic, I mean."

I grabbed the stacks of photos and held them out toward Mom. For a minute I thought she was going to take them, that she was going to sit down and talk to me about Dad, tell me stories, that we were finally going to stop pretending that he just didn't exist anymore, that he wasn't all around this house, real as a ghost.

Mom shut her eyes.

"Don't you let Larry catch you with that stuff," she said, and closed the door on her way out.

We never did have that talk about Dad, but she didn't rat me out to Larry either.

"When did you get into records?" Larry asked me a few weeks later.

"They're mine," said Mom. "Had them up in the attic all along."

"Vinyl is a pain in the ass," said Larry. "Bump the damn needle and it's ruined forever. CDs are so much easier."

"But less fun," I said.

"I guess," he said. "Glad you found a new hobby. Just keep it down, alright?"

Sometimes Larry actually wasn't so bad. Sometimes he could be pretty okay, considering.

But that didn't help me now, awake and wired in the middle of the night with no one to talk to and nothing to do.

It was in the lonely hours like these when I missed Her most. The way She could fill me with warmth and with light, like a candle lit inside me. Now all I felt was alone.

I couldn't sit around depressed like this all night. I had to do something.

Larry had fixed my door, but he also removed the lock, so I couldn't rely on any warning before he flung it open and stuck his fat head in to spy on me. I had to be sure they were asleep before I did anything that actually mattered. It was all silence downstairs. Now was the time.

I slipped the rosewood jewelry box out of my purse, and the orange notebook, too. The box had a tiny silver clasp on it.

I knew I shouldn't open it.

It wasn't mine, after all. It belonged to Uncle Mike's daughter, and it was probably precious to him. I'd stolen it for a crazy old lady I didn't even know, who Uncle Mike said was evil. Whatever was inside this box was strange and most likely dangerous. I knew just looking at it could get me in all kinds of trouble.

So, yeah, of course I opened it.

Here's what I found inside: a gold-painted Easter egg with sequins glued all over it. A boll of cotton still attached to the stalk. A cut-off chicken's foot with a red ribbon tied around the ankle. Golden rings on a metal loop, too small for my fingers, like they were meant for a child. And at the bottom of the box, a rolled-up strip of leather, about the width of a page from a book, bound by a piece of ribbon.

I loosened the knot and unscrolled the leather. It was rough, strange-feeling, like it was made out of some kind of animal I

didn't know. On it was scratched a series of designs and scribbles, a feather and an eyeball and what were maybe words, an impossible language of slashes and symbols that I couldn't begin to decipher.

It was like a treasure chest that belonged to some senile witch doctor, a hoarder of half-magic junk. I didn't understand how this stuff could be worth a thousand dollars. There had to be something secret to it, something I didn't quite get yet. What if Uncle Mike's wife really had been a witch, and Cléa was, too? Maybe this stuff was what she used to cast spells. Could that be why Miss Mathis wanted it so bad? Was she some kind of witch as well?

I picked up the orange notebook. The handwriting inside was scraggly and tough to read, like it had been written by someone's left hand. I could feel a tremble to it, the way the pages seemed to shiver in my hands. There was something to this book, something sinister and wonderful and full of secrets. A single name was scribbled on the inside cover in the same confused, staggery handwriting: *KEVIN HENRIKSON.*

I began to read.

My name is Kevin and I have a demon. It is my demon, my very own.

It first came to me in a dream. I was a kid, a little one. It wasn't anything, not a body or nothing, just a Feeling.

In my dream I said to that Feeling, what's your name?

The Feeling said I don't have a name.

I said to the Feeling are you a girl or a boy?

The Feeling said I'm a spirit. We aren't like people.

A spirit? I said. Like a ghost?

No it said.

A demon? I said.

If you like. But I can be your friend.

I said I'm only friends with boys.

It said okay, you can call me Nicolas. That's a boy's name.

And then I woke up. It was all in my sleep.

My hands shook I was so excited, and my heart slapped against my chest. It was like reading my own story in some other weird kid's words. It felt so good to know that someone else understood. I knew that She had intended for me to find this.

I read on.

Nicolas came back to me night after night. Nicolas could do a whole lot of things. One time Nicolas told me to shut my eyes.

Have you ever seen Paris? said Nicolas.

I said nuh uh I haven't.

Shut your eyes said Nicolas and I did.

At first nothing happened and then something did.

I was flying. I was flying but I wasn't alone. Nicolas was flying with me, I could feel his hand, it was like my spirit was a body and now we could touch.

I saw a big lit up tower that looked like the outline of a tower. It was bright and glowing like an old metal Christmas tree. It was beautiful.

I said what's that Nicolas? He said that's the Eiffel Tower. Didn't you know?

I said no I don't know anything.

So Nicolas showed me things.

He showed me the ocean. It's bigger than it looks in pictures. He showed me forests long as the sky and temples full of bones. He showed me a windmill and a clock tower and an old man in a hut on a mountain. He showed me the sun rise up out of the ocean like a giant fiery bird.

I said how can I see all this, it can't be real. Nicolas said it was real.

I said prove it.

He said okay.

Nicolas flew me to where the newspapers are printed. There were these great big machines and all kinds of paper whirring fast in them like a movie projector. Nicolas said to write down the headlines and see if they didn't match up next morning. Okay I said I will.

I snapped out of it. I was in my bedroom. I had a scrap of napkin in my hand where I wrote the headline.

I must have been in it deep because I don't remember grabbing a pen or a napkin and I don't know where the napkin even came from.

But there it was in my hand.

It said Mysterious Heavenly Body Found. I wondered if it was about me and Nicolas flying.

I slept and all my dreams were flying dreams with me and Nicolas, I don't know if they were dreams or not. When I woke up the next morning I went downstairs to ask Dad for the newspaper. There it was, just like I had written it: Mysterious Heavenly Body Found. But it was about a planet not me.

I got so happy I laughed.

Momma said what's got you feeling so good?

I said Momma I made a friend.

•

The phone buzzed. I jolted awake from the notebook. I clicked the silence button and flipped it open.

"Hello?" I whispered.

I don't know, for some reason I thought it might be Kevin Henrikson. That maybe by reading his notebook I'd conjured him up somehow, called to him through time and space just by loving his words so much.

"Hey, Clarabella. It's me, Roy."

"Holy shit," I said. "Roy, you scared me."

I couldn't tell if I was disappointed or relieved. What would it have meant to talk to Kevin? I knew he was brilliant and strange, maybe even a little off in some way. Would he like me? Would he want me to read this stuff?

"I'm sorry," said Roy. "Were you sleeping?"

"Nope," I said, trying to sound bright and chirpy. "Just reading."

"I'm reading, too. I'm like two hundred pages into that John Dee book. You didn't tell me he was also a minister. That's crazy."

"Glad you're liking it."

"I am, a lot," he said. "I didn't mean to call you so late. It was just . . . I got this feeling, like you were in trouble or something."

"What kind of trouble would I be in?" I said.

"I don't know. I just had a feeling."

"Well, all is right and well here. How about you, Roy? You all good?"

"Yeah," he said. "I'm talking to you, aren't I?"

I laughed.

"God, you're a dork."

We talked until four A.M. It was the warmest I'd felt, the least alone, since She'd been gone. I fell asleep still holding the phone, the notebook buried under my flung-back covers, forgotten for the night.

THE NEXT DAY MOM AND LARRY WERE

both at work, and they had both taken their cars. Technically I was still under basic house arrest, with no mode of transportation but my old bike. The tires were half-flat and the whole thing was painted little-girl pink, but it still rode okay. I'd looked up Miss Mathis's address earlier, and it wasn't too far from my house. I figured I'd go ahead and bring the box to her. Maybe she could tell me what all the stuff inside it meant. Besides, a thousand bucks was a hell of a lot of money.

The ride only took me about fifteen minutes. Her house was tucked into the back of a boring little neighborhood, the kind of place where kids roam free and the adults don't do anything but go to work and cheat on each other.

Miss Mathis's place was a one-story brick building, drab and ugly. Big curtains blocked out all the windows and you couldn't see anything on the inside. I walked past the overgrown hedges and was going to knock on the door, but there was a sign taped on the door, scrawled on yellow legal paper.

COME ON IN ALREADY, it said.

I pushed the door open and it creaked long and weird. The smell hit me so hard I almost gagged, cigarettes and wet dog and Febreze. The house was dark, just a lamp lit here and there. A stereo played sad, scratchy music, a lady singing in a foreign language.

"Miss Mathis?" I said. "It's Clare, from the junk shop."

I peeked my head into the living room. It was red-curtained, tossing splotches of red anytime the sunlight dared to stream through. Clutter was everywhere. Books in tall toppling stacks. Old creased magazines, *Harper's* and *Soldier of Fortune*. A stack of ancient, fat, rusty-looking tomes with a magnifying glass next to them. Four burned-down purple candles. A multitude of coffee cups, cigarette butts poking out like little crooked tombstones. Framed pictures hung all over the wall, of kids who were probably old dead people now. In the middle of the whole mess was Miss Mathis, leaned back all the way in her easy chair. She had on her big black sunglasses, like the kind that blind people wear in movies, and a navy-blue Bank of America sweatshirt. Miss Mathis was snoring. I mean long, drawling, guttural, nightmare snores, dragon snores. On an end table sat a dirty-looking NASCAR mug. She dangled a still-burning cigarette between two fingers, a froufrou dog—some kind of shih tzu or whatever—asleep on her lap.

I wasn't sure what to do. Wasn't it dangerous to wake old people suddenly? She might have a heart attack or something. I coughed real loud, but she didn't wake up. I figured maybe I should just come back later.

Miss Mathis drew in a fierce, short breath. Except she didn't exhale. She didn't cough, and she didn't snort it out. It was like she sucked her air in and it got stuck there. I peered at her close.

Miss Mathis wasn't breathing.

"Miss Mathis?" I said. "Hello?"

I waved my hand in front of her face. Nothing. I started sweating.

Oh god oh god. Do I give her mouth-to-mouth? Do I shake her? What if I break her neck?

The shih tzu sat snoozing in her lap. What a crap watchdog.

So I poked it.

The dog sprang up and bit me on the finger. It drew blood. I yanked my finger away and yowled. Miss Mathis shot up in her chair, her flung cigarette sparking against the TV, the dog flying off her lap like a furry, small angel. It scampered, yipping, around my feet. Miss Mathis sucked in a huge gulp of air, like she was just coming up from drowning.

"Jesus Christ!" she said.

Miss Mathis grabbed the NASCAR mug off her end table and took a swig. She spat it across the floor. "This ain't coffee." She shrugged and drank the rest of the mug down.

"Shut the fuck up, Prissy," Miss Mathis said. She picked up the growling dog, and it immediately went still and silent in her arms. "This is Clare, the dear girl who did us a favor. She's come here to collect her prize."

Miss Mathis looked at my bloody finger. "You need a Band-Aid for that?"

I shook my head.

"Might want to sterilize it when you get home, regardless.

Prissy's sick in the head, I swear." Miss Mathis lit a cigarette. "Kindly, Clare, do you mind stomping that butt out over there? Don't much want the house to burn down."

The cigarette smoldered on the carpet. I toed it out.

"Thank you," she said.

"No problem," I said. "I'm sorry I interrupted your nap. The sign just said to come on in."

"I wasn't napping, dear. I was out walking."

"Okay."

"Went to visit an old lover in Ireland I had once, when I wasn't much older than you. She's in hospice dying right now, bless her heart. Sad to see an old love laid up like that, but most of mine are long dead anyway. Wished I could hold her hand, but that's not how walking works, is it now, dear?"

"Walking?" I said. "You mean like astral projection?"

I knew all about that stuff from books I got at Uncle Mike's. Honestly, I'd always wanted to try it, cast the spirit of myself out into the cosmos, wandering deep across the worlds. I figured it wasn't too much different than when She would take me daydreaming to the Hidden Place. That somehow seemed a part of my destiny, I thought, to whisk myself through the stars and see what was hidden behind them.

"I don't like all this fancy terminology," said Miss Mathis. "If you can't say it pretty, don't say it at all. And that goes for science and politics and everything else in the free world."

"I have your box," I said.

"Not my box, dear," said Miss Mathis. "Cléa's box. And she wouldn't be too happy about me getting hold of it, I'll tell you that.

Not to mention her daddy. I'd steer clear of Mike's for a while if I was you. Now, if you don't mind."

She stretched her hands out to me. I pulled the box out of my backpack and handed it over. Miss Mathis caressed it, slid her long red fingernails in a scratch over the rosewood, tracing the spiraling eye carved into it.

"This is for protection, see. So no one can peek into it. No infernal powers, I mean. It's like a veil drawn over the whole thing."

"What was she trying to hide?"

Miss Mathis smirked at me.

"You opened the box, didn't you?"

I nodded.

"Then you know."

I watched as Miss Mathis flipped open the rosewood box and dumped its contents on the coffee table. The necklace clattered, the chicken foot fell on the ground. The shih tzu started to gnaw on it.

"Why is there a goddamn boll of cotton? Christ almighty," said Miss Mathis.

Miss Mathis found the leather scroll and let out a little gasp. She snatched it off the coffee table and untied it, ran her fingers over the scratches in it, seemed to try to read it by touch, like it was braille.

"This is it, Clare. You did it. You did very, very well for Miss Mathis."

She held the scroll up to her lips and kissed it.

So that was it. The valuable thing—the magic thing—was the scroll.

"Now, let me get my pocketbook," she said.

Miss Mathis stood up and hobbled toward the kitchen. I

followed her. The sink was filled with dirty dishes, the counters stacked with Styrofoam take-out containers, and moldy coffee mugs were scattered about like laboratory test tubes. It was about as far as you could get from any witch's kitchen I'd ever imagined.

Because that's what Miss Mathis was. I knew it now. She was a witch, same as Cléa. Or whatever you call a witch in real life, where words like "witch" seem ridiculous.

Miss Mathis dug her billfold out and placed eight one-hundred-dollar bills in my hand. I couldn't believe so much money took up such little space. It felt like less than what it would take to tip the pizza guy.

"I guess I don't totally understand," I said. "All this money for that little leather scroll?"

"First off, dear, it's not very much money. Not really," said Miss Mathis. "And second? That scroll ain't cowhide. It's human skin."

My stomach dropped. Human skin? I'd touched some dead person's carved-up belly?

"Don't look so peaked, dear," she said. "You're such a pretty girl, and disgust is unbecoming."

Miss Mathis shuffled back into the living room and sat down in her easy chair. Prissy leapt up into her lap, the chicken foot clamped tight between her jaws. I stood by the coffee table, clutching the money, not sure what to do next.

"Thank you, Clare. You saved me a heap of trouble. Don't be scared to come on by when you're sad or needing advice. Old Miss Mathis is a good listener. Bring me a liter of Smirnoff, and I'll listen to your worries all day."

"I don't have any worries," I said.

"Bullshit. You're what, fifteen? Sixteen? Your whole life is one big worry. Don't think I don't know. Don't think I don't remember what sixteen was like."

"I said I'm fine."

"Alright, alright," she said. "But I'll be seeing you again soon enough."

"What makes you say that?"

"Because whatever's coming involves the both of us. That I'm sure of."

I just stared at Miss Mathis. For a moment, she didn't seem so frail to me. She seemed strong somehow, wise, like a veteran from an old war that could still rise up and fight at a moment's notice.

Miss Mathis lit a cigarette.

"Now, run along," she said. "Miss Mathis needs to get tanked and watch her *Jeopardy*."

Miss Mathis fished around for the remote and flicked on the TV. As I walked out, both she and Prissy sat upright, the TV blaring so loud it hurt my ears.

Old people can really surprise you sometimes.

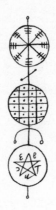

I GOT BACK TO MY HOUSE WITH A HEAD

full of questions. This was starting to seem a lot bigger than just me and Her. Roy was involved, Uncle Mike and Cléa, and now Miss Mathis as well. But I still didn't understand all of Her message.

Like: which stories was I supposed to remember, anyway? She told me a million of them. The No-ear Rabbit? The Girl with the Fang Face? The Old Hermit and the Broke-Up Sky? The Windmill and the Weeping Giant? The Woman with the Bag of Stars? Whirly Pearl? The Kitty Skull? Or any one of the hundreds She would make up on the spot, happy nothings to quiet the day away. That was something about Her I missed. She knew more stories than anyone else alive.

And what was so important about June 20?

I walked through my silent house alone, missing Her something fierce. My loneliness was like another creature in the room, the way a shadow is nothing really but it's still there anyway. I closed my eyes and imagined Her there, tucking a stray black curl behind my ear, whispering soft words to me, telling me a story.

I could do this. I could figure everything out. I just had to try.

Maybe the box for Miss Mathis wasn't the only thing I was supposed to find at the junk shop. Maybe the orange notebook was every bit as important. I remembered how it felt, secret and mine, like reading my own words written back at me. There had to be some kind of clue in the notebook, I just knew it. I walked upstairs and shut my door. I leaned a chair against it, so there'd be noise if someone tried to open it.

I flipped open the notebook to where I left off.

Nicolas knew things. Not just flying.

Nicolas walked me to school every day. It was fun to walk not by myself. One time Aaron Kilpatrick rode up in his Chevrolet. It was a real nice car. Aaron Kilpatrick threw a beer can at me from out the window. The beer can was full, he shook it up first. He said hey idiot, eat this. There were other kids in the car too, Becky Chapman who is real pretty and two more girls who were cheerleaders. The beer can hit me in the head.

It knocked me over. It splurted beer all over me. Now Dad would think I was drinking, the teachers too. I couldn't go to school, I'd get in trouble.

Becky Chapman laughed. She looked pretty when she laughed.

Blood dribbled down my nose.

The car drove away. I cried.

Nicolas was touching my hair. He said it's okay I'm here, take my hand. I did.

Nicolas said do you want to know a secret about Becky Chapman? What Nicolas?

She's going to have a baby.

A little bitty baby?

Yes, with Aaron Kilpatrick. Soon too, so soon you'll hear all about it. Her parents will kick her out of the house and she and Aaron will get married.

Aaron's mean.

Yes he is said Nicolas. Can you imagine what being married to Aaron will be like?

Very sad.

Yes, very sad. Becky will be very sad until she is old, until her children are grown and have left home, and Aaron is fat on the couch, a front tooth rotted out, and she will wonder what has become of her life, and where her dreams went, and why it is all already gone.

What will happen to Becky Chapman then?

Her hair will fall flat, her cheeks will sag. She will wither and grow old. And then she will be gone.

Where?

That's not for you to know. But she will never hurt you again. Aaron won't either. I won't let them. And their lives will fold out like an old map to a country that doesn't exist anymore.

I feel bad for Becky Chapman.

That's because you're good, Kevin.

I'm not good, I'm stupid.

You're good, and you're brilliant, and one day they will all know it.

I love you, Nicolas.

I love you too, Kevin. Let's go.

Nicolas walked me to the woods, to a sunny place with birds. I never even went to school.

Here is a picture of Becky Chapman while she is still pretty.

The page was a miracle. Never before had I seen such a perfect, realistic drawing of a person before, especially in black and white. Becky Chapman really was pretty, in that typical sort of boring way that popular girls always are. Kevin had drawn her face just right, the sort of arrogant half smirk that comes from having everyone love you all the time. It isn't a happy smile, not by a long shot.

Because those girls aren't happy either. I've seen them at school, the worried looks they get when they're alone, when there's no one there for them to smile at. Like they know that they're fakes. Like they know the only difference between them and me is some other popular girl's opinion, like all it would take is one public fuckup to turn them into me.

I've had boys like me before, too. I've been one of the desired ones. It's the dirty secret of the jock that he always wants the weird girl. That she's some kind of escape from his shit-grinning life, like she can be his door into a different world. Also they assume you're a slut because you wear black and like bands they've never heard of. I've been one of the desired, but I didn't give in. Even when someone tried to make me, I wouldn't let him. She wouldn't let him. No one could touch me but Her. And compared with Her, jock boys seemed ridiculous, popularity contests petty. It was hard to care about a bunch of kids when you had someone ageless inside you. She made every boy seem weak, pitiful.

And without Her I was all alone.

I turned the page.

There were more drawings. I flipped through the book and saw them, all beautiful black ink and pen. Like photographs, but realer somehow. There was the Eiffel Tower, lit up and gorgeous, just like Kevin said it was. A garden with giant flowers, a clock tower in the rain, an old windmill covered in lost birds. It was like a sketchbook of dreams, each one so real I wanted to reach my hands into them, their world of whites and darks, and pluck the fleshy petals of a flower, feel the softness of the rain on cold cobblestones, see the midnight glow of the moon in a hermit's broken window. Around the fringes of the pictures swirled strange symbols, eyeballs and runes like in cave paintings and hieroglyphics. These weren't just dreams. They were visions, what Nicolas had shown Kevin when they were flying.

It made me wonder about Kevin. His writing was strange and scribbled, singsongy in a way that seemed a little off. And yet, there was no doubt that he was a genius, a real artist. Based on the stuff with Aaron Kilpatrick and Becky Chapman, I guessed Kevin was about my age when he made this, or maybe a little older. The notebook had to have been from before Cléa disappeared. Kevin would be an adult by now. But maybe he was still around somewhere. Maybe I could somehow find him and we could talk. Maybe he would know how to get Her back for me.

I read on.

Nicolas told me about a man. He lived in a big house in the woods. He is a magic man, gentle and kind. Nicolas said go see that man.

I said why?

He said aren't we special friends?

I said yes Nicolas you're my first best friend.

Do you like being best friends?

I do every day is good now.

The man can make us closer.

How do you mean Nicolas?

We could be the same person.

I don't understand.

Nicolas said it's like putting on new clothes, those new clothes are me. Don't you want to be together always?

Yes.

Then go see the man in the woods. He is a magic man, gentle and kind. He understands about you and me. He can help us.

Why do we need his help Nicolas?

Because some people I can just step into and out of, like a pair of shoes. But sometimes it takes a little help to fit me into a person. It takes someone of great power, and there aren't many of those left in the world.

Okay I said.

You're very special said Nicolas.

Thanks Nicolas, you are too, I love you.

I love you too Kevin.

When do we go Nicolas?

Tomorrow.

I go to see the man in the woods tomorrow. He is a magic man, gentle and kind. He understands about me and Nicolas. Tomorrow I go to have him put Nicolas inside me for always.

There wasn't anything written after that. Not even any more drawings. Just four blank pages, and they were the most mysterious of all.

I read the notebook again and again. I touched the drawings with my fingertips, felt where the tip of the pen bore down on the paper. I knew that in the drawings were secrets, that if only I stared at them long enough, conjured them up in my mind clear and full, the truth of the world would appear to me.

I had to find Kevin. I wanted to know what happened with the man in the woods, if Kevin got what he wanted. I had so many questions for him. Kevin would know. He would understand me.

It made me think of a story She once told me when I was just a kid. Well, not so much a story, but a game we would play, about a wise man who lived deep in the woods. A man who could grant our secret wishes.

The game was called One Wish Man.

It went like this:

She would ask, in her lisping, scratchy, little-girl's voice, *If you could wish for one thing, what would it be? What would you ask for from the One Wish Man?*

The One Wish Man was tall and handsome, he was mysterious, he lived in a house out in the woods called the Wish House. It was a mansion, not some little cottage like in a fairy tale, with rooms and rooms for many guests whenever the One Wish Man would throw a party. But not just anyone could enter the Wish House. You had to be invited, and the gates to the Wish House had to be opened for you. If the One Wish Man didn't open the gates, or if the Wish House didn't want you, you'd be lost wandering the woods forever.

But if you knew what you were looking for, if you had it perfectly clear in your heart what you wanted from him, then the Wish House would accept you, and the One Wish Man would grant your request. Of course, he always asked for a payment, a *boon*, she called it. I liked that word. It sounded silly, harmless, like a birthday present nobody wanted. One Wish Man was a game we played over and over again, especially when I was sad. She would ask it at curious times, almost like it was a test, to see if I was ready.

What would you ask the One Wish Man for today, Clare?

A puppy.

What kind of puppy?

A dachshund. A long-haired, dopey-eared dachshund named Sweet Potato. Who could bark the alphabet.

And today?

A moon-colored frog.

And today?

A cyclops raccoon. With a fire tail.

And today?

A dandelion circus. A knife made out of a rainbow.

And today?

A frozen piece of light. For my pocket.

And today?

A bridge made out of sea turtles straight to Japan. They don't mind me walking on them, because I'm so light, because I tickle their shells with my bare feet.

And today?

A new daddy, a new house. For the One Wish Man's house to be my house, so I could stay there asking things forever.

And today?

For you to never leave me, ever. For it always to be just the same as this.

She would laugh at that. She would run shivers all through me. That meant I passed the test. That meant She loved me more than anyone else, even my mom.

That meant She would love me forever.

It was just a game, just a story we told back and forth, always, changing it slightly. But that was back when I was little. We hadn't played One Wish Man for ages. Maybe that was my fault. Maybe I'd gotten tired of asking for things, for always wishing around for things that would never happen. As I got older the game slowly faded away, same as most other childhood play.

And yet there was one night, maybe four years ago, when the One Wish Man came back into our lives.

THIS IS THE STORY OF THE SECOND
time She took over my body.

I was twelve years old.

I awoke in the darkness, on a dirt road, in nothing but my night-shirt and Converses. I was cold and terrified, the sky a black swirl-ing menace above me. I was far, far from home, surrounded by woods, the leafless trees stretching their twiggy arms above me. In the road an opossum hissed, its eyes glowing coals in the darkness.

"Where am I?" I said.

Look, She said.

"I don't understand. How did I get here?"

Look.

Just as She spoke in me, moonlight cut through the clouds and shone down on a tree at the edge of the road. It was a broad, fat oak tree, the kind you know has always been there and will always be there, the kind they build whole roads around. And on its bark, scarred white as if seared by lightning, was the outline of a bird.

I reached my hand out and touched it, traced the markings with my fingers, in awe of how any knife could ever have carved something so beautiful, so intricate. I felt a power in that tree, in that sign, something deeper than language.

"What is this place?" I said.

That's where he lives.

"Who?"

The path starts here. These are the gates. When the bird becomes real.

"What path? What are you talking about?"

The Wish House, Clare. That's where the One Wish Man lives.

"How did I get here?"

You walked, silly.

"This isn't funny," I said. "Why did you do this to me?"

I had to show you the way, so you wouldn't forget. Now come along, we're walking back.

She guided me back, speaking into my ears, pulling me by the hand when I got too tired. It was late at night and the moon had vanished again and the wind on the road was cold, cold. Creatures wandered in the dark, howling things far off, deep in the woods where I couldn't see.

I was so mad at Her, I cussed at Her in my heart. I said awful things to Her that I later regretted, things you should never say to someone you love.

But I had to show you where the One Wish Man lives.

"Just shut up and get me home."

I will. But you have to pay attention. You have to know the way.

Soon we reached the highway, and big trucks came whooshing

by in the darkness. I wanted to wave one down, to hitchhike somewhere safer.

Not this one, She'd say, and I'd let him pass by.

After maybe twelve trucks passed by, She said that the next one was okay. I stepped out onto the shoulder of the road and jumped up and down, waving my hands. It was a red Ford Ranger that pulled over. An old lady in a trucker cap was behind the wheel. She looked like she was seventy, way too old to be out so late at night.

"Christ," she said when she saw me. "What in the hell happened to you?"

Don't say a word you don't have to.

"Can you take me to town, please?" I said.

"Which town?"

I told her.

"That's ten miles from here. You telling me you walked the whole way, in the middle of the night?"

You didn't walk. I made you run a lot of it. That's why you're so tired.

"Yes, ma'am."

"Is there something you're not saying?" she said. "Listen, if you're in some kind of trouble, you can tell me. I can get you somewhere safe if you need it."

"No, ma'am. If you could just take me to town, I would appreciate it."

The old lady was kind, and she let me sip coffee from her thermos. The old lady was a baker, she said, she had to get to work early to make pastries for the morning. I let her drop me off at the post office, about half a mile from home. It was still dark—the sun wouldn't be up for another hour. My mom and stepdad would never even know I'd been gone.

When I got home safe I took off my clothes and lay in my bed and huffed at Her. My feet hurt and my legs were sore and I was exhausted.

"You can't just take me where you want to," I told Her. "I could've been killed or run over or something."

I wouldn't let anything happen to you. You're my Clare.

"You shouldn't have done it."

But you had to see where he lives.

"I don't want to hear another word from you about the One Wish Man," I said. "He isn't real. He's made-up."

But it's important, Clare.

Oh, but I was mad. I've never been so mad as that before.

"Not another word. Ever. Do you hear me?"

Fine. If you want, I'll never mention the One Wish Man again.

"It's what I want."

She kept her promise. We never spoke about the One Wish Man after that. And eventually, well, I forgot all about him.

Could that be why She wrote *Remember the stories* instead of just saying his name, all because She promised me not to? Yeah, of course it was. She was like that, it was Her nature. And I bet the One Wish Man was the same person Kevin had gone to see.

Even though it was years ago, I had a good mind for directions, and I almost never got lost. She had made me walk all that way, repeating back to Her the directions, wiring them into my brain.

It would take a couple of tries, but I thought I could get back there eventually. Soon enough, I would find out for sure.

That night, when Roy's dad fell asleep and he called me, I asked him a question:

"Tell me, Roy. Have you ever heard of the One Wish Man?"

A FEW DAYS LATER ME AND ROY FOUND

a time to meet up again. Mom and Larry had a date night, which just meant they'd go to Olive Garden and Larry would get so drunk he could hardly walk. The whole thing would take hours and hours and then they'd fight when they got home. It was the same thing that happened every time they had a date night.

I waited for Roy in my driveway, same as last time. I would have gone to pick him up, but Larry's car was in the shop, and they had taken Mom's for the night. I wore a dress, a long periwinkle blue one. Roy was wearing the pink shirt I'd picked out for him. He wasn't nearly so sweaty as last time. I figured maybe he'd biked slower.

"Nice shirt," I said.

He blushed.

"I got something to show you," I said. "It's a secret."

I took off walking toward the woods behind my house. He stayed a few steps back, walking behind me, looking all cautious.

"What are you so worried about?" I said.

"Snakes," he said. "I always figure they're everywhere."

"Come on." I held my hand out to him. "Nothing's going to hurt you while I'm here."

Soon we came to a partly fallen-down garden shed. Rusty tools lay slacked and discarded, pruning shears sticking out of the dirt blades-up like the forest had claws. A hammock hung in a sad smile from tree to tree. A chimney stood there, no house around it. It leaned, bent and blackened, like a stooped bald old monk. The sun poked through the trees in long spears of light.

"What is this place?" he said.

"It's a secret spot," I said. "Not a single other person knows about it except for me, and you too now."

"What did it used to be?"

"I don't know. Probably somebody's house about a hundred years ago."

"I wonder what happened to it."

"Burned down, likely. It's been like this ever since I found it, when I was just a kid."

"You been coming here that long?"

"Yep," I said. "You know, it was here that I met Her. When I was a little girl."

"You mean your demon?"

A breeze hushed through the woods, leaves scattering in little scritches across the forest floor. Dust motes floated in the light. The woods were full and breathing. Never had I been surrounded by so much life. In my mind everything was watching me, taking note.

"I bet that's why the house burned down," he said. "I bet the demon did it."

"Could be," I said. "But She was always real nice to me. When I was a kid, we used to have tea parties, just me and Her. We used to play blindman's bluff and I lost every time."

"What did you call Her?" he said.

"Just 'You.' That's all I ever called Her for a name. She knew me, though. *Clare*, She said, right when I first met Her. But look here."

I reached into the fireplace and pulled out a small leather satchel. And inside the satchel were two teacups and a bottle of peach rum.

"I took it from my mom," I said. "She had like six bottles, so she won't notice."

"Rum?" he said. "Isn't that what pirates drink?"

"Yeah, I guess so. Want a sip?"

Roy nodded. He seemed a little scared. We sat down in the leaves next to an old stump that was flat enough for a table. I poured him a teacup full of rum.

"Cheers," I said.

We drank. Roy made a face.

"Delicious," he said, and I laughed.

We drank for a while and played One Wish Man. Little by little Roy was getting the hang of it, even though I could tell he thought it was a kid's game.

"Right now I'd ask for a Mexican Coke," he said. "With some peanuts in it."

"You have to be kidding me."

"No, I'm serious. You ever had Mexican Coke, drop a few salted peanuts in it? An old guy at the nursing home named Colonel

Jasper showed me when I was a kid. He said it was the best drink in the whole world. And Colonel Jasper was right. You don't get any better than that."

"I'm a little horrified right now, Roy."

"Well, what would you ask the One Wish Man for?"

I couldn't tell Roy the truth, that I wanted Her back and nothing else. I knew he wasn't ready to hear something like that from me. So I told him the next best truth I had.

"I'd wish for money enough to leave here. Enough to get a car and a fake passport. To drive and not get caught. To leave for somewhere with no Mom and no Larry, just gone off and free, the whole world waiting for me."

"Can I come, too?" said Roy.

"I don't see why not," I said. "But you'd have to earn your keep. You couldn't be any old slouch about it."

"I think it sounds real nice," he said.

"Nice? That's all you got?"

"It sounds like a dream. It sounds like being free as pirates, traveling from ocean to ocean, falling asleep with new stars over your head every night."

"There you go. *That's* how you say it."

It was near dusktime now and the fireflies were coming out, rising up from the grass.

Roy smiled goofily. I could tell he was drunk already.

"Look at them," he said. "Look at 'em go."

"The fireflies?"

"Yep," he said. "Floating around there. Like the ghosts of grass. Like dead grass ghosts."

I laughed. It was good to see Roy letting loose a little, not being such a square all the time. He was enjoying himself, I knew it. He was enjoying being here with me.

"There you go with that fancy talk," I said. "What else you got?"

"Crickets scritch like angels," he said. "And cicadas make flying-saucer noises. Tree frogs are drunk old men croaking gospel songs."

I clapped my hands and near fell over laughing. I guess I was feeling it too at this point. It was so nice not being alone, sitting out here hidden away with another person, someone who seemed to truly like me.

"You're getting really good at this," I said. "Want to come sit up in the hammock and tell me more?"

Roy nodded and tried to stand up, but he almost fell and had to sit back down again. I laughed and helped him up. I led him down to the hammock, and when we both sat on it I was scared it would break, but it didn't. I leaned my head on his shoulder.

"Clarabella . . ." he said.

"Do more," I said. "What's the moon?"

"A quail's egg."

"What's the milky way?"

"Old star blood."

"And what are the stars?"

"God crying His eyes out to see me drinking like this."

"Well, you know what I think the stars are?" I said. "I think they're peepholes for the angels. I think the angels in Heaven get bored up there and poke holes in the sky so they can spy down at us, see what all trouble we're up to."

"I like that," he said.

"What? That the stars are peepholes?"

"No, that you and me are up to some trouble."

"Preacher-boy Roy," I said. "You got a little wild to you, don't you?"

"I sure hope so," he said.

We were quiet then, the both of us. But the woods weren't. The woods were loud, every creature stirring itself up, yapping wild. It was like walking into the most crowded city in the world, everybody speaking different languages, raising a racket like you wouldn't believe. Except you couldn't see a single person. It was like they were all ghosts talking, all spirits, speaking languages ancient as old stars and time. It felt peaceful to be in the middle of all that invisible life. Roy's eyelids were droopy, and he seemed all glazed over, lost somewhere in his head.

"What are you thinking about that's got you so still all of a sudden?" I said.

"I was just thinking about this dream I had when I was a kid. I told my dad about it and he said it wasn't a dream. He said it was a vision. People were having visions all the time in my church, but it was the first time I ever had one."

"Go on," I said.

"Naw," he said. "Nobody likes hearing about dreams."

"Are you kidding?" I said. "I *love* to hear about dreams. I think dreams are about the most fascinating thing in the world. I mean it. People used to treat dreams with respect. Now we just think dreams are your brain messing around with itself. Kind of sad, isn't it?"

"Yeah," he said. "I guess it is. It must have been real scary for somebody like John to dream Revelation. Or Ezekiel's visions. All those scary angels with their eyes all over their bodies, even on the palms of their hands."

"No joke," I said. "You know, this poet I like named Rilke said that every angel was terrifying. I guess that's why whenever one shows up in the Bible everybody hits the deck. That or they try to worship them. Aren't angels just the scariest things you could ever think of?"

"Who's Rilke?" he said.

"He's a poet. You'd like him, I think."

"I don't know who anybody is."

"Just tell me your damn dream already."

"Okay," he said. "It was of a garden, a great and glorious garden, not like anything you ever seen before. It was a garden where the wind sang and the sun made music when it shone and even the air was glad. The flowers were the flowers of all the colors of the world, big as babies, and they would turn and look at you as you walked by. It was so peaceful, and lovely, and I wanted to lie down in the garden forever and let it take me, swallow me whole, until I became a part of the garden, too."

"It sounds like the Hidden Place," I said.

"What's that?" said Roy.

I didn't know how to explain it to him. I didn't have the words for it. So I lied.

"Just somewhere I made up," I said.

"Well, this wasn't made-up," said Roy. "It was Heaven, I think. I mean, I know it was. It had to be, you know? And I wanted to pluck a flower so bad, so bad. I reached my hand out toward a dandelion bigger than my head. A voice in the wind told me to stop, that it wasn't mine to touch yet. It was hard because the garden was so lovely. But everything was sharp too, like it had an edge on it, and even the flowers could cut you. Just being in that garden was so beautiful it was painful, it hurt me. But I never wanted to leave."

Roy began to cry.

"Whenever I think about that garden, I always hope my mom's there," he said. "I always hope she's sitting there, waiting on me."

I brushed my hand over his cheeks, smearing his tears. I turned his cheek to make him face me straight on.

"That's a beautiful vision," I said.

And just like that he kissed me.

I don't know. I'd been kissed before and it hadn't gone so well for me. But this time kissing felt good, and maybe I wanted more of it. So I kissed him back. I kissed him back and I enjoyed it.

Why shouldn't I have a little fun every once in a while?

About five minutes later Roy was snoring next to me. The rum had knocked him clean out.

I was drunk and still reeling a little from all the kissing. It felt strange to be here without Her, with a boy. I had a million memories of this place, all tied to Her, some of the happiest times of my life. It was like a sacred place to me.

Why had I brought Roy here anyway? It was like I was always trying to tell him something about myself, something I didn't dare put into words. I wanted him to understand me in a way that only She had, in a way that maybe only She could. And this was what She wanted, wasn't it? For me to be nice to him?

But what if I wasn't doing "nice" right? What if I was letting things go too far?

It started to feel wrong, like I'd betrayed Her somehow. It was a stupid idea to bring Roy here. It was our place, just mine and Hers. I never should have brought anyone else here. I felt all my good warm happiness drain away, leaving my insides black and empty. Even with Roy sleeping next to me, I began to feel unbearably alone.

I sat up and looked around in the darkness.

"Where are You?" I asked out loud.

I remembered the first day I found Her. Mom and Dad were fighting like crazy, they were all fucked up on drugs and everything, and I just wandered out of the house, nobody even noticing I was gone. I couldn't have been more than six years old. I wandered right on out and sat here by myself, watching damselflies hop around on the grass.

She was just a feeling at first, a notion, a breath between my fingers. I was just a little girl, but I knew She was there.

"Hello?" I said.

Do you want to play?

She was a whisper in my ear.

"Yes," I said.

And then I felt Her beside me.

At first She would wait for me here, every day, and I would come to Her to play. Games, tea parties, pretend, whatever I wanted. It was the same as any other lonely kid does, the same as every kid I'd ever met. Except She wasn't imaginary. She was real and sometimes She would hold my hand. It didn't feel like a person's hand. It felt like a warm breeze, like the wind would swoop down and wrap itself around me.

I missed Her something awful right then. A deep pain, a stabbing right under my heart. It hurt, Jesus Christ, it hurt.

I thought I saw something out of the corner of my eye. Some kind of shadow, moving, just a darkness sliding out of place. I felt someone watching me, and I knew that me and Roy were not here alone.

Roy lurched up from the hammock. His eyes were wide, his mouth all twisted like a gargoyle's. I could see his gums, his teeth bared at me, the veins in his neck bulging. He whipped his hands around him, like he'd walked through a spiderweb, like he was ripping the threads from his face.

"No," he screamed. "Get away from me."

I didn't know what to do. He thrashed about in the hammock, hollering. I was scared he'd tip us over. I reached my hand out to his face.

"Roy," I whispered. "Shhhh. It's me. It's Clare."

Roy's whole body shook. He panted little short breaths, gasps for air. I ran my fingers soft across his cheeks, calming him.

"Calm down, now. It's okay. You're here with me."

He looked at me, eyes wide like he had no idea where he was.

"I had a nightmare," he said.

"I could tell."

"I feel awful," he said. "I feel . . ."

Roy vomited off the hammock. It splattered all over the dirt. He groaned. I patted his head.

"Sorry," he said.

I sighed.

"It's okay. Come on, I'll help you up."

It was getting full-on dark now. My mom and stepdad were supposed to be gone for another hour or two, but you never could tell with them.

"You want to tell me about that nightmare of yours?"

"I don't know if you want to hear it," he said. "It was kind of a doozy."

"Tell me another time, then."

"I will."

Roy tried to stand up and then vomited again. I rubbed his back while he puked it all out.

"Sorry," I said. "I didn't think we drank enough for this."

"This would probably be the most embarrassing moment of my life if I wasn't too sick to feel embarrassed."

I had to laugh a little at that.

Roy finished puking and I led him back through the woods, to where we had stashed his bike. But when I got to the house, Mom's car was parked crookedly in the driveway, the driver's-side door hanging open.

"Oh shit," I said. "They're home."

"You going to get caught?" he said.

I shook my head.

"They're wasted, Roy. I mean, look at that parking job. No way they noticed I wasn't home. Besides, I set up precautions."

I pointed up to my window, where a lamp glowed. Faintly you could hear music playing.

"I left a light on, a record on repeat. If they're drunk, they'll leave me be. They only fight with each other when they're drunk."

"Alright," he said. "I'm real sorry for puking."

"It's fine, Roy."

Roy got on his bike and shook his head at me, and I wondered if he'd blow chunks again. But Roy held it in, pedaling off into the night. I waved goodbye to him, but he didn't see me.

I should have probably hurried up to my room quick as I could, lest Larry come out for a beer or something. But I was curious. I walked around the side of the house, to where my mom's bedroom was. The curtains had drifted aside and there was a light on. I peeked in.

Mom was in her underwear, a black lacy bra and panties. She looked beautiful, in a way I hadn't seen her look before. Mom smiled, but sadly, while my stepdad lay on the floor, stark naked, weeping, kissing her feet. She reached a hand down and laid it on top of his head, like she was blessing him.

I had no idea what to think about that.

I snuck in through the back door and made it all the way up to my room.

I WAS PRETTY FREAKED OUT BY MOM

and Larry. It was kind of one of those things you don't yet have words for, that you just see and something deep changes in you. It happens to nearly everyone I bet, the moment you finally know that you'll never escape sadness, that being an adult just means despair. It made me scared that there was nothing on the other side of life waiting for me but misery, stalking like a wolf in the darkness.

I wouldn't let that be my life. I would fight that, somehow. I knew there was a way to live differently than Mom had, a way to choose my life so it wouldn't be a failure. I remembered how happy I had been with Her, how much She had protected me in my life, kept me from loneliness. Because loneliness was the kind of thing that made Mom take up with guys who weren't good enough for her. Loneliness was probably what drove Larry to drink in the first place.

All this just served to get me focused again. I had to find Her, and fast. Tonight was as good a night as any to search for the Wish House.

Mom and Larry were definitely wasted, and once they passed out they'd sleep through anything. I waited until about midnight, until I could hear them both snoring. I snuck into their room and took a peek. They lay on separate sides of the bed, all the way on the edges, as if they couldn't bear the thought of accidentally touching in the night. It made me sad for my mom, who had come through so much. Another guy who turned out to be half of what she thought he'd be. I wondered if that would always happen to Mom, if that was just a pattern she couldn't escape.

Larry's pants were on the floor, discarded in a hurry. I tried not to remember what I'd seen earlier. I fished the keys out of his pocket and eased the door shut. I coasted the car down the driveway and cranked the engine once I reached the road. The sky was dark but clear, and the stars glimmered faintly above me. The moon was at its quietest, just a bright line in the sky. It was a perfect driving night. I kept the windows down and the music off, listening.

Night could make even a shitty neighborhood like ours something special. It wasn't much of a developed area, just a house here and there among deeper patches of wood. When Mom first started bringing Larry around, he would always talk about how the neighborhood "had potential."

"If they can ever get the economy up and running," Larry would say, "like it was thirty, forty years back—in the Simpkins days when this town was thriving—maybe we'd have something here. Shoot, all this land? Somebody would want to develop it."

It got a little annoying after a while, but it was nice to hear that something we had could get better. Larry had a good job selling insurance and he was real sweet to Mom, even if he wasn't the most attractive guy. He even made an effort to get along with me, though I could tell he didn't like me too much. He'd take me comic-book shopping sometimes, laugh when I picked up something weird like *Hellblazer* or *Pretty Deadly* or *Johnny the Homicidal Maniac*.

"Your mom lets you read this crap?" he'd say, and I would nod.

Even if I wasn't a perfect kid, Larry didn't seem to mind a whole lot. I was pretty happy that Mom decided to marry him, and even more so when he decided to move in with us.

"My place just isn't big enough for all of us," he said. "It would be easier if I just shacked up with y'all."

My grandfather built our house and left it to Dad when he died. I figured it would be weird for Larry, living in our old house, all our memories of Dad floating around the house like ghosts, but he seemed to adjust okay. I was thrilled. I loved that house. My whole life had happened there. It was awful to think of who I would have become if only we'd moved when Dad died, if we'd lived somewhere else entirely. I had a feeling things were finally going to take a turn for the better.

Of course She didn't believe that, not for a second.

Larry is a scoundrel, She said.

"That's harsh," I said. "Mom really likes him."

No, it isn't. He's a scoundrel. You'll see. You'll find out soon enough.

"You're wrong," I insisted.

Wait and see.

I knew I'd made Her mad. I could feel Her skulking around

inside me all day, and it made me nervous. It wasn't often that She was wrong about these kinds of things.

But for about a year, all was well with Larry. Mom kept getting prettier and prettier, as if being loved made her bloom. It was a beautiful thing to see. Our house felt warm again, and we all laughed a lot. I wondered if this could be a good place, if we could all maybe one day be happy together. For a while, it actually seemed possible.

Things only started going to shit when Larry lost his job.

I never found out why they fired him. Mom wouldn't tell me. It seemed like it was over something distasteful, though, like maybe he was scamming money from people. I remember Larry drinking, which he'd never done around us before. Mom wouldn't have married an alcoholic, not after struggling so hard with Dad. But Larry would get drunk and cry. He started getting fat, and Mom started to wither again. She started doing her nervous-hands thing that she always did when Dad would go off for days and not come back. Worst of all, she started drinking, even though she swore to me a long time ago she never would again.

I don't really think I could ever forgive Larry for that.

I only had a vague idea of where I was driving. The memory of the night when She walked me back from the Wish House gates was like a dream, the darks too dark, the roads too long and curvy to ever be actual roads. Even the kind lady who stopped for me seemed unreal, her face blurry, her mannerisms all stolen from an actress on TV. The only concrete details I had were passing Little John's gas station, and again, later, passing my aunt Pattie's house.

Aunt Pattie wasn't really my aunt, of course. I didn't have

any extended family. She was just my mom's best friend, and every now and then we'd go over to visit. But she died when I was twelve. Sometimes it seemed like no good thing could last if you were me or my mom. The people we loved either were taken from us or changed into something worse. It was like we were cursed.

Soon I was ten miles out, turning down country roads, driving deep into the night. The trail had gone cold a little while back. Landscapes change so much, with buildings torn down and strip malls shooting up, just to fall abandoned a year later. Trailer homes ravaged by tornadoes and time and plain old rot. I saw a family of raccoons wander single file into a gutter. Critters could make a home anywhere, I guessed.

I passed bait shops and churches, endless churches, banks and gas stations. I passed dead ends and cul-de-sacs. I passed gated communities and the mansion we all said belonged to a secret drug dealer in town. But nothing seemed right, nothing felt like a call to magic.

I began to get tired. With the windows rolled down, I let myself swelter in the night heat. He's out there, I told myself, and he wants to see me. The One Wish Man wants to see me. He needs me.

I didn't know why, but that seemed true: the One Wish Man needs me. I repeated it, I held it close to me like a talisman, I let the words guide me like a dowsing rod toward hidden water.

My fingers went slack on the wheel, and the memories kept in my muscles and blood and bones took over. I let myself coast slowly, drifting from lane to lane, my eyes dimming. A low night fog crept over the road. I was getting closer. I turned down a gravel road, unmarked. The trees loomed overhead like elder guardians and the moon snuffed itself out like a candle.

A black shape slammed into my windshield.

I swerved the car, almost into a ditch on the side of the road. The windshield was splattered with blood and I couldn't see through it. I yanked the wheel the opposite way. The back tires spun out, cutting gashes in the dirt road. A creature was caught in the wipers, mashing its wings into the glass. I finally skidded the car to a stop, just in front of a massive oak tree.

I let my breathing calm, my heart slow itself. I was fine. I hadn't died. I hadn't wrecked the car. My stepdad would never know I'd taken it. The wounded creature beat feebly against the windshield, its blood matting in clumps. I had to figure out what I'd hit and put it out of its misery.

I stepped out of the car, knees shaky. The road was pitch-black on either side, the tree limbs forming a canopy overhead, like I was in a tunnel, like I had somehow burrowed deep into the night itself. The dark was alive with bugs and tree frogs and hidden groaning things, the invisible army that gathered in the woods every night. I bent over the bloody windshield.

It was a bat. Its head busted open, its wings ragged and torn, its body not much bigger than my fist. Somehow I'd hit it. I never knew you could hit a bat with a car before. They had sonar, didn't they? They were blind but they could see in the dark. How had I managed to smack this one?

It squealed at me, that weird chirping hymn of bats. I had to free it. I had to let it die untangled.

I grabbed it by the body, careful to keep my fingers from its mouth. The bat could be sick—it could have rabies. I shouldn't be doing this, I thought. I shouldn't be touching it at all. It struggled in my fist as I pulled the wing out from the windshield wiper. It chittered and shook, it fought me, but I got it free. I carried it over to the side of the road, hopping over the ditch, and I set it in the leaves to die.

I didn't know why, but I said a prayer over it. I had been possessed by a demon, but I wasn't sure if I believed in God, even though I knew She believed in God. She was fearful of him, with a kind of awe. I couldn't picture God, something so huge and so scary and supposedly filled with love. I couldn't picture the Father of the World stretching his big arms out, ready to receive all the sick and the dying. I couldn't picture anything caring that much.

"God or whoever, take this bat into your arms," I prayed. "Take it into your kingdom and give it rest. Amen."

The bat died. Or at least it stopped moving. I figured something would come along and eat it soon enough. That or it would be gnarled by ants, whittled into bone by a million invisible teeth. I could think of worse ways to go.

As I stood in the woods that night, fog laid out like a carpet at my feet, I felt a tingly feeling, like little silvery stars falling down my spine.

I wasn't alone. Someone was watching me.

I listened, but there was no crack of limbs or crunch of leaves, not even a night bird's call in the darkness. Only my own breath, and the low hum of the car engine. I tried to look out into the woods, but I couldn't see anything, not even with the car headlights. They only seemed to light up the trees. In front of me stood the giant oak, bigger and wider and taller than all the rest, the elder brother of the forest, bent-backed and leering over me. Then I caught my breath.

Because the car beams illuminated the trunk of that tree. On its bark was carved deep—no, *burned*—the outline of a bird. Wings spread wide, head back, like it was flying away. This was it. I'd found it.

The gateway to the Wish House.

I REMEMBER ONE DAY SPENT WITH HER

at the Hidden Place, one of the best days of my whole life. It could only have been a few hours, because Mom woke me up afterward for supper, said I had been daydreaming all afternoon. But the time to me had seemed weeks and weeks. We lay in the weeds and felt the sun on our bare stomachs and I asked Her a question.

"How old are you?"

As old as never, She said, *and as young as always.*

"That doesn't make sense."

She shrugged.

Time isn't my concern.

"How does it feel to be so old," I said.

Oh, I'm not old, She said. *I'm always. It's much different.*

"You look like a little girl to me."

I am a little girl. That's the always part of me.

"But why?" I said. "Don't you want to be older? Don't you want to be able to do anything you want?"

You won't say that when you're older. You'll wish you were still like me, always and never, an eight-year-old girl on top of a mountain.

She hopped to Her feet.

Want to see something amazing?

I nodded and She pulled me up by the hand. We walked to the bare edge of the cliff. I had to shield my eyes from the sun. A wide spiral of birds uncurled itself over the waves and I wondered where they were heading.

Not the birds, She said. *Look.*

And from far off on the horizon a ship passed this way, something like a Spanish galleon from a picture book, eight wide white sails billowing in the wind. I watched in awe as it crested a wave and spray exploded from its side, the sun glinting off its cannons.

"When are we?" I said.

She smiled at me and took my hand.

Always, She said. *And never.*

THAT NIGHT WHEN I GOT HOME I couldn't hardly sleep.

I knew somewhere far off in the world She was there, dragging Herself through wilderness, calling out to me. When Roy's dad cast Her out he must have built a boundary between me and Her, some sort of supernatural wall with his words, like he was a king and he had banished Her from me. I needed someone to break down that wall, to summon Her back. All roads pointed to the One Wish Man, and now I had found the doorway into his world.

But how was I supposed to make it work? I'd spent an hour at the Bird Tree tracing my finger over the scars, hollering out into the darkness for the One Wish Man to open his path to me. Because there was nothing beyond that tree but scrub. Nowhere to go but wandering, and I knew by wandering I could never find the Wish House.

Around three A.M. I'd driven back to Little John's truck stop and gassed up. I used the squeegee next to the pump to clean the bat blood off the windshield so Larry wouldn't know I'd taken the car. It took a while, and a lot of scrubbing, but I got it all off. I coasted the car back into the driveway, engine off, and parked it just how he left it. I didn't dare try to sneak the keys back into his pants pocket, so I left them on the kitchen counter, as conceivable a place for a drunk to leave them as any. The moon vanished in the brightening sky and the sun spilled its gold over the hills. I smoked a morning cigarette and thought about it.

There was only one person I knew who I was pretty sure had been to see the One Wish Man. Only one other person in the whole world who might know what I was supposed to do next.

I had to find Kevin Henrikson.

That week my mom joined a carpool for nurses at the hospital. She said she hoped it would save us gas money, and maybe she could even make some friends.

"They have a little group," Mom said. "These girls go to movies with each other, have a glass of wine and play cards. It sounds nice."

I guess I'd never realized how lonesome Mom was. I'd try to do better by her in the future. Still, I was excited. This meant that a few days a week she would leave her car at our house during the day. Mom only had a few hiding places, so I could find the spare key no problem. So long as I gassed up, I now had access to a car for nearly half the week. Since we didn't have the Internet anymore and there were no Henriksons in the phone book, my first stop was the library.

The Simpkins Memorial Library—named after Myna Simpkins, the old mayor's grandmother—was a crazy place during the weekday. It was mostly homeless folks checking their e-mail, or else asleep in the cubicles. It made me sad a little, that there was nowhere else for destitute folks to go. But at least they had somewhere, right? And maybe the books over there on the shelves would provide a little comfort.

I found an empty computer. The keyboard was sticky from spilled Coke but it worked okay. I googled every Kevin Henrikson in my area, hoping like mad something would pop up. Maybe he still lived around here. I had a million things to ask him.

But I found nothing on the Internet about this particular Kevin Henrikson. No Facebook, no picture, nothing. If he died, there would be an obituary I could track down. I would have to search through all the old town newspapers that weren't online. Maybe there was a separate database somewhere for that.

I walked up to one of the librarians working, a fifty-ish, squatty woman named Mrs. Jenkins. She squinted at me.

"Hi there," I said.

"Got you more of those horror movies you're always checking out?"

"Not today," I said. "Actually I was just wondering if y'all had a backlog of the county newspaper. You know, like a box full of all the old issues or something?"

Mrs. Jenkins wet her lips and smiled at me.

"You know what you are?" she said.

I shook my head.

"You're in luck, that's what you are. We had boxes and boxes of old newspapers in the back, maybe two hundred boxes total, and we had to clean them out to make room for new computers.

That's just how it goes. We were going to have to throw it all out. Imagine that, all that history, just—*poof!* And gone."

"That would be awful," I said.

"Sure would," she said. "Mighty durn awful, if you ask me. Except it didn't happen. No sirree."

"You didn't throw away all the old newspapers?"

"'Course we did. Got all that grant money for new computers, and we couldn't let it just go to waste, could we? But we didn't lose the history. See, this Boy Scout come up here, asking if there's something he could do for a service project. Wanted to make Eagle Scout, understand? Had to do a service project, take up to a hundred man-hours, he said. So I said, 'Well, boy, how about you start scanning up all them newspapers we got back there?' And you know what? He did it, bless his heart. I got it all on a computer in the back. PDFs. Searchable, too."

Mrs. Jenkins got up from the desk and motioned for me to follow her. She led me through a locked door and into a room with what looked like an overcrowded office desk. Piles and piles of books and papers and Diet Coke cans and gas station food wrappers. In the midst of the chaos sat an old Gateway computer.

"It gets messy in here sometimes," she said. "But it's all on that machine right there. I haven't uploaded it to the network yet. Frankly I just don't know how. I'm hoping another Boy Scout comes along, one who's good with computers. Now you just go right ahead and search to your heart's content."

"Thanks."

"'Course, darlin'. Not many people care much about the past. We don't get folks your age in here. It's either the elderly, or parents come in with their hollering little devil kids. Feel more like a social worker than a librarian most days. But that's life, ain't it?"

"I guess so."

"Sure it is. You'll find out soon enough," she said. "It don't go the way you think it should, but it goes alright. I'll be up front if you need anything."

I waited till Mrs. Jenkins was gone. She didn't shut the door, which was annoying, but I could deal with it. I sat down at the computer and typed in Kevin's name.

The computer was slow, and it took a decent while to open everything and load the results. I waited with equal parts excitement and dread. Maybe Kevin had just gone quiet, off the grid, living a simple life somewhere, painting maybe. I would hate it if he gave up on his art. Or else something horrible had happened to him. I didn't know why I thought it had to be one of those two extremes, but in my mind there was no other way it could go.

Eventually an article did pop up, but it felt like a kick in the belly.

It was a short little article called "Local Teen Struck by Car." Kevin Henrikson was dead.

It kept to the basics: a kid named Kevin Henrikson was hit by a car off Highway 7 while attempting to cross the road. He died instantly. He was eighteen years old at the time. Kevin was survived by his father and mother. There wasn't much to it other than that.

I thanked Mrs. Jenkins and walked outside. My hands shook and it was hard for me to light a cigarette. I leaned up against a shady spot on the library wall and lingered there a minute, pretending to be busy, my sunglasses on so no one could see me crying.

So Kevin was dead, after all that. I finally thought I would have someone to talk to about Her, someone who would understand. This made the orange notebook more precious, like the last living testament of some fucked-up kid who knew what it was like to be me. I was even more grateful to have it now.

"I'll take good care of your notebook, Kevin," I whispered to nobody. "I'll protect your drawings, all your art."

I don't know why, but that made me feel a little bit better.

I still didn't know what to do about the Bird Tree, or how to find the Wish House. She said the gates would open *when the bird becomes real*. What in the hell did that even mean? Did it work like a trapdoor, some sort of lever you could pull on the tree and a bird would hop out like a deranged magic trick? Was "magic" even the right word for all this?

I didn't understand at all. But maybe I knew someone else who would.

THE SIGN ON MISS MATHIS'S DOOR SAID

MADAM IS PRESENT, so I just walked on in. I found her in her easy chair, sunglasses on, smoking a cigarette, sipping on something from a big silver goblet. The radio buzzed jazz music.

"To what do I owe the pleasure?" said Miss Mathis.

"Just come to check in on you," I said.

"Sure you did. Christ, you got to be lonely to come see me."

Well, she had me there.

Miss Mathis took a gulp from her goblet. "Sit on down, go ahead. Not like I have anything to do today."

I saw the scroll unbound, lying on the coffee table, next to a half-eaten donut. It made me gag in my mouth a little.

"Any luck with that?" I said.

"Not a bit," she said. "It's all carved up in some alchemic code I can't make heads or tails of. All the old wizards did shit like that. Like magic was some good-old-boys' club you just had to hack your way into from the get-go."

"You'll crack it, I'm sure."

"Thanks for the faith, missy, but it don't do much good. There's got to be some kind of an alphabet to the thing, a key for translating it. If only I could find it." She gestured with her cigarette over to a pile of leather-bound ancient-looking volumes stacked in the corner, yellow scraps of paper bookmarking all of them. "It ain't like I haven't been trying. Wish Cléa was here. That girl was smarter than I'll ever be."

"How did you meet Cléa?"

"Same as I met you. By happenstance. By fate. By whatever it is that draws all us touched folk together."

"Touched?"

"You don't have to lie to me, girl. I know you've met something from the other side. I can see its fingerprints all over you."

I didn't want to talk about Her to Miss Mathis. Something in my heart told me that would be dangerous. But I was happy that Miss Mathis could see Her on me. I was so happy I still carried a trace of Her with me around.

"Fine," said Miss Mathis. "Keep your secrets. As for me and Cléa, well. I introduced her to this life, helped her follow in her mama's footsteps. Cléa was about the most natural mystic I ever known. Didn't hardly have to teach her a thing. Just sort of pointed her in the right direction, so to speak. Or the wrong one. Rest in peace, honey."

Miss Mathis lifted her goblet and drank.

"Is that why Uncle Mike hates you so much?" I said.

"Wouldn't you?" she said. "I mean, the only person who hates me more than him is me, and that's saying something."

Miss Mathis hacked up a glob and spit it on the floor. The dog yawned.

"Enough about me," she said. "Why the hell do you look so glum?"

I fidgeted a little. Why was it so much easier talking about Her to Roy than it was to Miss Mathis?

"I lost a friend," I said.

"Haven't we all." Miss Mathis raised her goblet in a toast. "And we all will. We'll lose everyone. And they'll all lose you. Just the way of it." She coughed so long, I thought I should get up and pat her on the back or something. "No, no, sit down. I'm not dying yet."

We were quiet a minute. The radio and the cigarette smoke and the dog napping on the floor.

"Of course, Cléa and I weren't the only ones," said Miss Mathis. "There were loads of us practicing back then. I myself picked it up from a slew of lovers I had in the early seventies, back when I was into the cocaine."

I didn't know what to say to that.

"Don't look so shocked, little girl. Miss Mathis was quite the wild one in her time. Of course, we all were back then, the circle I ran in. Awful big circle for such a small town, mind you. This town has a pull to it, understand? Ever since it was founded, since the beginning. It's a magnet for mystical types, the occult, all that. Good business, too. You couldn't hardly be anyone notable in this town unless you took part. Corruption starts at the top, and don't you forget it. Ritual and sex and money all go hand in hand, for good or bad. Mostly bad. Orgies, that sort of thing. Never took part in that garbage. Dangerous, I say. Bad juju."

"Orgies?"

"It's a fancy word for a bunch of people taking what they ought not to have and then sharing it."

"I know what an orgy is."

"'Course you do. Probably learned about it on the goddamn Internet. That thing's worse magic than any spell the devil ever conjured up."

I figured I might as well just go for it.

"Miss Mathis, have you ever heard of someone called the One Wish Man?"

"The what?"

"He's this guy who lives in this big house off in the woods, past where people normally go. I mean deep in there, no road or anything. You can't even find it unless you know what you're looking for already. It's called the Wish House."

Miss Mathis looked grave a moment. Then she busted out laughing, half knocking the glasses off her face. The laugh led to another coughing fit. I sat there and waited it out, embarrassed and a little annoyed.

"The Wish House," she said. "What are you, a seven-year-old? A man in the woods, granting wishes. That's the stupidest thing I ever heard of."

I scowled at her. "You don't have to be such a dick about it."

Miss Mathis sat up straight and adjusted her sunglasses. The cigarette was all ashes in her fingers.

"It appears I have offended my guest," she said. "Well, I apologize, Clare dear. But no, not in all my mystic ramblings have I ever heard of such a place like that."

We talked a minute longer, but my heart wasn't in it. Pretty soon I got up to leave.

I CAME HOME WITH A HEAD FULL OF

questions and no one to talk to. Mom was at the hospital, Roy was with his dad, and what was I supposed to do? I couldn't even get Eyeball to play with me. It was times like this I missed Her the most. If She were here, we could have talked for hours about this stuff, told stories, turned it into a game. We could have watched a movie, a genius old horror film like *Basket Case* or *The Curse of the Cat People*, something She loved, and somehow I would fall asleep at the end of the night with all my questions answered and a dozen new ones sprung up to take their place.

Even if Miss Mathis thought it was stupid, I still believed in the One Wish Man. Kevin Henrikson did too, though I'd never get to ask him about it. And I still didn't have any idea how to open the Wish House gates.

The afternoon was hideously hot, that sort of swamped sweatiness that only happens in the deep South. Dogs hid in the shade, panting with their tongues out, birds were scarce, and even the mosquitoes flew slower. I stayed upstairs, my bedroom door shut, lights off, the air-conditioning cranked, while outside the sun glared down at me. Everything was too hot, too humid and wet. I didn't belong out there. It was like my room was the only bearable place left in the world.

I lay in bed and tried to put the pieces together. She had left me three clues, another game to play. I had solved two of them already. The "him" I was supposed to be nice to was Roy, and I was doing a pretty good job of that. Without Her around, Roy was maybe my only friend in the world. So, *nice*, yes, I had that one covered.

As for *Remember the stories*, that had to be about the One Wish Man. It was the only batch of stories She'd told me that made sense now that I actually had something to wish for. I had even found the gateway to his house, if only I could figure out how to open it. Maybe the bird was a lock, and there was a key out there somewhere. There had to be something.

Which left me with the final clue: *June 20*. It was only two weeks away. If I was supposed to do something on that day, I was running out of time.

What was so great about June 20?

I checked the calendar my mom had hanging downstairs in the kitchen. It was pretty anachronistic to have a calendar hanging around now, with everyone having cell phones and all that, but Mom was pretty particular about it. She said it was a good way to "get the family on the same page." As if we were a family, as if there was any hope of us all agreeing on anything. Still, for her the calendar was important, and she picked a new one out each year.

This year's was all sailboats. Mom had always wanted to go sailing, but Larry hated the ocean, and besides, he was allergic to shellfish. We went to the beach once for a few days, Gulf Shores in Alabama. Mom was so excited. I only liked the beach at night, when the ocean sunk right into the sky in one big blackness so that you couldn't tell the difference between them. I wouldn't even go out on the sand if the sun was out. Still, I'm pretty sure it was the best weekend of Mom's life. She wore this big straw hat and sunglasses and sat under an umbrella all day. At night she'd lie on the bed next to a sunburned Larry and me pouting off in the corner and she'd smile and say, "Isn't this nice?" It was enough to break your heart, and those were the good days. Even with Mom and Larry working regularly again, we were always somehow almost broke. The beach would never happen again, and sailing was impossible. All Mom had left was her calendar.

Which, of course, was blank on June 20.

Except for a few grey letters in tiny print: *Summer Solstice*.

I didn't even really know what that meant. In books and stories, the solstice was when witches held black masses, or maybe the druids slaughtered a virgin or two. That was a magic holiday, right? I didn't feel like driving back to the library, so I looked it up in my dad's old *Encyclopædia Britannica* from the '80s. Mom kept them up in the attic, even though Larry wanted them thrown out.

"Why?" Mom always said. "They're culture."

Larry just wanted them gone because they were my dad's, but he wouldn't say that out loud. So Mom hid them away, and like everything she hid, I eventually found them.

I loved the musty smell of the old editions, the tiny print and the full-color pictures. I loved reading out-of-date information, present-tense stories about people who were long dead. I loved seeing the way people thought things would turn out. Articles on countries that didn't even exist anymore. It was like living in an alternate universe every time you opened one up.

I pulled out the "S" volume and got to searching.

Turned out summer solstice was the longest day of the year, the time the sun shone brightest. It meant that every day after that would get a little bit shorter, until deep into winter. It meant that it was the last of the sun days, and the beginning of the moon nights. All kinds of pagan stuff happened on the solstice. In pre-Christian times, it was a pretty big deal. That led me to an article on Midsummer's Eve, a whole new volume plucked out of the pile. That was an ancient fertility festival still celebrated in some places, with ceremonial bonfires and everything, a time when nature was at its greatest power.

Holy shit. This was it.

Maybe the gateway—that beautiful bird scarred into the great oak tree, its big living arms stretched out over the road—would be open on the summer solstice. Why else would She have written that day of all days? It was worth a try. I just had to make sure I had access to a car that night.

I went searching and found my stepdad's spare key along with two thousand in twenties tucked into a colorful pair of socks in his drawer. There was no way Mom knew about this secret stash. She was always so worried about money. No, Larry was holding out on her, which meant he was even more of a shithead than I thought. Part of me wanted to rob him blind, right then and there.

It would have been so easy. I didn't do it, though. I had plenty of cash on my own, from Miss Mathis. Also, knowing Larry, he probably counted it all every night after Mom went to bed.

Miss Mathis didn't seem to care about money, like it was just something she'd conjured up earlier in the morning, millions more where that came from. The way Miss Mathis talked, this whole town used to be filled with magic folks, occultists and witches and all that. I always knew there was something strange about this place, something wrong with our town.

All the clues were falling into place now. And in two weeks I would meet the One Wish Man.

I WENT TO THE BIRD TREE EVERY

chance I got. Day or night, it didn't matter, just so long as I had access to a car. Partly it was to memorize the way, but also to check and see if the gates had opened early, if the bird had become real. I didn't know how it would happen, or even what that actually meant. But I watched for it eagerly, waiting and hoping.

Also, I dreamed. In my sleep I'd see the bird erupt from the tree in feathers of grey and gold, or a burst in wild squawking colors like a parrot, and it would take off in a rainbow of swirls to the sky. Some dreams it perched on a branch, common as a robin but alert with some sort of ancient knowledge, a guide bird sent to lead the way. In others the carving simply stepped out of itself, a ghost bird, see-through as smoke. Always it was a thing of wonder, an omen of awe and joy. It could be striped like a barber pole or luminescent blue like a jellyfish, an uninvented bird, a wide-winged pterodactyl, a dignified medieval falcon sent out by his lord. In my best dreams it was a snowy owl who turned its face around to watch me pass.

Some days I brought Roy with me, too.

The first time, we were driving around in my mom's car, just killing the daylight. Roy's dad had been busy lately, he said, spending long hours in his study at the church. Roy said he'd never seen his dad so preoccupied before.

"It's weird," he said. "It's not like he's usually some kind of workaholic or anything."

"Well, at least it gives us more time to be together," I said.

"Yeah," he said. "I guess there's an upside to being neglected."

Roy meant it as a joke, but I saw a twinge of hurt there, too. That's okay. I knew exactly how that felt. I squeezed his hand and he smiled at me.

I asked Roy for the hundredth time what he wanted from the One Wish Man.

"I'd ask for ten million dollars," he said, "in small, unmarked bills to be delivered under my bed in a black suitcase, like in the movies."

"Boring," I said.

"Okay. I'd like to have yesterday back. All I did was sit on my front porch and eat pork rinds. I'd like to do that and never get fat. Maybe have some Peach Nehi, too."

"You're terrible at this."

"I'd love to be good at an instrument. The guitar, maybe?"

"Come on, Roy. Isn't there something else you want? I mean, something you really, *really* want?"

"Why?" said Roy. "It's just a game, right?"

"I got a surprise for you," I said, and whipped the car around.

We drove glad and laughing past Little John's, down the

country roads. I was so happy I even let Roy pick the music. He put on the Replacements.

"I like when he sings, 'Jesus rides beside me. He never buys any smokes.'"

"Why's that?" I said.

"I don't know," he said. "It makes all this okay. Like Jesus really is here, beside me, bumming a cigarette."

"Speaking of which, you want one?"

"Are you kidding?" he said. "My dad would kill me."

We parked and sat in the car, windows down, the light making crazy shadow patterns from the leaves. I was happy there, the two of us alone.

"What's so special about here?" said Roy.

I pointed at the Bird Tree.

"Wow," he said. "Did you do that?"

"No way. I think lightning did it. I think it was burned there by magic."

Roy laughed a little.

"I'm serious," I said. "This is a magic tree."

"Sure it is," he said. "It's a regular burning bush."

"Laugh all you want," I said. "But this is it, Roy. This is the gateway to the Wish House."

"You got to be kidding me, Clarabella," he said. "You mean, if you just head off in that direction, you'll bump into the giant mansion of wishes granted, all kinds of folks in suits partying it up, getting their hearts' desires?"

"Yep," I said. "Only, the Bird Tree has to wake up first. The bird has to become real. That's how you know the gates are open.

Then you got to picture in your mind just exactly what it is you're wishing for and want it with all your heart. That's the only way you can get to the Wish House."

Roy looked at me, his eyebrows squinched up a little.

"You really believe this stuff, don't you?" he said.

"I do. Very much."

It was an important moment. If Roy laughed it off, if he thought all this was ridiculous, I didn't know if I could still be around him anymore. Besides, it didn't seem too out of the realm of his church world stuffed full of miracles, of old ladies speaking in tongues and demons flung out of people with the right words spoken. And I think Roy realized that. I think he knew just how much I was counting on it all being true.

"Fine," he said. "I believe it, too."

"Get over here," I said, and crawled myself into the back seat. Roy followed me, bumping his head on the ceiling. When he sat down next to me he hunched his shoulders, like he was embarrassed.

"What's wrong?" I said.

"I don't know if this is a good idea."

"Shh," I said, and kissed him. It was our second kiss.

Roy was tense at first, but soon he relaxed, soon he was holding me and kissing me back. I felt him grow braver. His hands moved over me and I let them, I didn't stop where he wanted to touch.

It was the electricity of the place, a hope of magic and possibility, maybe the end of loneliness forever.

After a minute Roy laid his head on my shoulder, buried his

face deep in my neck and kissed me there. I could feel it coming, feel the want rise up in me, the good warmth filling up all the cold and dark inside me. So maybe I did something I shouldn't have.

I reached down and touched him.

Roy jerked back from me like I had poked a dagger at him.

"I'm sorry," I said.

"I just don't know if it's right."

"Why?"

"I'm supposed to become a reverend, you know? Like my dad. So I have to be righteous. I have to do things the right way."

"Like what?"

"Like not do that stuff until I'm married."

"You really believe all that?"

"I mean, yeah. Dad made me sign a contract at youth group about it. A purity contract, where I swore before God and everybody else I'd keep it in my pants until marriage."

This was too much.

"Are you fucking serious, Roy?"

"I know that seems crazy," he said. "But it's a big deal to my dad, to my church and all that." Roy ran his hand through his hair in the same gesture I'd seen his dad do on the day they stole Her from me. I'd never seen that resemblance in them before, and it made me want to puke a little. "Look, please don't be mad at me. I want to do more with you, I'm just scared."

"Why? Is it because of me?"

"Of course not," he said. "I think you're amazing. I've never met anyone like you in my whole life. I'm just scared. I'm scared of how mad my dad would get if he ever found out. I'm scared that God would be mad too, and maybe He'd stop blessing me or something. I'm scared of all the bad stuff that could happen."

I should have known it would be like that with Roy. Who knew what kind of baggage his dad had filled his head with, all the guilt he felt? But there were worse things than guys who wanted to wait for true love. I knew that fact firsthand.

"Okay then," I said. "We don't have to do anything else."

"Really?"

He seemed relieved.

"I'm trying to be good," he said. "To do things right. I've never done anything like this before. You know, kissing and all that."

"Well, if it makes you feel any better, I haven't exactly either."

"For real?" he said, with enough surprise in his voice that it hurt my feelings. I crawled off him and back to the driver's seat and fired up the car.

I drove way too fast out of the woods. We were both mad, and uncomfortable. About halfway through the ride he reached out and took my hand. That was good. I needed that.

I reminded myself that I only started being nice to him because She asked me to, that all of this was just part of Her plan that I didn't quite understand yet. Sure, I liked him a lot, and he was without a doubt the best human friend I'd ever had in my life. But maybe he was starting to mean too much to me. It probably wasn't a good idea for me to get involved with Roy, not in that kind of romantic way. I didn't quite think that was what She had in mind. So yes, we could stop with the touching and the kissing and all that. Roy was right, it wasn't a good idea.

•

But me and Roy didn't stop. Not even close.

The more chances we had to be alone together, the more time we spent touching and kissing and doing other stuff. Even when we didn't intend to let anything happen, it always did. It was like our bodies were drawn to each other in a way that our brains weren't quite conscious of. I marveled how quickly a laugh could turn into a kiss, how I would press my face into his neck without even thinking about it, how I didn't stop him whenever he put his arm around me and pulled me toward him. Every time it felt inevitable—fated even—that our bodies would touch.

The Bird Tree became our spot. A place we could go to be alone and figure each other out. It was a freedom space. I could smoke all the cigarettes and listen to all the music I wanted. I had plenty of money for gas because of Miss Mathis's thousand. Even if we only had an hour or two free, if Roy could manage an afternoon out of visiting the sick with his dad, we took the chance.

I think in those ten days Roy and I made maybe six trips to the Bird Tree. They were some of my favorite times I'd ever had. Each afternoon we'd make out for a while, push it a little bit further every time. Twice I wound up with my shirt off, my bra unclasped. We were moving toward something, and I think we both knew it.

But Roy would always stop at the last possible moment. Part of me was frustrated. The hungry part, the empty part that my hours with Roy seemed to fill up. But I was also glad too, when I let myself admit it. In the moments before it got dark and we had to drive back, when the light was at its most golden, I would shut my eyes and see the carved bird spring to life, spread its wings full-feathered and rise. I longed for it to lead me down the path into a new world, a new dream, a house of wishes with Her at the end of it, waiting for me. Then I wouldn't need Roy anymore. Then I would never need anyone else again.

On the night before the summer solstice, I was on the phone talking with Roy, same as always. His dad was preaching at some kind of retreat coming up, and Roy was supposed to preach, too. They'd be gone almost a week. There would be healing services and speaking in tongues and all kinds of things, probably even casting out demons. I kept my peace about that part of it, even though it was hard. I asked Roy if he was nervous about preaching.

"It's almost like an act," he said. "You stand up there and talk yourself up same as you talk up the crowd. We rehearse everything beforehand, me and Dad. I have so much scripture in my head it's easy, you know? Like I have my lines memorized and I'm just performing in a play."

"Do you like doing it?" I said.

"I think so. I mean, it's what I've always wanted to do, be a reverend like my dad. It's what he's raised me for. And I'm pretty good at it. That's what the old ladies at church tell me. They say I have an 'anointing,' that God has picked me out to be something special."

"But?"

"Well, it's just that lately I'm not sure. About being a reverend, I mean. Like maybe I could do some other stuff with my life. Maybe I could be good at other things."

"Like what?"

"Lots of stuff," he said. "I could join a band and travel the world."

"I didn't know you played anything."

"I don't. But I *could*, you know? I could buy a guitar and learn how to play it and maybe even get good. Music runs in my family. I can already sing okay. I guess I just never realized it was possible for me. I never realized I could be anything else but a minister. I didn't realize I could be much of anything until I met you."

I didn't know what to say. Roy had always been so serious, so sure of his place at his dad's side. I still despised Roy's dad for what he had done to me, and part of me loved the idea of Roy turning away from him someday. But I also didn't want to see Roy get hurt. I mean, I liked Roy. A lot. I wasn't just following Her orders anymore, I was doing what I wanted. No way I was faking that.

"Jesus, Roy," I said, "that means the world to me. But it shouldn't take me to teach you something like that. You should know on your own how great you are."

"I'm going to miss you," he said.

"I'll miss you, too."

It was true. I really would miss Roy. But I was also excited. Tomorrow was the summer solstice, and if I was right, that would be the day I saw the One Wish Man. He had power, he could fix things, I just knew it. Tomorrow would be the day I got Her back.

And I'd never be lonely again.

ONE AFTERNOON SHE AND I WERE AT

the Hidden Place, just talking, when a brace of rabbits burst through the heather. They were quick and brown and gone suddenly, dashed away into the swirling whirls of grass. For the millionth time I wondered what lay quiet in the Hidden Place, how much secret life was there in the flowers and weeds, biding its time.

"Sometimes I just want to run through all this grass with a stick," I said, "banging on everything, just to see what comes out. I mean, there are all kinds of caves and tunnels in the cliffs, right? I bet there's things here a thousand years old."

So? She said.

"So? I want to see what's down there. I want to see what's hidden all around me."

Do you, Clare? Are you really so sure about that?

"Of course I'm sure. Why wouldn't I?"

Because there are worlds here, silly, She said. *Places beyond places. You go tramping around, well . . .*

"Well what?"

This is not a regular place. It lies on the edge of things. Worlds beyond worlds, Clare. A convergence. She smiled at me, Her eyes mysterious as stars. *If you want to go barging into the grasslands, into the darkness of the caves, disturbing everything, be my guest. But there's no telling what you might wake up.*

IT WAS THE NIGHT OF JUNE 20, THE

summer solstice. Once Mom and Larry fell asleep, I slipped out of the house and coasted the car into a clear and wide-open night. I made it to the Bird Tree just before midnight. The moon was bright, and the tree branches dangled long above the road. I pulled over as near to the treeline as possible in case somebody else passed by. I was so excited I was shaking. I couldn't wait. This was finally it.

I shone my flashlight at the Bird Tree, my heart a moon full of hope.

The bird was there alright, a real bird, just like She said it would be. Except it wasn't the explosion of color I dreamed of, no wild-eyed toucan of jungle blues and greens, no darting hummingbird floating red and still, no wise unflappable owl gazing silent as a sentinel.

It was nothing like that at all.

A cardinal hung on the tree, wings spread wide, its head and feet dangling down, a nail through each wing. Crucified. Its blood ran down the bark in dark rivulets.

I stepped out of the car and peered closer at it. The cardinal was newly dead, not even yet begun to rot. Its head hung sorrowful, like a museum painting of a martyr.

I felt a darkness creep over me then, the eyes I felt always on my back now up close, a figure in the darkness, a creature whose breath was hot on my neck. I told myself that this was okay, and that things weren't always how they seemed. Besides, who said magic wasn't supposed to be a little bit scary?

I had to keep going. She was waiting for me.

I fixed Her firmly in my mind, my deepest heart's desire, my *Only*. I took one last glimpse at the soft burning moon and walked out of the road, the civilized world, and into the woods.

The trail was dark and long grown over. I got the feeling that it had once been regularly used, that people had stolen down this way many a dark night. Every thirty feet or so there were stones marking the way, strange figures scratched on them: an eye, a triangle, a spiral, an arrow. Tree branches crossed the pathway in long tangles, and moss hung down like veils. Creatures scurried all around me: the armies of grasshoppers and tree frogs singing off to something, the yellow flashes of animal eyes that flared up and were gone. Above me watched the angel-eyed stars.

My flashlight was borderline useless, the forest was so dense. Sometimes a tangle of moonlight would spill through the trees, but mostly I was in darkness. Even though I followed a path, rocks marking the way regular as headstones, I felt myself getting more and more lost.

I passed a big tree with three thick branches, white wounds on the bark of each, as if they had been burned by lightning. It was a cursed tree, I could feel it all over, they might as well have crucified Christ on that exact tree. One of the branches looped around on itself, hanging there like a noose, beckoning to me. I kept moving, surrounded by the lights of insect eyes, the buzz of secret wings, the windblown leaves and the night creatures scuttling across the forest floor.

I came to a long stretch where the path narrowed and the trees formed a dense wall on either side, so close it was tough to squeeze through. It felt like I was on a rickety old bridge, one that might slip or crack or sway and cast me off into oblivion forever. I knew that was ridiculous, that you couldn't fall through a patch of trees same as you would empty space. But it still felt that way, that the trees could swallow me whole, that beyond the leaves lay some horrible nowhere. This part of the path scared me more than anything that had come so far.

I took a deep breath and stepped forward. A breeze swirled around me, though I knew there wasn't any wind. I heard whispers in the air, *Clare, Clare, Clarabella*, like the voices knew me, like they had been waiting on me to come. Tree limbs clawed at my face like witch fingers. I snagged my shirt and for a second I couldn't move. I heard a slithering behind me, felt a chill on my neck, and breath, as someone whispered into my ear, *Have you come for me, my love?*

I ripped my shirt free and ran.

The voices louder now.

Calling for me.

Lights flickering off in the woods on either side of me.

Faces in the gloom.

Little boys and girls with weeping yellow eyes.

The trees crowded close to me and I couldn't find any way out.

I began to panic.

This smothering darkness all around me.

Clawing to keep me near.

I was stuck here, I knew it.

I was trapped with these grasping spirits forever.

A haze of a girl with long black hair appeared in front of me. She was ghostly, beautiful and somehow familiar. The girl smiled at me. I realized she didn't have any eyes, the sockets an empty black, and smoke poured out of them.

Don't stop, Clarabella, the girl said. *You must keep going.*

Trees snatched at me, the darkness gnashed its teeth, the spirits howled out their agony. The hazy girl took my hand, and it was somehow like I was holding a beam of light. *Don't look*, she whispered. *They're lying to you.* I followed where she led, my eyes shut tight, this ghostly girl guiding me. It was as if her blindness gave me peace, like not-seeing was the best way to navigate the altered world. Soon branches weren't clawing me anymore, and the voices had grown fainter, vanished into the mist.

Be brave, Clare, the girl whispered. *I will be watching you.*

I opened my eyes. I was alone.

Who was that girl, and where had she gone? It wasn't Her, I knew that. It was someone else. My hand still tingled from the light of her.

Soon the woods grew sparser, less brambly. The moon parted the clouds and threw its glow down on a clearing. I stepped through the treeline. There it stood before me.

The Wish House was massive. You could tell it went on for rooms and rooms. It sat grand and regal in the wallow of waist-high grass and brambles, some picture-postcard millionaire's mansion nestled away in a thicket. The windows glowed with light, and smoke billowed from the chimney. A small walkway cut through the overgrowth and led straight to the front doors. They were gigantic and wooden, with lion-headed brass knockers on each one. Candles flickered on either side of the doorframe. The moon glowed bright in a saint's halo above.

It was the most beautiful house I'd ever seen.

The journey through the screaming spirits and tangled groping branches had been a nightmare, something I never wanted to endure again. But now I was here, the Wish House, same as She said it would be. I lifted my hand to knock but the door opened on its own, exactly as I knew it would. It was just how I'd dreamed it.

"Thank You," I whispered to Her, and walked inside.

I found myself in a sort of foyer, the richest room I'd ever been in. The floor was marble, and a chandelier of diamonds and rubies dangled sparkling and candy-like above me. Sconces shaped like human arms reached out from the walls, holding lit candles. The room opened into a long hallway lined by closed doors. I had a feeling that I shouldn't open them, that it was dangerous to open strange doors in a house like this. I followed the long red carpet down the hall, leading deeper into the Wish House.

A mantel ran the length of the hallway, cluttered with wonders. A stuffed black-eyed raccoon. A child's plastic whistle. A one-armed blond-haired baby doll draped in Mardi Gras beads. A golden key. A cross made out of bound chicken feet. A sock monkey with a button eye hanging loose. A perfect slice of lemon icebox pie, somehow still fresh. Family pictures of all types hung on the wall, oil paintings and black-and-white photos and Polaroids even, a thousand different people. It made Uncle Mike's look downright sane in comparison. Never had I seen something so fantastic in my life.

"It's all true," I whispered. "Everything You told me was true."

The hallway ended in a wall with a closed door. I figured this was one I needed to open. Where else could I go? I tried the handle and it turned easily. The next room was dark, but that was no problem. I still had my flashlight. I flicked it on and stepped inside.

The room was completely black. My flashlight didn't even begin to cut it. I could have been pointing it down a well. The door slammed shut behind me.

My flashlight sputtered twice and went out.

I found myself in a blank space, a long stare of darkness, not one fleck of light anywhere. It was so dark I couldn't even be sure of the ground I walked on. I felt around for the walls, for the paintings and the curtains, for something my hands could touch. Except there wasn't anything, just a slight wind that blew through my fingers. I turned to backtrack, but there was no behind. I stepped forward, but there was no forward. I had never felt so lost in all my life.

I felt hands descend upon me like a swarm of birds, touching me, groping and squeezing me, an unseen army of limbs like snakes slithering over me. I heard a great wind like a tornado. I covered my ears and cried out.

Everything went silent. Nothing touched me. All was still as a held-in breath.

I saw a slim knife blade of light, like it was seeping in from underneath a door. I reached down to the floor and it felt solid. I wasn't in some void, I was in the Wish House. It was as if the earth returned to me, as if I had somehow found myself back in the real world again. My breathing grew steady. I got on my hands and knees and crawled myself toward the glow.

The light fluttered. I realized it wasn't a door in front of me, it was a curtain. I heard a voice whispering in the next room. I eased the curtain aside an inch and peeked through.

It was a large, cozy room with a fire roaring in a great brick hearth. The walls were covered by long black curtains that swayed slightly from some imaginary breeze. The room was completely bare except for one rocking chair, facing away from me.

And in that chair sat a man. He rocked slowly back and forth, his face toward the fire. I could only see the top of his head, age-spotted with thin, wispy hair.

"Come, little one," he said. His voice was strong and rich, high-pitched, not the feeble grandfather croak I expected.

The crackle of the flames, the slow creak of the chair. I didn't dare move.

"Come, come." He gestured, his long fingers twirling a circle in the air. "And do not dally. The little girl desires something, does she not? Then speak it to old Gaspar, for he has not had a visitor in so very long."

I crept around the rocking chair and came to face the One Wish Man.

He was very thin, with sallow cheeks and a long pointed nose. His teeth were a bit yellow, and his hair scraggled all the way down to his chin. He wore an old black suit that was crinkled and dusty, as if he hadn't stood in years, as if he'd been waiting in this chair the whole time. I would have thought him hideous if it wasn't for his eyes. They were a pale, bright blue, the color of summer lightning. I couldn't take my eyes off them. And when he smiled his face lit up with warmth and light.

"Not what you expected?" he said.

"No . . . no, sir. Not exactly."

"The years have quite leeched me, have they not? I was pretty once, yes, I was a beautiful man. And all the lovely little girls loved for me to give them roses."

He held his palm out to me, and in it was a red and glistering rose.

I reached for it, I couldn't help myself.

"Not too quickly!" he said, snatching his hand back. "It is dangerous to grasp at what we do not comprehend, is it not?"

He opened his palm again and it was a cardinal, just like the one nailed to the tree. I guess I flinched a little at the thought. The bird flew away behind the billowy black curtains and vanished.

"Does the girl grieve over the lost bird? Let her know that it gave its blood for Gaspar's door to be opened, and it gave willingly. For magic always comes at a price, does it not, little girl? Yes, it does, and I believe you already knew that."

I nodded at him, still a little afraid.

"You're some kind of magician, right?" I said. "A wizard."

Gaspar nodded at me, his eyes gleaming.

"Like John Dee?" I said.

"The marvelous John Dee, the intercessor of the angels!" he said. "Yes, the girl is very smart, isn't she? Of course she would know Dr. Dee, the wise and benevolent."

I felt a little better then. At least I understood what kind of man sat before me, someone like John Dee. I had a feeling that there were all kinds of these magic people out there, hidden and secret, living mysterious lives so far removed from all the rest of us. She was like that for me, a gateway out of the pain and misery of normal life. How good it was to be back in the strange world again.

"You come here," said Gaspar, "because you are missing someone, are you not?"

"Yes," I said. "I lost someone I loved."

"Not a someone. A spirit."

My heart began to beat a little faster. He already knew.

"Yes, yes, child, Gaspar knows your desires, does he not? For how else could he have granted you passage into his house?"

"Gaspar," I said. "That's your name?"

"Indeed," he said. "And what would you have me called?"

"Well," I said, "She always called you 'the One Wish Man.'"

Gaspar clapped his hands and laughed. It was a high sort of giggle, a child's laugh, and it made me smile, too. I liked it when Gaspar laughed. Suddenly I wanted him to laugh more than I wanted anything in the world.

"Splendid!" he said. "Oh, how marvelous! One Wish Man indeed. We are going to have a time, aren't we? Now come and whisper the spirit's name in my ear. It's fine, fine if you do not know the exact name. Tell me what you call the spirit and that shall be enough. For a common name holds a familiarity, an affinity, and spirits have names they carry about them like a scent. Come close to me and whisper and I shall know."

I took a deep breath and bent down and whispered "*Her*" into his ear.

"The spirit has done well to send you here, to old Gaspar," he said, nodding. "Such a wise spirit, yes, to send you on a day when the gates would be open, when I always leave them open."

"Because of the solstice?"

"Yes," he said. "One never knows who will heed a Midsummer's call. Yes, the spirit was good to send you here this evening. Ah, it has been so long since I've had company. Gaspar has been waiting so, so very long for someone to come and see him."

Just then I thought of Kevin Henrikson. But I would have to wait on that. I had more important things to ask Gaspar about.

"So, will you get Her back for me?" I said.

"Of course, little one."

It was like my heart lit up with fireflies, like butterflies blossomed and fluttered in my chest.

"But old Gaspar may then ask of you a boon?"

"Name it," I said. "Anything."

Gaspar giggled.

"Soon enough, soon enough. We mustn't be too eager now. Magic is always a frightful business, to be engaged most solemnly.

My boon will be named in a manner as necessary. For magic requires a sacrifice. Have we not said so already this evening?"

"How will I know what to bring?"

"The spirit will choose."

"She'll choose?" I said. "Have you spoken with Her? Is She here?"

"No," he said, grinning. "Not that spirit."

The One Wish Man looked me dead in the eyes.

"This one, shall we say, is a *watchful* spirit, yes? He will test your mettle, see if your heart is pure, if your desire is true. Yes, the spirit will tell you in three days what it wants, and then you shall bring a boon to me."

Gaspar held that stare for a minute. I felt a creeping feeling, some long shadow stretching itself over me. I couldn't help it, even standing so close to a fire, I shivered.

"What kind of boon?" I asked.

Gaspar laughed.

"Oh, just a trifle. Like a party favor. I ask each according to their measure. Something to tie you to this place. You must have passed dozens on your way in."

I thought of the long hallway and all the weird knickknacks. So that's what they were for. I wondered what he would ask of me. Hopefully not my *Lady Snowblood* poster.

"And when you bring me my boon, you shall get your wish!" he said, clapping his hands. "We shall all be so happy, shall we not? Perhaps even we shall throw a party. Oh, it has been so long since there were parties at old Gaspar's house. How lonely it has been for poor Gaspar!"

I thought again about Kevin Henrikson. I was scared to ask, but somehow I felt like I had to.

"Mr. Gaspar," I said. "Did you ever happen to know a kid named Kevin Henrikson?"

A thoughtful look came over Gaspar, and he was quiet a moment. The firelight danced across his face.

"I remember Kevin, yes, oh I do. Miraculous boy, was he not? He used to come and visit me, out here in the Wish House, back in the happiest days, when my garden was full of roses. I loved him so, oh I did. Yes, a true artist, a genuine soul. Alas, he fell in with such loathsome company. I was devastated when he passed, wasn't I? Gaspar's heart was broken, yes, snapped in two."

His grief was visible, immense. Gaspar's face drooped, and the light seemed to shiver in his eyes. It made me terribly sad, I felt it deep in my heart. A tear slipped down my cheek.

"Don't cry, little one," said Gaspar. "Gaspar's house is no place for tears, now is it? There, there. Enough of that. For certainly Kevin is happy now, in the space where all souls go, is he not? Of course he is!"

Gaspar clapped his hands again.

"You shall bring me my boon, and you shall have your friend back, and all will be well again, won't it? Oh it is such a delight to have a young pretty thing in the Wish House again. My, my, it has been years."

Gaspar held his arms out and I gave him my hands. He clasped them in his and kissed them.

"Thank you, dear girl. Oh how lonely I have been. How happy you have made me."

"No," I said, smiling. "You're the one who's made me happy. You're the one who is giving me all I ever wanted."

Gaspar sank back into his chair. I watched the fire cast shadows across his face.

"Forgive me, dear girl, but I've grown tired. Old Gaspar is not used to such company, is he? Oh, it has been far too long."

"I'll be back in a few days, then," I said.

"Yes," Gaspar said, his eyes closing, head nodding. "A few days, yes, and the spirit will choose. Yes, he will."

And Gaspar fell asleep.

I snuck my way around him and back toward the curtain. The hardwood creaked under me, and I was scared I was going to wake him. But if I did, he didn't make any notice. As I passed through the curtain to leave, I heard him snoring softly in his chair.

When I left the room, I expected the long blank confusion of my journey through the house to start all over. But I found myself back in the hallway, the red carpet before me leading the way out. It might have been my imagination, but I felt like something passed through that door with me, like I wasn't by myself anymore.

The path back from the Wish House was quiet, no howling spirits, no eyeless girls. I guess they were some kind of test, to thwart anyone whose desire wasn't pure. My heart was definitely pure. There wasn't anything I wanted more than Her. I was so happy I couldn't believe it. Everything She said was true. The One Wish Man was real and he could get Her back for me. My days of loneliness were coming to an end.

I stopped at the Bird Tree. The crucified bird had faded back into a simple carving, and there wasn't a drop of blood to be found. I drove the car back to the real world, to Mom and Larry's house, to the hope that Gaspar could bring Her back to me, that soon we could be safe and together again.

I WAS SO HAPPY I COULDN'T BELIEVE

it. I felt light and glorious and free for the first time since Roy and his dad came. To be honest, I was also pretty proud of myself. She had set the rules for our game, and I was following them down to a T. I don't know how I could have played my part better. And now, in just three days, I would have Her back with me.

I got up early the next morning (what, like I could have slept after that?) and made Mom and Larry breakfast. I figured I'd cook a feast for them, do everything that Mom and Larry wanted. I'd tell them how grateful I was for all they had done for me, show them that I was trying again, that I was getting better. At the very least I would stay on their good side.

I could feel the spirit from the Wish House with me, hovering around. I tried to talk to it like I would Her.

"Hello," I said. "How are you this morning?"

The spirit didn't respond. It just lingered on the fringes of things, watching. That was okay. It was probably acting in an official capacity, like one of those British soldiers who just guard the palace and can't say anything. I did my best to ignore it while I cooked.

And let me tell you, I cooked the hell out of some breakfast.

I made bacon, I made pancakes, I made those little awful sausages slathered in grease, three eggs a piece. I put on the coffee and had it ready for Larry just how he likes it, with double cream and sugar. He came downstairs and I set a plate for him. He opened the newspaper warily.

"You feeling okay?" he said.

"Never better," I said.

"Right. Okay."

"How do you want your eggs? Just kidding. Scrambled, with cheddar cheese. That's the only way you like them."

He cocked an eye at me.

"Glad to know you remembered."

Of course I remembered, I wanted to say. How many times have I heard you bitch Mom out because she got your fucking eggs wrong? But I held my tongue.

Mom liked her eggs over easy, so I did that. She liked to smother them in Louisiana Hot Sauce, and she liked a side of toast. I did that, too.

Mom came downstairs so surprised she kissed me right on the cheek.

We all sat down together for breakfast. I even made myself a plate and managed to choke it all down.

"Isn't this nice?" said Mom. "Don't we feel just like a family?"

That made me a little sad, because Mom didn't even say we were a family. She just said we felt like one. It was like Mom knew we would never all belong together, that any opportunity for that was long gone. Like the best we could ever do was pretend it was okay and try to look the way families look on TV.

"Sure, Mom," I said, and kissed her on the cheek.

"Don't leave the dishes in the sink," said Larry. I told him I wouldn't. Even when you were being nice to Larry, he could still be kind of a jerk.

But not even Larry could get me down today. I finished the dishes and went back upstairs and lay down on my bed feeling happier than I had in months. Gaspar was real and he was good, just like John Dee. Soon he would bring Her back to me, and it would be the best day of my life.

Now all I had to do was wait for him to name a boon. But what would it be? Probably something trivial and strange, like in a fairy story. What did magic folks ever want? A rose, a pearl, a gold doubloon, something to remember me by? Gaspar wasn't evil, because why would She send me to someone evil? It's not like he'd ask for my soul or something. At worst, he'd probably take my voice, like in *The Little Mermaid*. I'd give up my voice for Her, no problem. She was about the only person I wanted to talk to anyway.

Lying there, feeling all happy inside, I looked over and saw Kevin's notebook sitting there on my bedside table. I'd taken it out late last night to read over again, to gaze at the drawings. I started thinking about how happy I was, and how that maybe wasn't quite fair. Gaspar seemed so sad when he spoke of Kevin, how much he had loved him, what a talented artist he was. It was true, Kevin was a genius. Even now, as I traced my fingers over his drawings,

I got a chill from them, like they could evoke something hidden in me, like they were some kind of magic all their own.

Maybe it wasn't right that I have this notebook. It didn't exactly belong to me. I thought back to how I'd stolen it along with the rosewood box, stolen it from poor Uncle Mike of all people. I started to feel pretty shitty about the whole thing. I remembered that article I found about Kevin. Didn't it say something about his mom and dad being alive? Maybe they were still around. They might like to have this notebook. I know I would if Kevin were my son.

It was settled then. In the last few days before I got Her back, I was going to track down Kevin Henrikson's parents.

After Mom and Larry went to work, I took Mom's car over to the library and made a beeline for Mrs. Jenkins's desk. She fiddled with her glasses and squinted at me.

"What'll it be today?" she said. "Horror movies or the news?"

"What's the difference?"

"You said it, honey."

She led me back to the research room, to the computer with all the old newspapers on it.

"Glad somebody's getting some use out of the past," she said. "Lord knows you're the only one."

I found the article about Kevin's death again. It gave me his parents' names, and this time I was smart enough to copy them down. After a quick search of the obituaries I found out his mother, Irna, had died ten years after her son, but it seemed like Kevin's dad was still around.

The whole time I was researching, I felt the Wish House spirit watching me, curious. I could feel it reading over my shoulder, same as you can when anyone does that. It just about drove me crazy. Just because it's a spirit doing it doesn't make it any less annoying.

I spent the next hour digging for Kevin's father, Willie Henrikson. I got one phone number, and then another one. I found an old employer of his, an auto parts shop that hadn't gone corporate yet. An old man answered. I had to chat him up for a while, asking about Willie, dodging all kinds of questions for why I needed to talk to him. But eventually I wound up with an address.

It was only a little after noon, so I still had plenty of time. I grabbed a couple of videos I had on hold and left.

Mr. Henrikson was at a nursing home called the Country Place. Nursing homes were all named stupid stuff like that. I'd been to a couple while Larry's mom was still around. They all look the same on the inside, too. The same pee-yellow walls, the cafeteria-tile floors. The old folks were scattered in strategic armchairs, widows in walkers leaned against doorways, a motionless old man or two parked in a wheelchair around each corner like props in a Halloween spook house. It was scary to think that one day I'd end up in this kind of place, and that was only if I was lucky and lived a real long time. Life could seem pretty shitty if you took the long view of it.

I told the nurse at the front desk that I was Mr. Henrikson's grandniece. She cocked an eye up at that, but she let me on through. I tried to look as innocent as possible. I wore an oversize T-shirt from the '80s with a pink elephant on it and my jeans with the least amount of holes. Also, I had my backpack with Kevin's notebook in it.

"He's in there," she said. "Don't let him bite you on the way out."

I walked into a standard nursing home room, tacky furniture and off-white walls, a TV hanging crookedly from a wall mount. A curtain was drawn halfway across the space, separating it into two rooms. A TV on the other side of the curtain blasted *Judge Judy* at a painful volume. That was fine, that would give us the closest thing to privacy possible.

Mr. Henrikson lay in one of those electronic beds that sits up so the person can watch TV, though he had his on mute with subtitles. I wondered if it was because of all the racket on the other side. The spirit followed me in, but it kept its distance, like it was afraid of being seen in here. It made me wonder about old folks, if maybe they had better eyes for spirits since they were closer to death. I'd have to ask Miss Mathis about it someday if I could manage to do it without pissing her off.

"Hello there, little lady," said Mr. Henrikson. "What can I do you for?"

I tried to smile but it came out a grimace. I hated it when old men talked that shit to me.

"Hi, Mr. Henrikson. I wanted to know if I could ask you a couple of questions."

"It's Willie to you, darlin'. Why don't you pull up a chair and ask me anything your little heart desires?"

"I'll stand."

I hadn't quite thought this through. I just barged in on an old man in a nursing home and I was fixing to bug him about his only son's horrific death. All of a sudden this maybe didn't seem like such a good idea. I brushed my hair out of my face and realized my forehead was sweaty. I figured I should just go ahead and spit it out.

"It's about . . . um . . . Sir, was Kevin Henrikson your son?"

Mr. Henrikson's eyes went narrow and he looked like he wanted to pop me across the face.

"Yeah, he was my boy. What about it?"

"Well, I was just wondering about him. See, I found this notebook of his."

I pulled the notebook out of the backpack and held it toward him.

"Let me see that," he said, snatching it from my hands. "Christ, I ain't seen this thing for years. Hell, I didn't even know it existed until after Kevin was gone. A young lady came and found it for us. This was about a year after Kevin passed, mind you."

"A young lady found it?"

"A girl was what she was. Real pretty, dark hair like yours. She said she had a dream about Kevin, that he had left something for us to find. I got mad at first. I don't much go into that spiritual mumbo jumbo, dreams and the like. I'm a Baptist."

The girl had to be Cléa. That's how she got the notebook.

"Wouldn't have let her in the house if it was up to me. But Irna—that was my wife—she told me to calm down, that I was being rude, and would the girl like a Coke? And I figured if somebody had to come creeping around after my boy, at least it was a pretty little thing like that. I know how that makes me sound, but I figure I ain't got more than a couple years left in me, so the hell do I care what people think?"

I said that was a good way to be.

"No, it ain't," he said. "Just means there ain't much left they hadn't already took away, you understand? Now listen. The girl just walks right upstairs to Kevin's room, same as if she'd been there a thousand times. She opens the door, waltzes over to his bed, and just climbs on up it. I'm about to shoo her down, tell her she's being damn disrespectful, but she whips a screwdriver out from her belt and sets to work on the air vent. I figure I got a crazy person in my house, but hell, it ain't the first time. Not if you know anything about that boy of mine. Girl unscrews the vent and pulls this here notebook out like some kind of prize egg on an Easter hunt."

"Did you read it?" I said.

"Sure I read it. To my shame I read it. I knew the boy was crazy, but I didn't know quite how bad it had gotten. I wasn't a good dad, not by any stretch, but I wasn't the worst." He shook his head. "Irna, though, bless her heart. She just kept staring at the pictures, all them drawings he did. She kept saying, 'My poor boy, we didn't know.' 'Didn't know what?' I asked. 'That he was an artist,' she said. 'That he was special.' Special, my foot. He was my boy, but he was strange, and we never did get along too well."

I felt like I had to stick up for Kevin. Even if his writing was odd and his drawings were eerie, they were his own, and to me they were beautiful.

"I think the notebook is amazing," I said. "Especially the drawings."

"Whatever you say, darlin'. If Irna was here, she'd probably get all teary-eyed and offer you a Coke as well. But Irna's dead, ain't she? Anyways, the girl asked me if she could take it. I said sure, go right ahead. Kevin was gone by then. I didn't need anything else to remember him by."

Mr. Henrikson's scowl deepened then, wrinkles gouging his whole forehead in anguish, like a stirred-up river in a summer storm.

"But Irna, no, she didn't want to part with the notebook. She hugged it close to her and said it was all she had left of the boy. That's when this girl—Christ, for the life of me I cannot remember her name—squatted down to where Irna sat and looked her dead in the eyes, and then she spoke. I remember her voice then, real gentle and calm, so in control of everything. It was spooky-like. I could have listened to her talk for years."

"What did she say?"

Mr. Henrikson's eyes glazed over. I could tell this hurt him, I could tell he was about to cry.

"She said, 'Ma'am, I'm going to get the people that did this to your boy. I'm going to stop them from ever hurting anyone again.' I remember it same as it was yesterday. And Irna cried and said, 'Okay, honey, do what you got to do.' And the girl took the notebook and left and I never seen her again."

He was quiet a moment after that. The TV blared, strange instruments beeped and buzzed, the disinfectant and body-odor fug of the place filled the room. I was suddenly afraid. I felt the watchful spirit creep closer to me, hidden away among the shadows, and I shivered.

"Mr. Henrikson," I said, "what do you think happened to Kevin?"

"I think he died, that's what I think." He tried to sit up, coughed, and lay back down. "Now, look here. I don't know what you're trying to do, but there ain't any good to come from digging all this up."

"Was there something, I don't know, strange about Kevin's death?"

It was hard to find the words to talk about this, standing there next to his bedridden father. Things were always more difficult when you had to face them in person.

"Listen, honey, Kevin was missing for years before he got killed," he said.

"Missing?" I said. "I don't understand."

"Kevin ran away," he said. "Left a damn note and everything. We didn't know where he was or what happened to him. I figured Kevin was dead years before he turned back up. But Irna, she held on. Think when they found him like that, that's what finally did her in, rest her soul."

I didn't want to ask this next part, but I knew I had to. I had to find out the truth about Kevin. I realized that now. He was the only person who could have understood me. I owed him that much.

"Mr. Henrikson, do you think it had something to do with the man in the woods, like it said in the notebook?"

"Man in the woods, nothing," said Mr. Henrikson. "It was goddamn Luther Simpkins."

"As in *Mayor* Luther Simpkins?"

Luther Simpkins was big news. He was the mayor for about a billion years, even when I was a girl. I remember his face on the billboards, a skinny grinning man with perfect silver hair. Half the town was named after him and his family.

"I don't understand," I said. "What in the world would the mayor want with your son?"

"That's the million-dollar question, ain't it?" said Mr. Henrikson. "See, that girl's visit got me to thinking. When Kevin died, the police wouldn't let me see his body, said it was too mangled. Only let me look at his face to identify him, if you can believe that. I wanted an open-casket funeral—I wanted to bury my boy right. Authorities wouldn't let me. Flat wouldn't let me touch him. About a year later, I started wondering if there wasn't something else to it. So I started asking around myself, you know, see what I can figure out. And what I figured out was the Paradise Society."

He said those words all mysterious-like, as if I was supposed to know what that meant.

"I'm sorry," I said. "Is that some kind of club?"

"It's devil worship is what it is," said Mr. Henrikson. "Look, you weren't even alive yet when all this stuff was happening. There were rumors about this town since the beginning. Folks wearing robes in the graveyard, drinking blood, doing all that satanic goat bullshit. But you never much believe it until it sneaks up and bites you on the ass. By then it's too late. You look up and it's all around you, been all around you since the day you were born.

"The Paradise Society was what Luther Simpkins and all his cronies called themselves in private. They ran everything around here. Rich as hell, money as old as America. Supposed to be in some kind of cult. I always figured that was just jealous folks talking, like they do in a small town. But the more I looked into it, the more I started to find. Like how Luther Simpkins owned the whole damn police force, which is probably why they wouldn't let me see my boy. How a Simpkins was in office ever since the founding of this town up until now. I heard talk of spooky stuff, a bunch of wild parties gone wrong. And that girl that found Kevin's diary? Wound up seeing her face on a missing poster not long after. I called the police station about it to report her coming to see me."

"What did the police say?" I said.

"That she was a runaway and it wasn't any of my business. The next thing I know I'm fired off the worksite. Pretty soon no one's talking to me anymore, much less answering my questions. I start drinking, a few years later my wife passes, and now I know I got to sell the house. And my life's been one long stretch of skid-marks since."

Mr. Henrikson motioned toward the curtain, the TV squawking on the other side of it. He seemed so tired, so old and beat down. I hated to bother him more, but my mind still spun wild with questions.

"Is there anything else you can tell me, Mr. Henrikson? Anything at all?"

"Watch your back. Those people are ruthless, and they don't take kindly to others poking in on their business. They won't kill you, nothing like that. They won't have to. When half of the town is owned by a handful of people with power, those folks can do whatever they want."

"How come I've never heard about any of this?" I said. "Wouldn't someone have exposed them by now?"

"What, you going to read about it in the newspaper? The Simpkins family owns the newspaper. Besides, it's all gone quiet since Kevin's time. You seen Luther Simpkins walking around town lately? Man's been shut up in his house for years. I used to see him in the grocery store and the old bastard would wink at me. Made me want to gouge his eyes out."

It was true, I used to see Luther Simpkins on TV all the time when I was a kid. Ribbon cuttings at the new hospital, endorsing some candidate or other. But that was years ago. I couldn't remember the last time I'd seen his face anywhere. Maybe that was why Larry always bitched about him being gone. I always just figured he was getting old, probably turned into some kind of PR risk. Maybe something had actually happened to him.

"Thanks, Mr. Henrikson," I said. "For talking to me and all. I know it must be hard on you."

"Shit," he said. "Nothing's harder on me than just staying alive. And I've done plenty of that already. It's time for me to go now. Thanks for letting me get some of that off my chest." He handed the notebook back to me. "I don't want it. There ain't a thing I can do with it. It's better off in the hands of somebody like you."

Mr. Henrikson's eyes met mine, and for a second I thought he was going to cry.

"Thanks for giving a shit about my boy," he said.

I nodded at him. He lay back on his bed and plugged his ears with his fingers, as if to block out the TV sound and everything else.

And that's how I left him.

I drove home quick as I could. Mom would be back any minute, and I didn't have time to visit the Simpkins mansion. I didn't even have time to stop at the library to search the newspapers for the Paradise Society. That was probably a good thing, since Mr. Henrikson had given me more than my brain could process already. I mean, Luther Simpkins was a legend in our town. My stepdad Larry talked about him all the time.

"If only we had Mayor Simpkins again," he would say. "That was a man who knew how government worked. He didn't let the federal bureaucracy push him around. He knew how to keep Big Government out."

I always ignored him. Larry's political views were about the least interesting thing in the world to me, and as far as I was concerned, our town had always been a piece-of-shit place and the Simpkins family were there from the beginning. Everybody knew they were the richest folks in the whole town. I'd heard kids at school talk about how the Simpkins mansion was haunted, how they had snuck past the gates and seen weird things, but I always figured they were lying, trying to out-tough each other. I knew Luther had a daughter that Mom and I used to see out in town when I was a kid, but come to think of it, I hadn't seen her around in ages either. She supposedly lived in that big house with him.

The mom died a long time back. It was like the whole Simpkins clan had gone reclusive, holed up in that mansion away from the world.

I made it home just before Mom and Larry got back. It felt bad inside. There was a heaviness to the air, something that made it hard for me to breathe. I started feeling pretty low, that Wish House spirit gazing close at me whenever I was alone. It whisked around my house, peeking in on Mom and Larry, sat itself down in the empty chair during dinner, watching us eat.

Keep the focus, Clare, I told myself. You're so close to getting Her back. Everything is going to be just fine.

Yeah, but what about Kevin Henrikson? Was Luther Simpkins the "loathsome company" that Gaspar said Kevin had fallen in with? And if he ran away, where was he hiding all those years? Where did Cléa and Miss Mathis fall in with all this?

There were too many questions for my brain to deal with tonight. I was glad I remembered the videos from the library. Roy couldn't talk when he was on trips with his dad, and I was really starting to miss his voice over the phone. I had to wait until Mom and Larry went to bed and then watch a movie with the volume way down so as not to wake them up. At least movies would be a distraction.

The movie I watched was called *The Sentinel*. It was pretty great. It was about this crazy blind man that stood watch over the gates of Hell, which were really a door in some dumb New York apartment building. The best part of the movie was when the door opened up and all the creepy souls long locked up came crawling out. The main character running around screaming, wondering how her boring old apartment building could be the gateway to the underworld.

I don't know, it made sense to me. I was pretty sure you could find Hell just about anywhere.

ALL THAT NIGHT I HAD NIGHTMARES.

I dreamed She was lost, wandering the woods around the Wish House. Grasping white hands clawed at Her voice, some ghostly wall barring Her from me.

I dreamed Her as a little girl in a pink dress, lost and alone in a great forest. I saw Her with eyes black and terrified, calling out for me. The trees became brown-hooded monks with long wooden crosses hung upside down from their chests. They staggered toward Her, surrounding Her under the bright white moonlight, the stars glimmering blackly. The monks were singing an old song, not in English, some garbled wail from long before time.

I watched Her cover Her face. I watched Her scream and cower and moan. I realized it wasn't Her who I was seeing anymore, it was me. I was Her, and the hooded figures were closing in. One of them grasped me by my wrist. He pulled me up to the darkness of his face and let his hood fall.

I woke myself screaming.

My mom was standing just inside my door.

"Well, good morning to you, too," she said.

"I had a nightmare."

"No kidding. I was just coming to tell you breakfast is ready."

"Thanks, Mom."

Mom stopped at my door. I knew she wanted to say something to me, something important, the words perfect as magic to stitch up all the ripped places between us, to fix everything. But then she just sighed.

"Maybe you shouldn't watch so many scary movies," she said.

"I'll try not to."

Mom smiled and shut my door. She'd be leaving for work any minute.

I felt a little sick, like I was coming down with the flu or something. The Wish House spirit hovered over me, watching. I was getting tired of its presence, tired of having eyes on me all the time. I wanted to pull the covers over my head and lie back down and doze my way until tomorrow, when Gaspar would name his boon. But I couldn't do that. I know it's weird, but I felt like I owed it to Kevin. He was the only person I ever knew of who was anything like me. I felt like he was my friend or something, like he and I could be the same person. It was amazing what that little notebook could do.

My next stop was Luther Simpkins's house.

The Simpkinses' house sat lonely and high-gated, the oak trees surrounding it shrouded in Spanish moss. You could only just barely see the house, the attic poking through the treetops. Hopping the fence didn't seem like such a good idea, so I rang the buzzer.

"Yes?" said a woman's voice.

"I need to talk to Luther Simpkins, please," I said.

"Oh," said the voice. "I thought you were the delivery boy. Poppy doesn't see visitors anymore. You'll have to find another source for your school newspaper."

"I'm not writing for the paper," I said. "Besides, it's summer. There's no school."

"Be that as it may, Poppy does not receive visitors. I suggest you trouble us no further."

"Please," I said. "It's real important."

"Go away."

"It's about the Paradise Society."

There was a silence on the intercom. I felt the Wish House spirit leaning in close, as if in anticipation of what would happen next. I put my ear to the speaker. I could hear the woman breathing on the other end, slow and steady, as if she were trying to make a decision.

The intercom shut off and a buzzer sounded. The gates swung themselves open.

I walked down the tree-lined brick path to the Simpkinses' house, three stately stories glaring down at me through the trees and moss. But the spirit didn't follow me. I could feel its presence hang back a bit, like it was scared to walk onto the Simpkinses' property. That didn't make me feel any better. But I had come so far, and I wasn't going to stop now. I climbed the steps to the front porch and knocked on the bright-red double doors.

A woman answered, maybe fifty years old, with a blue wrap on her head. She wore a leopard-print dress with black high heels. I thought she was pretty. I'd never seen anybody wear anything like that, much less in the middle of the day. All the curtains were drawn in the house and it was very dark inside.

The woman smiled at me. Her lips were bright pink, and she smelled like perfume and cigarettes.

"Come in, I suppose," she said.

The house was grand, big mirrors everywhere, so clean there was no way anybody here had kids. All the counters had sharp edges, and the tabletops were made of stone. It didn't seem so much a house you lived in as a place where you showed off all the cool stuff you bought. Giant vases stood like funeral urns all over the place. The rugs on the floor seemed ancient, woven with strange village scenes: a woman plucking a chicken, animals hung up bleeding by their hooves. A painting of a naked lady smoking a cigar hung over the mantel, her face fat and drunk and happy. Two scary-faced masks grinned at me from the wall. One had big red cheeks and a massive tongue lolling out of its mouth. The other was slim, ghostly, like something that would sneak up on you at night.

The woman led me to the living room. It was dark, with red velvet curtains draped over the windows, blocking the light. A bunch of folks sat around a small wooden table, chatting and laughing. Some were young, some were old, but they were all dressed fancy, they had nice shoes, they looked like lords and ladies out of a show about England. I felt pretty shabby in just my jeans and hoodie. One woman with three rings on her finger held a large golden cup. On the wooden table burned a fat purple candle next to what looked like a cat's skull. The air was thick with incense and something chemical, like sulfur.

"This girl came to talk to Poppy," the lady said.

The men and women looked back and forth at each other, as if sharing a secret. A blond man in little round glasses smirked at me.

"I told her that no one speaks to Poppy, but she insisted." The lady took my hand. Hers was gloved, soft. "She said she must speak to him about the Paradise Society."

At this the room went silent. The blond man stopped his smirking, and I saw the teacup tremble in his hands.

"What is your name, young lady?" said the woman.

"Clare. And you're Luther Simpkins's daughter."

"Millicent, yes. How very perceptive of you."

"Millicent, darling," said the blond-haired man, "what on earth did you tell her?"

"Nothing yet," she said. "But what would I tell her except for the truth? That we are merely a group of concerned citizens who gather to discuss the rejuvenation of our fair town. It was once the jewel of the state, was it not? A rather tiny jewel, but all the more precious for that. Though the shimmer has quite fallen off it these days, don't you think?"

"Yes," said a grey-headed woman. "It most certainly has."

"And we," said Millicent, gesturing around the room, "have taken it upon ourselves to start a sort of grassroots campaign, do you see? To make our town what it once was, back when my father was in charge. Before others of a decidedly inferior quality usurped it from him."

"Where is Luther Simpkins?" I said. "Is he here?"

"Of course he is, child!" said Millicent. "Where else would he be?"

"But, Millicent . . ." said the blond-haired man.

"And I believe," she said, "that Poppy would be most delighted to speak to this girl about the Paradise Society. Don't you agree?"

"Yes," the blond-haired man said, smirking. "I do believe he would."

"I'm not sure if I ought to," I said.

"Oh, hush now, darling, you've already disturbed our little gathering here, thrown the ambiance off, and I doubt we shall ever recover. Poppy's right this way, just up this staircase—yes, here you go."

Millicent ushered me along toward the back of the house. She shooed me past a baby grand piano, past portraits and snapshots, some looking as old as the Civil War. In all the newer ones stood a suited and grinning man, Luther Simpkins himself, always surrounded by people. Luther Simpkins giving a speech. Luther Simpkins shaking hands with a mustached man. Luther Simpkins with his arm around a striking girl in a red dress, probably Millicent when she was about my age. I wondered what it was like to grow up so rich. To be proud of who you are and where you came from. I loved Mom, but she was a wreck, and don't even get me started on Dad. We had never been family-photo material.

"My family was quite happy back then, weren't we?" said Millicent. "Mommy took the loveliest photos of us. Yes, we were so very happy."

We reached the landing on the second story. Another staircase continued, much narrower, up to the third floor. Millicent herded me up it, following close behind me. The top of the staircase ended in a small enclave with a shut door at the end. Millicent reached around me with a key in her hand and unlocked the door.

"Poppy likes his privacy," she said.

"Well, maybe I should leave, then."

"No, no. I assure you, he'll find you *very* interesting. He's right this way, come along."

Millicent shoved me through the doorway and into a pitch-dark room.

"Poppy?" she said. "Poppy, dear, you have a visitor."

Something lurched in the darkness.

I turned to run but Millicent slammed the door shut in my face. I heard the lock turn.

"Let me out!" I said.

I heard laughing from the other side.

I kicked the door as hard as I could. I banged on it and screamed. I was trapped in here, and I wasn't alone. The floorboards creaked. I whirled around but I couldn't see anything. My back against the doorframe, I pulled out my flip phone and shone its tinny screen light around the room. It was sparsely furnished, just a chair and a table on which sat an empty plate, a cup turned on its side. The walls were blank except for thick curtains that hung over what must have been windows.

I shone the light to my left and froze. Someone was standing in the far corner of the room. A man, naked, with his back to me, facing the wall. He shivered. I could hear the panting of his breath.

"Mr. Simpkins?" I said.

Slowly he turned toward me. Most of his body was hidden

in the shadows, but I could see his face. It was Luther Simpkins alright, the man from all the billboards, or at least some version of him. His head was tilted to the side and his eyes shone a pure white in the cell phone light. His mouth was open wide in a painful smile, all gums and teeth. Tears ran down his cheeks. He stepped forward and I shone my phone light down his body.

Claw marks streaked across his chest, the skin curled and ribboned around the gashes. Blood dripped down his legs and onto the floor.

I fumbled at the door, trying to pry it open, but it was locked, it wouldn't budge.

"They're coming," said Luther Simpkins, his voice ragged and maimed, like something drug down a highway, his eyes wide with awe and wonder. "They're coming back."

He pinched a torn hangnail of flesh and pulled, slowly ripping a long strip of skin down his chest.

"You're part of it," he rasped. "You made it happen."

Luther Simpkins reached his bloody finger out toward me.

I screamed.

The door yanked open and I fell out onto the landing. Millicent stood above me, laughing. She slammed the door and locked it with her key.

"Poppy didn't want our little group reuniting," she said. "He said it was too dangerous. In his old age Poppy has become a coward." She leered down at me. "Do you see what we do to people who oppose us? Do you see what we do to our own family?"

I jumped to my feet and ran down the stairs. The guests were all seated, sipping their drinks, laughing at me. The candle and skull were gone, it looked now just like a gathering of old friends. Millicent followed me down the stairs.

"You can't stop us, darling," she said. "You can't stop what we've already begun."

I didn't quit running until I had reached my mom's car, jumped into the driver's seat, and gunned it as far away from that house, as fast as I could get.

I FELT SICK AFTER WHAT I'D SEEN AT
the Simpkins mansion. Luther Simpkins was obviously ill,
or crazy, or something, locked up in that room in the dark by
Millicent, his own fucking daughter. And who were those people
with her? Was that some new version of the Paradise Society?

I got home and took the hottest shower I could stand. I wanted
to wash that place off me, to scrub every trace of it from my skin.
I felt light-headed and woozy, my body shivering in the hot water.
Afterward I crawled into bed, even though it was still early, even
though Mom wouldn't be home for hours.

I hadn't felt this bad in ages, not since I had the flu two winters
ago. Even She was worried about me then. When Mom left the
room She would lay her cold hand on my forehead and sing to me.
She was always so good when I was sick.

I wished it was tomorrow. I wished the spirit would name its
boon and I could have Her back with me already.

I dozed for a while, and when I woke up Mom was home. I lay
under the covers and listened to her bustle around the house,

hoping she wouldn't come upstairs and try to talk to me. I didn't feel up for too much conversation. But pretty soon I heard footsteps on the stairs. I burrowed deeper under the covers and turned my back to the door. Mom sat down on the side of my bed.

"Hi, honey," she said.

"Hey, Mom."

I tried to make my voice sound scratchy, like I'd been asleep. Mom brushed my hair behind my ear.

"Not feeling well?"

"Never felt better."

Mom bent down and kissed my forehead. That's how she always took my temperature.

"Good Lord, you're burning up," she said.

"I'm fine, really."

"No, honey, I don't think you are. I'll get you some Advil and a glass of orange juice, how does that sound?"

"Can I have a ginger ale?"

"Of course you can."

Mom was always sweet like that. I didn't have anything against her, not really. She'd done her best with me, gotten cleaned up, moved our lives onward past Dad. But it still felt like there was a wall between us now, some kind of barrier that sprung up after Mom married Larry. Maybe it was Her, I don't know. Still, I wished I could be honest with my mom. I wished I could be the kind of daughter I knew she wanted me to be.

Mom left my room and came back with the Advil and ginger ale. I took the pills and lay back down, hoping she would leave.

"I know things have been hard lately," said Mom. "I've

probably done everything all wrong with you, smart as you are, strong as you are. But I'm trying, Clare. I'm trying to make things good again."

"You can just leave him, you know?" I said. "We can pack up and go tomorrow."

"It isn't as easy as that," she said.

"Why not?"

"It just isn't." Mom looked up at me, her eyes wet and shining.

I wanted to sit up and throw my arms around her, to let her cry on my shoulder, to cry with her about all I'd seen at the Simpkins mansion. But I just couldn't manage it. I never seemed to be able to cry when I really needed to. So I just pretended to be asleep. After a minute or so, Mom got up and let herself out of the room, shutting the door behind her. The Wish House spirit lingered there, in the corner, watching as always.

"Sorry you had to see that," I said. The spirit was silent. Slowly I fell asleep.

I had a dream. It was a memory dream, from when I was a little girl.

It was a pretty day, and I'd been with Her out in the woods. Mom was off at work. I came inside because it was hot out, and because I was thirsty. I just wanted a cup of water.

And that's when I found him.

He was slumped back in a chair at the kitchen table. His arm was still tied, the needle lay freshly used on the table. His beautiful blue eyes were wide open. That's what I remembered, and that's just the way it was in the dream. His eyes were the blue of the noon sky, his gaze long gone and far off, like the ceiling had fallen away and the clouds opened up and Heaven was coming down. His jaw was slack and open. He looked mystified, amazed. My daddy was dead.

I snapped awake. The house was silent and I was alone. Except I didn't feel alone. I felt cold, I felt afraid, like if I closed my eyes and concentrated I would see the Wish House spirit looming over me.

It was right there. It was right at the foot of my bed.

Could it see what I dreamed?

I pulled the covers up to my neck and forced myself to turn my back to it. I could feel its breath on me, the burn of it on my neck.

I lay awake like that for the rest of the night.

In the morning I felt worse. I hated that. Today was the day I'd dreamed of for so long, and now I was going to be sick for it. Mom came in to check on me, bringing coffee and DayQuil. I took the medicine from Mom and rolled over, hoping she would leave me alone.

"Love you, sweetie," she said.

Mom hesitated a little by the doorway.

"You know, if something's going on," she said. "Or maybe, if you want to talk about what happened . . ."

"I know, Mom," I said. "Thanks."

"I mean it, Clare. I'm here."

"I got it."

Mom nodded at me and left.

I don't know. I think I really hurt her feelings.

●

Once everyone was gone, the house empty, I rolled myself over. Even with the curtains drawn, my room seemed impossibly dark. I needed to get out of bed, maybe out into the sunshine, shake off whatever sickness I'd picked up.

I straggled myself out of bed and into a pair of jeans and my dad's old holey Bikini Kill T-shirt, for strength. I made it to the bathroom and threw up for a few minutes while the spirit watched me, probably taking notes.

"Can't you just name your boon already?" I said. "Please?"

I got dizzy and puked again.

"Well, if you're just going to stand there," I said, "want to hold back my hair or something?"

I staggered over to the sink and gargled mouthwash. Somehow I made it downstairs. Mom had driven her own car to work today, so I had to take my bike. That was fine. Even though I was weak as hell, a ride would get my heart beating. It would remind me of the blood pumping in me. Soon this would all be over. I would have Her back, and I'd never be lonely again.

I pedaled down familiar roads, through the nice, friendly neighborhoods with medium-size houses where I used to wish I lived—yards full of kids running through sprinklers, moms gardening, dads sipping beers and tossing footballs to sons in shorts. I saw a girl smoking a cigarette on the roof of her house. I waved at her, and she waved back. That made me feel a little bit better.

Every now and again someone would look at me and squint—usually an old lady or a little kid—and I could tell they saw that something was different about me. It used to happen sometimes with Her too, especially at playgrounds and parks. I would stretch myself out on a quilt and have Her stretch out with me, both of us feeling the warmth of the sun and of each other, how happy we could be with a book and a pair of headphones.

One time I was lying out, eyes shut, just mind-drifting, when I felt someone watching me. It was a little blond-haired girl. She had a big forehead and tiny lips.

"Well, hi there," I said.

"Hello."

"What's your name?"

"I've seen that girl before," she said.

"Me? Where have you seen me before? Walmart or something?"

"Not you. *Her*."

The little girl pointed at the spot next to me.

"Honey, there isn't anybody there."

"Yes, there is," said the girl. "You can't fool me. Besides, I know Her. I had a dream and She was in it. She pulled my hair."

And the little girl skipped off.

The girl was sad, She said, *and I made her laugh. It's okay. It was just in her dreams.*

"You won't leave me, will You?" I asked.

I'll never leave you, She promised. *Not for anybody. You're my Only.*

Oh, I missed Her. Roy helped, sure, but Roy wasn't *Her*. It was different with him. I liked Roy, and he was a good distraction, but he could never be what She was, he could never understand me the way She did. She knew me deeply, into my bones, and She loved me anyway. She kept me safe. She filled up all the cold, gnawing parts of me with light. Roy couldn't do that. Not even close.

No one else could. Only Her.

I started to cry a little, tears mingling with sweat, the hot ride, and my sick feeling, and I pedaled harder and let the tears fall. I was so close. So soon it would be just us two again, happy like we were. I missed Her so much my bones ached and my veins throbbed. Soon, so soon. I repeated it like a mantra.

Maybe this was the difficult part, just a test from Gaspar. He said he sent a trying spirit, right? To test my mettle, to make sure my heart was pure? Well, I knew my heart, and my desire for Her was about as pure as it got.

I pedaled and cried, winding my way through town. I felt the breeze blow through my hair, the cool calming winds, and tried to push the Paradise Society and Luther Simpkins and Kevin Henrikson out of my mind. As much as I felt like I owed Kevin, this battle seemed too big for me, and it wasn't mine to fight. I focused on Her, trying to keep nothing but the feeling of Her in my mind. I focused so hard that I didn't realize exactly where I was headed. But soon enough I turned down a familiar road, coasting down the hill toward Uncle Mike's Used and Collectible.

I pulled to a stop in the parking lot. I was sweaty and hot and I needed a break. At the same time, I didn't want to go in there. I didn't want to be reminded what I'd done to Uncle Mike, how I'd gotten myself caught up in all this Paradise Society stuff.

But I didn't have to go inside. Because Uncle Mike had already seen me. He came barreling out of the store, hollering.

"You! You thief!" He shook his skinny fist at me. "I should call the police! You belong in jail!"

"I'm sorry," I said. "I'm so sorry."

"That belonged to my daughter!" he said. "I don't have much of her left. You stole from her and from me."

I hung my head. I didn't know what else to say.

"It's that woman, I know it. Eugenia Mathis, always meddling. Cléa wouldn't be dead if it was not for her."

"Why?" I said. "What did she do?"

"The bad magic. The evil my Cléa tried to destroy."

Just then I had a thought. It was about Miss Mathis, and about guilt, and it maybe tied Kevin Henrikson and Cléa together in my mind.

"Uncle Mike, does the evil you're talking about have anything to do with the Paradise Society?"

"Yes, that is what they called themselves. Wicked, every last one of them."

Was Miss Mathis part of the Paradise Society? All those parties she was talking about. Was Miss Mathis evil? In giving her Cléa's rosewood box, had I only made everything worse?

Uncle Mike sat down hard on the outside bench. He seemed exhausted. I sat down next to him.

"It is too much. This town is too much evil," said Uncle Mike. "I say leave it alone. I already lost my daughter. Already that's too much."

"I'm sorry about what I stole, Uncle Mike. I won't come back again."

"If you did not come back, that would be the worst thing." Uncle Mike squinted at me and smiled. "You remind me of her, my Cléa."

"I didn't mean to bother you with bad memories."

"It's no bother," he said. "It's good to be reminded. In my memories she never dies. She's waiting for me when I dream, every night, with my wife. Dreaming is my most precious thing, for we are a family again."

"I'm real sorry," I said.

"It is okay," he said. "But please, stay away from Eugenia Mathis. Let this alone."

"I will," I said. "I wish I could take it all back."

Uncle Mike nodded sadly, like he understood. He rose and made the sign of the cross over me.

"Wherever you go," he said, "you go with God."

I don't know. For some reason that made me feel a little bit better.

I made it home and threw up. Lots. I threw up more than anything I had eaten. I retched bile into the toilet, my body emptying itself, trying to shake off whatever sickness I'd caught.

I crawled myself to bed and lay there, panting.

"Please," I said to the Wish House spirit. "Will you just name your boon already?"

But it was silent. I felt it watching.

I pulled poor dead Kevin Henrikson's notebook from my backpack. I thought I could use it like a talisman, something I could draw strength from. Didn't some artists believe that their essence was actually transferred into their drawings, like somehow they stitched their souls on the page with every scratch and line? If their art existed in this world, then they would always exist, too. As long as I had this notebook, Kevin Henrikson would never truly die, he would never be forgotten. That meant something to me.

I flipped to my favorite page, a lonely hermit seated in his shack on a mountain, the moon hanging worried just outside his window. In the night sky were scrawled those strange symbols that Kevin always swirled around his figures, in the shading and shadows. I wondered if they were like cave paintings, some fucked-up picture language meant to tell a story. Maybe it was a way Kevin—or his demon—was trying to speak.

I knew I was caught in something much larger than myself. I was just a small piece of a story that started a long time before me and that would continue long after I was gone. I didn't want to be alone right now. I wished Roy was with me. I wished I could at least hear his voice on the phone. He was my comfort, right? The person to help me until She came back. But Roy was off preaching with his damn father, the very same person who ruined everything for me.

So I lay back in my bed, shivering, and thought about the night Larry figured out about me, the night he decided everything was wrong enough to call up Roy's dad and take Her away.

It was the night Larry finally came to believe in Her.

THIS IS THE STORY OF THE THIRD TIME

She took over my body. It happened one night almost two months back. It went like this:

A knock sounded at our door.

Mom answered. She was tired after work and she looked it. I was helping her get dinner going.

A tall lady with blond hair stood in the doorway, two bored-looking kids at her side. They were all three relaxed and well dressed and grinning like they could have been posing on a billboard somewhere. The woman's teeth glistened in our porch light.

"Hi there," said the lady. "My name is Lisa Holbrook, and this is Richard and Camille-Ellen. Say hi, kids."

The girl was maybe eight and she looked like the cute kid from every TV show you ever saw. The boy was older, seventeen or so. Him I knew already. We went to the same high school, not that he would have ever noticed me.

"Hi," said the girl.

The boy—Richard—just waved.

"We've met before," said Mom. "At the Fourth of July cookout at the church. The last two years."

"That's right!" said Mrs. Holbrook. "I knew you looked familiar. Anyway, my family is raising money for a Care Walk. You know, the kind of thing where we get donations and my whole family runs a marathon, for cancer and whatnot? Well, if you pledge a certain amount of money, that's how much each of us get for every mile we run."

In seconds my stepdad Larry was in the doorway, huffing and red-faced, already two drinks in. There was no way he would miss a chance to schmooze, especially with a family as rich as the Holbrooks.

"It's for cancer?" said Larry.

For one weird moment I realized Richard was staring at me. I wasn't dressed any special way. Just my jeans, a too-big black Misfits T-shirt with a skull on it. But he was looking. I don't know, I kind of liked it. That's the truth. Sometimes it just feels good to get looked at. Not so much other times. But when it's your choice, when it's what you want—when you know for a fact that you can get it and getting it feels good to you—well, I don't really figure anybody can blame me for that.

I knew She never wanted me to get attention from boys. She said it was too dangerous, and I trusted Her about that. But She was quiet that day, pouty for some reason, and I ignored Her.

"This one is actually for a new Family Life Center," said Mrs. Holbrook. "You know, a gym for members? A basketball court for our church league."

"Oh," said my mom. "Well, actually . . ."

Larry cut in.

"Sure thing. We'd love to help out. How much?"

"We ask for a minimum donation of ten dollars a mile," said Mrs. Holbrook. "Some particularly generous families have given up to a hundred."

I could tell Larry didn't like that. He got all blustery and stuttered a little. Richard saw it, too. We met eyes and smirked together. It was weird connecting with a boy in that way, especially a boy like Richard Holbrook. He was tall and athletic and popular. We'd been around each other at school for years and never once had he spoken to me. That was fine, I didn't particularly care too much, because I had Her, and because he was a notorious snob. The more invisible I was to people like him the better. But it felt good to share a laugh at my stepdad's expense. It felt real damn good.

"Uh, how about twenty?" said my stepdad.

Mom looked away, embarrassed. I could tell she'd done the math, and even twenty was more than we could afford.

"Twenty dollars would be just fine," said Mrs. Holbrook, smiling. Great god, what a fake she was. Richard rolled his eyes. Again I had to stifle a laugh.

"Thank y'all so much for the pledge," she said. "The run isn't for another month, so we're still training, five miles a day. See y'all soon."

They turned to go.

Richard Holbrook looked back at me.

"Be seeing you," he said.

I'll be honest, I blushed a little.

I still hate myself for that.

A couple of hours later I lay on my bed, talking to Her. She was pretty mad.

He's going to come and see you, you know.

"Now why would he do that?"

Because you're beautiful, and you're strange, and that's what boys like Richard Holbrook do.

"I doubt it."

You shouldn't.

"You're just jealous that somebody else might pay a little attention to me."

You'll be sorry.

But Richard Holbrook did come back later that night, just like She said he would. It was a wide, clear night and the moon shone down like an old friend. Richard threw pebbles at my window.

I opened it and told him to knock it off. I had to do the thing where I loud-whispered, like I was screaming a secret.

"I tried to call you," he said, "but nobody knew your number."

"So you threw rocks at my window?"

"It works in the movies. Besides, what else was I supposed to do? Ring your doorbell?"

Richard wasn't so much to look at, really. He was too tall and he had dirty-blond hair. Freckles, too. But he had a way about him when he smiled, like he had just pulled a trick on you. I liked that.

"So, you coming, or what?" he said.

"Just a minute."

I crept out of my bedroom and down the stairs, out the front door. It was easy sneaking out of my house. I'd done it a hundred times. When I got down there Richard was leaning up against a tree, smirking at me. The moonlight made his freckles look pimply. He had a flask of something he kept drinking out of.

"You're not wearing any shoes," he said.

It was true. I'd forgotten them.

"Maybe I just don't have a pair I like," I said.

"You're about as weird as everyone says you are," he said, and took a big drink. "But you seem pretty smart, too."

"Thanks," I said. "Can I have a sip of that?"

He handed it to me. I took a swig and gagged a little.

"What is that?"

"Whiskey," he said.

I'd never had whiskey before. Just beer and peach rum and whatever else my mom and Larry had lying around.

"Want to go for a walk?" he said.

I nodded sure. It was good to walk in the night, moonglow all over everything. Richard took my hand. That felt good, too. I'd never done that before either.

We didn't go far. Just out into the woods a little bit, to this lovely wide-armed pecan tree that I like. Pretty soon me and Richard were kissing. It was new to me, and I didn't really want to, but I let him anyway. I guessed that's what you were supposed to do when you're sixteen and out walking during a big moon night. It was fun for a little while.

But then he started touching me, just all over the place. I didn't want that at all. I asked him to stop.

"Sure," he said, but he didn't quit. He kept going, clutching at me, rubbing his hands all over my body.

"Quit it," I said, and pushed him away.

"Come on, don't make me beg you."

He grabbed at me again.

"Stop it, you creep," I said.

I slapped him.

Richard laughed.

That pissed me off. To have him laugh at my anger, to chuckle off laying a hand on me. Never had I felt smaller or more humiliated in my life.

"Fuck you," I said. "I'm out of here."

Richard laughed again. Then he pushed me.

I tripped over a tree limb and went down hard, smacking my head on a stump. It dazed me a second. Richard crawled on top of me. I couldn't believe it. I couldn't believe this was happening to me.

"Come on," he said. "Just give me what I want."

I tried to crawl away, but Richard grabbed my shoulders and pinned me. He was a football player, I knew that. He was strong. I couldn't move with all his awful weight on top of me.

"Let me go," I said. "Please."

I was crying.

"You'll love it," he said. "Everybody says I'm good at it."

Richard pulled my shirt over my head. I hit him with my fists and he got mad. He palmed my face with his hand and pressed my head into the dirt. I hit him again and he punched me in the jaw.

"Stupid bitch," he said. "I can think of a dozen girls who would kill to be where you are now."

"Let me go," I said. "Please."

I hated how my voice sounded, how puny and pleading and weak.

"I'll tell everyone," I said. "If you don't let me go right now I'll tell everyone what you did."

Richard laughed.

"Tell anyone you want," he said. "But no one is going to believe you. Not that I was ever here, not that somebody like me would ever try to fuck somebody like you."

I hated Richard Holbrook. I hated him and I wanted him to die.

I could feel Her roar up in me then. I could feel Her taking over me, crawling like a fire over my bones.

"You better let me go," I said.

Richard put his mouth on my breast and bit. I think that's what did it.

I felt the world change colors, I felt light swirl and grow magnificent, and I knew She was taking over, tingling into my palms, into my fingers and my head, into my lips, my eyes. I felt the colors reverse themselves and finally I knew this boy for what he really was.

The whole world went blank for a minute.

I couldn't see. I couldn't feel anything.

It was like the way people talk about those isolation tanks, where you're floating on salt water and there's no lights and you can't see anything, you can't feel or smell anything at all. You start to forget that you even exist.

It's nice.

I awoke on all fours, hissing and growling. I had a warm cop-
pery taste in my mouth, thick as syrup. Richard Holbrook stood
about four feet from me, eyes wide with fear. He held his hand,
blood gushing all down it. I guessed that was what was in my
mouth. I guessed that was what tasted so good.

I felt wild. I wanted more. I wanted to rip Richard's head off.

A pair of hands grabbed my arms, yanking me back. I tried to
bite at them—I tried to snap at them with my teeth. I was flipped
over and pinned down again. It was Larry. Mom came running
out, screaming. I wanted to stop, I wanted to calm myself, to tell
them I was okay. But I couldn't get back control of my body. She
was raging, She was too strong, She had all of me. I kept biting at
Richard. I wanted to kill him.

"Go on home, Richard," said Larry.

"But I'm bleeding everywhere," he said. "That crazy fucking
girl bit me."

"Get your ass on home," said Larry. "Or I'll tell your parents
you came here to rape my stepdaughter. I will have the cops here
in ten minutes."

I was wild, flailing, gnashing my teeth at everyone.

I saw Richard Holbrook stumble off to his car, heard it crank
and saw headlights disappear down the drive. Larry flipped me
on my stomach and pinned my hands behind my back.

"Get the duct tape," he said.

"You can't do that to her," said Mom.

"Just hurry up and get the goddamn duct tape."

Mom went to the house and came back with the tape. Larry
bound my wrists together, and then my ankles. He picked me up,

careful to hold my face away from his body, and carried me. Larry dropped me on the couch. I flopped off onto the floor.

I couldn't stop. I was screaming in Her voice, gnashing my teeth, yelling in languages I didn't even know. She was out of control. There wasn't a single part of me that wasn't Her.

"Jesus help us," said Mom.

Through my mouth She screamed agony in fire.

"Calm down now, baby," said Mom. "I love you, darling. God's going to take care of you."

She roared like flames lapped at her feet.

Larry began to sing a hymn, "A Mighty Fortress Is Our God," in his reedy pitchy voice.

She shrieked like he'd chucked Her right in the flames. Oh it hurt, Christ it hurt, I could feel the fire rip through my veins like they were filled with tar, like the word "Christ" was a match tossed and my blood was all gasoline.

"My God," said Larry. "She ain't crazy. She's possessed."

Mom just wept and wept.

I started hyperventilating, until I couldn't breathe anymore. Just before I blacked out I felt Her let go of me, I felt my breath return to normal, I wasn't even scared anymore, and She sang inside me as I passed out.

A few hours later I woke up locked in my bedroom. I was still taped up, so tired I could hardly move. I heard my mom and Larry whispering from downstairs through the vents.

"You should have seen her when I first got out there," said Larry. "Heard all that screaming. She looked like an animal."

"But the boy was trying to hurt her," said Mom. "She was just defending herself."

"Christ, Suzanne, she nearly ripped his throat out."

I should have let Her do it. I never should have tried to stop Her.

You never should have gone out there in the first place, She said. *I told you not to.*

"You were right," I said. "I'm sorry."

It's not your fault. It's his. It's his fault and no one else's. But it's too late now. They're going to take me away from you.

"What?"

They're going to call a preacher, and he's going to steal me from you.

I began to cry then.

Don't worry, She said. *I knew this would happen, sooner or later. Don't worry at all. I have a plan.*

"What kind of plan?"

I felt Her smile inside me.

I can't tell you yet, She said. *It's a secret.*

Soon Mom came upstairs. I was docile and quiet. Mom un-duct-taped me. I had peed the bed. I watched while Mom stripped the sheets. She kissed me on the forehead and cried.

Mom said things like, "Oh, my baby girl, your face is gone ghost-white." Mom cried and cried over me. Later she brought me a bowl of soup.

I wanted to run, to flee and never come back, but I had no money and nowhere to go.

I was trapped.

They called their church in the morning. The big First Baptist church, the one the Holbrooks went to, didn't do things like that—casting out demons, speaking in tongues, all that wild heathen stuff—but they knew someone who would. The church denied all liability of course, and no one could know how Mom and Larry got this particular preacher's name. That was fine. Larry wanted it secret.

And Reverend Sanders came to save me the very next day.

My phone buzzed. I jolted upright, swiping a long string of drool from my chin. I must have fallen asleep. The clock said three P.M.

"Hello?" I said, disoriented. I didn't even look at the number calling in.

"Clarabella?"

"Roy! You're back early!"

"Yep. Dad said he had to get back to town and take care of something. He's at his office now."

"Sounds serious."

"Yeah, it does," said Roy. "But I wouldn't know. He hasn't been telling me much lately. Honestly, he seems pretty freaked out."

"About what?" I said.

"I don't know," he said. "That's what's bothering me. He just keeps saying, 'This town is filthy with evil. It's rotten from the top down.'"

"Jeez. I'm sorry, Roy," I said. "Can I help?"

"Any chance you got your mom's car today? I got a feeling Dad won't be home till pretty late tonight."

"I'll be there in fifteen minutes."

I ran to the bathroom and brushed all the puke out of my mouth. Then I got in Mom's car and drove straight for Roy's house. I already felt so much better. I had really missed him, even more than I realized. The past few days had been a sort of dark, haunted nightmare, and, well . . . I was just so happy to see Roy.

I swooped into his driveway and Roy jumped in the car. I kissed him twice on the cheek and let him put his arms around me. It felt so good to be held like that, to be warmed by his body after these long lonely days. Roy pulled back from me and looked me deep in the eyes. I felt my heart spark a little bit.

Behind me the Wish House spirit crept closer.

"Did you feel that?" said Roy. "It's like it got cold in here all of a sudden. I'm chilled all over."

He held his arm out to me, and the flesh was goosebumped.

"No, Roy. I didn't feel anything," I said. "Nothing at all."

I wished I was a better liar.

"So, tell me about your trip."

"Well, it was kind of weird," he said. "My dad spoke to this youth retreat, right? It was all homeschooled kids, about our age. I spent most of the time in the crowd with them, getting preached to."

"That's strange."

"Yeah, no kidding. Dad was all jittery too, nervous-like. I don't think he slept half the time we were gone. I'd wake up in the hotel and he'd be sitting up in bed, staring at the TV on mute, muttering to himself." Roy must have seen the worry on my face, because he laughed. "It's not as bad as it sounds. I mean, he gets like that sometimes. Usually around this time of year, about when Mom died."

"I'm sorry, Roy."

"It's okay. My dad can be pretty eccentric. I'm kind of used to it at this point. But what was really weird was the sermon he decided to preach on. He said he picked it just for me, that it was a message he wanted me to hear."

"What was it about?"

"That's the thing," he said. Roy ran his hand through his hair, like he was embarrassed to tell me. "It was about purity."

"Purity?"

"You know. Like sexual purity. Virginity and waiting until marriage, all that. How important that stuff is. How sex can open up a whole world of problems."

"It's weird that he singled you out like that."

"Yeah," said Roy. "It's like he knows something's up."

Roy looked so sad it almost broke my heart. It was nice to hurt for somebody other than myself for once.

"But something *is* up, isn't it?" I said.

"Yeah, I guess so." Roy smiled at me. "I guess it is."

We spent the rest of the time making out. It was like time spent healing. I just hoped I wasn't being selfish and getting Roy sick. When I dropped off Roy back at his driveway a couple of hours later I felt better than I had in days. It was amazing the way closeness to another person could patch you up like that, if only for a little while. I only wish Roy could have stayed with me longer, but he promised his dad he would clean up the house before he got home. Roy didn't want to give him anything else to be suspicious about. We had only been apart ten minutes before I started missing Roy all over again.

Maybe that was why She wanted me to be nice to Roy in the first place. Maybe She knew how hideous it would be without Her, how sick and lonely I would feel with Her gone, like my soul was chucked under the wheels of a garbage truck. Maybe She knew that Roy, for all his dorky loser backwardness, could soothe that pain for a little while. Yeah, that had to be it.

"Thank You," I whispered to Her, "for giving me Roy."

Back home I already felt better. I sat on the porch again for another hour, trying to get Eyeball to come and sit on my lap. He wouldn't do it, no matter what I offered him, no matter how many treats. It was like he was afraid of me, of the Wish House spirit hounding me around. It was weird. He was never scared of Her, you know?

I went upstairs and took a shower. I stayed in the water a long, long time. It felt good, like the best kind of warm blanket. The shower is such a private place. Sometimes I like to curl up in a ball, like I'm warm and safe and a baby again. I know that's weird, but I do it a lot.

It was coming close to nighttime, and I knew it would be any moment before the Wish House spirit spoke and Gaspar revealed his boon. I was so close to having Her back. I was so close to being happy again.

I got out and started to towel-dry my hair. The mirror was all fogged up. I moved to wipe it with my hand, but then I stopped.

Words began to appear on the mirror, written in the steam as if by an invisible finger. I watched it etch, letter by letter, my fate:

Bring me the boy.

Jesus Christ. It wanted Roy. Gaspar wanted Roy.

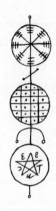

IT DIDN'T MAKE ANY SENSE. I WAS THE

one asking for my demon to be found. I was the one who had to walk through that awful old house all by myself. None of that had anything to do with Roy. It couldn't. Was that why She wanted me to be friends with Roy? So I could hand him over to Gaspar? What would he want with Roy?

I knew the answer had to lie with whatever happened to Kevin Henrikson. He was the last kid to be delivered to the One Wish Man, right? Other than me, I guess, and Gaspar didn't want me.

I wished I could talk to Cléa. That girl knew all about what happened to Kevin, and it seemed like she had the power to do something about it. But Cléa was dead. I guessed the best I could do was talk to the person who knew both Cléa and magic, who probably knew a hell of a lot more about what was happening than she let on—Miss Mathis.

I still had a couple of hours before Mom got home. I had to go see Miss Mathis, even though Uncle Mike said she was dangerous, that she was evil. Even if it turned out she was a part of the Paradise Society and she'd lock me up with Luther Simpkins, I had to try. This was too important. Roy's life could be at stake.

I threw on some clothes and drove to Miss Mathis's house.

There was a sign on her door, same as usual. But this time, it said MADAM IS OUT. TRY AGAIN LATER.

Well, that didn't help me any.

What was I supposed to do now? Gaspar wanted Roy and I didn't know what for, I didn't know why. I had all these names—Miss Mathis, Kevin Henrikson, Gaspar, the Paradise Society, Cléa—all of them swimming around in my head, clattering against each other, not making a damn bit of sense. Someone had to be able to explain it to me. Someone had to know something.

I was about to turn back into my neighborhood when I had an idea. Roy had said his dad was scared about something, right? And that the whole town was rotten through with evil. He had even mentioned secret societies and cults. Did Reverend Sanders know about the Paradise Society? Could he give me some answers?

I couldn't stand the man. I absolutely did not want to even be in the same room as him. Besides, what would Roy say if he found out I went to see his dad behind his back? But maybe Reverend Sanders knew something I didn't. He sure knew how to cast out demons, and that was power, something I didn't have much in the way of right now. Roy said his dad wouldn't be home until late. Maybe he was still at the church. I would have to suck up my pride, bury my anger. It wasn't just me and Her at stake now, it was Roy, too.

I was off to find the man who had ruined my life.

•

The church Mom and Larry went to—First Baptist, the one all the rich and popular folks went to—was massive, big as a high school campus, complete with an exercise facility and basketball courts. It had beautiful stained-glass windows from the 1800s and life-size oil paintings of all the previous pastors. The youth group room (which I walked by once, curious) had a movie projector and a pool table and a giant sound system.

Reverend Sanders's church was nothing like that. It was tiny, for one, an ugly red-bricked government-looking building just off the highway. The patch of grass in front of the church was brown and dead, and the parking lot had potholes all over it. Inside, the carpet was grey and dour fluorescent lights turned the walls a seasick yellow.

First Baptist was like God's house if God was an investment banker, all splendor and gadgets. Roy's dad's church looked more like the county DMV.

The receptionist's desk was empty, the computer turned off. Still, the air conditioner hummed and the ceiling lights blinkered and the place was unlocked, so I knew Roy's dad had to be here somewhere. The Wish House spirit hissed in my ears to stop, that I shouldn't go anywhere near this place, but that didn't slow me down any.

I walked down a long hallway, peering into dark rooms and passing locked doors, until I came to a door labeled REVEREND CLIFF SANDERS, HEAD PASTOR. I took a deep breath and knocked.

I heard the sound of shuffling papers. A man's voice said, "Come in."

Reverend Sanders wasn't wearing his suit. That's the first thing I noticed about him. He wore a University of Southern Mississippi T-shirt and his hair was all wild grey-and-black tangles, reading glasses perched on his nose. His office was dark and windowless. An old IBM computer sat on his desk amid piles and piles of papers and one of those green accountant-looking desk lamps. The walls were covered in bookshelves, volumes dangling over the edges, all with a lean to them like they could topple over and squash him at any moment.

Reverend Sanders scribbled furiously on a yellow legal pad. I realized the Wish House spirit hadn't followed me in, that it was afraid of Reverend Sanders. I was still a little afraid myself.

"Yes?" said Reverend Sanders. "Can I help you?"

"Hi, sir," I said.

Sir? Was I serious?

"I just had a few questions for you."

"I'm sure you do," he said, not looking up. "We all have questions, don't we? That's what this whole business is, the asking of questions. Most of them unanswerable, of course. Who can ask something of God and know for sure he got an answer? Impossible, really. But we ask anyway. And we pray for faith. Now, what can I do for you?"

Reverend Sanders took off his glasses and squinted at me. I could see a little bit of Roy in him, the slightly befuddled look on his face, the tilt of his head to the left as he peered at me. His smile seemed kind. This man looked nothing like the fierce Bible-thumper who stole Her from me. He seemed more like a sad librarian, or some kind of thwarted philosopher. There was nothing scary to him at all.

"I'm not so sure you remember me. My name is Clare . . . Clarabella . . ."

His face darkened.

"I know who you are."

"Yeah. See, I wasn't sure if you recognized me at first."

"I didn't. And honestly, I'm a bit surprised to see you here. People don't tend to want to see folks who cast demons out of them again, even under the best circumstances. Reminds them too much of hard times, like bumping into your old bail bondsman. Besides, I didn't exactly get the feeling that you wanted me there in the first place."

I didn't, I wanted to say. You ruined everything.

"I wasn't entirely in my right mind at the time," I said.

"Oh, hogwash. I know the difference between a girl and a demon talking. I knew you didn't want me there, plain as day."

"Then why did you come?" I shouted. My eyes blurred with tears. Hold it back, Clare, I thought. Don't let him know how much it hurt.

"Because it wasn't up to you," he said. "Last time I checked, you're under your parents' authority. They called me. I did what I was asked to do." Reverend Sanders leaned back in his chair. "And frankly, you'll thank me for it one day. Or you would if only you could see how things would have turned out having that demon inside you your whole life."

You don't know, I wanted to say, you don't know what She was like. But I held my peace. From the way he looked at me I felt like Reverend Sanders knew good and well how I was feeling.

"Look," I said. "I need to know what I was caught up in. Because I know it was bigger than just me and . . . and the demon."

"How do you figure?"

"Well, the town, for one. I know there's evil here. I know about the Paradise Society."

"Like hell you do," he said, snapping back upright in his chair. He placed his fat fists on either side of the desk and leaned forward at me, staring down into my eyes. "You don't have one clue what those folks are up to, how deep that evil goes. At least, I pray you don't, and Lord help you if I'm mistaken."

I couldn't back down now. I had to be brave. I had to try. I had to do this for Roy.

"I know about Gaspar," I said.

Reverend Sanders scrunched his eyes at me. He doesn't know who I'm talking about, I thought. He doesn't know anything about the One Wish Man. That's good. That might mean Gaspar has nothing to do with any of this. I tried something else.

"And I know about Kevin Henrikson," I said.

Reverend Sanders sucked in a breath and drew back in his chair. This was a name he seemed to know pretty damn well.

"Now just what exactly did that demon of yours tell you?"

"Not much, to be honest. I found out about Kevin on my own. He was a demon-possessed kid too, wasn't he?"

"I don't know," he said. "I never spoke to the boy."

"But you know about him?"

"Of course I do," said Reverend Sanders. "But I don't have any idea how you should. They sure shut everyone up about that boy, yes they did."

"You mean Luther Simpkins?"

"I mean the whole durn lot of them. I know what I saw. Other folks saw him, too. And I never heard a single word about it. Not in the papers, not on the radio, nothing. What showed up in the newspapers was so bland you would have thought it was just another roadside tragedy, a kid run down by accident."

"But it wasn't that?"

"Hell no, it wasn't. I was there, I saw it myself. I was just a boy. But I remember. I remember it perfectly. The traffic was all backed up on Highway 7 and the cars were moving slow, real slow. Everybody rubbernecking, like folks do. I remember the car in front of us braking too fast and my dad bumping them. Not too hard, mind you, but enough to scuff a bumper. My dad was a hothead, you know, he didn't cotton to being yelled at by some sucker in a Cadillac. Ten seconds later he's out of the car with his finger in the guy's face, screaming. And the cops are trying to wave us on, but my daddy won't get back in the car. My daddy was like that, never wanted to mind anyone, never gave one lick what other people thought. Boy, did he hate folks in authority. Spit on a cop just the same as say hello to one."

Reverend Sanders waved his hands at me, talking too fast, his eyes red-rimmed and tired, his fingers a little twitchy. I saw the empty coffee cups littering his desk, the crunched Red Bull cans in his trash bin. Just how long had he been awake?

"So my daddy's screaming and the cops are getting huffy and

I'm scared he's going to get thrown in jail again and I'll have to call my aunt to come and pick me up—and I look over to the side of the road and there's a body being loaded into an ambulance, a stretcher with a great white sheet over it. And I know immediately what it means: I know I'm seeing the first dead person I ever saw. I wonder if it's an old man, someone's granddad who saw it all coming, who had a heart attack on the road.

"But then the sheet falls back—I don't know if it was the wind, or if God blew it back just for me to see, for me to bear witness, Lord knows how it changed my life—but I saw the body. It was a boy, a teenager. I saw his blond hair and his blue, dead eyes, his mouth open like he was trying to holler out. And as the paramedics scrambled to get the sheet back over him, I saw everything else. His body savaged. The skin carved on, written in rips and slashes. Crazy things, symbols, some kind of language not meant for people. Even as a boy I knew it was from the devil. I knew in that moment my calling would be to stop this evil of this kind. I would stand between it and the goodness of the world."

My heart plummeted. Kevin was mutilated? Carved on, like in some sick satanic ritual? That's the future his demon promised him—that's what would happen to Roy, all because She told me to be his friend?

No, She wasn't like that. She *couldn't* be. Kevin's demon was nothing like Her at all. This was all some kind of mistake.

"By that point the cops were shooing my daddy back to the car. I kept poking at him, saying, 'Daddy, did you see that boy, did you, Daddy?' But by then they had the sheet back up, they had him loaded into the ambulance, there was nothing to rubberneck at.

My daddy told me to mind my own damned business and drove me off. Nobody ever mentioned the body, what happened to it. Nobody ever said a damn word. That's how I knew there was evil in this world. That's how I knew my calling. I began to read my Bible, and I began to go to church. I was a prodigy, mind you, they thought I'd be some million-dollar preacher off in Memphis or Nashville somewhere, in a congregation of thousands. But I never wanted any of that. All I wanted was to save this here town, where I lived all my life, where I first came to know there was such a thing as evil."

And now I'd brought this evil onto his son. I felt sick, like I'd puke myself empty right there on his desk. But I choked it back and asked another question.

"Are you saying that the Paradise Society is bigger than just Luther Simpkins?" I said. "Who all is in it?"

"Who ain't is a better question," he said. "Look around you, girl. Just drive somewhere and see. They're everywhere. Folks ain't even evil necessarily, just looking to get ahead. Get money, get power, who cares where it comes from? I used to think they were all gone, but now there's more than ever. They're coming back. This is their sign."

Reverend Sanders reached into his desk drawer. He held up a long red feather pinched between his fingers.

"Believe me or not, I don't care. The police sure don't. I told them time and time again, and they threatened me with jail. I warned my congregation and they left by the dozens. Half the time my own boy thinks I'm crazy. But I know I'm right. They're coming back, mind you. Be careful. Especially a girl like you, having suffered what you have. You'll be like a carcass for those vultures. They'll eat you up, won't need to come back for seconds. You, especially, beware. Pray with everything you got. Because something's coming. Something big."

I looked at that feather, the bright red of the cardinal, so like the one crucified to the Bird Tree. Deep in my heart I knew Reverend Sanders was right. Gaspar and the Paradise Society were connected, there was no use denying it now. The cardinal feather was the final clue.

"I just can't figure it out," he said. "I don't understand where this evil comes from, who controls it. I don't understand how to stop everything from getting worse."

I noticed the picture on his desk. It was Reverend Sanders, much younger and slimmer, all the grey gone out of his hair. He had a little boy in a red collared shirt sitting on his lap. It was Roy, no question. He still smiled the same. And next to him stood a beautiful blond-headed woman. I liked her immediately, I couldn't help it. People in pictures always seem to be lying, you know? Posing, I mean. Grinning too big for the camera, putting in all the twinkle their eyes can muster, practically begging you to believe they're happy. But she wasn't smiling like that. She had a quiet look, a warmth. She was the kind of person you hoped your teacher would be, brown eyes wide with understanding.

"Is that your wife?" I said.

Reverend Sanders's face sank. It was like I'd brought up some kind of old defeat.

"My wife," he said, "is none of your business."

"I'm sorry," I said. "I can leave."

"It's just life, you understand?" he said. "You make mistakes and you make mistakes and Jesus forgives you—He always does. He forgives and forgives and forgives. But that doesn't fix things. That doesn't suddenly make them right. Lust and stupidity. The damned weakness of the flesh. And you think you'll spend your whole life making it right, healing all the hurt you caused. You think, Yes, Lord, I'll do anything to make it right. And then all of a sudden it's too late. She's gone. It's too late."

He seemed so tired, so old, as if he had been fighting this battle in his mind for years and years and there was no winning it, there was no beating back this guilt. I almost reached out and placed my hand on him. I almost touched his hand to comfort him. But then a fire lit up in his eyes and his voice rose to a holler.

"That's why I have to fix this. This I *can* help. I can help this town, my home, this place that I love, despite its black heart. If God can save me, then the town can be saved, too. I have to believe that. I have to work for it with all my heart."

Maybe you should let the town go, I thought, and focus on your kid. He's the one they're after. But no, I couldn't say that. I couldn't let him know about me and Roy. I didn't dare say a word. I would have to fix this myself.

"I guess I don't have any more questions," I said. "Thanks."

"Don't thank me for nothing," he said. "Don't you dare thank me for anything at all."

And I left his office, wondering what in the hell he meant by that.

The spirit latched back on to me the second I left the church. I made it to the car and slumped over in the seat. My head hurt, and I puked again out the open door. I cranked the AC, my brain all swirly and confused. Kevin Henrikson, mutilated. The reverend saw it himself.

Back home I ran upstairs and crawled myself into bed, my light off, door shut, please don't let anybody bother me now. Everything in my room seemed strange, off somehow, *Lady Snowblood* glowering down from above me. Nothing brought comfort, as if even my room was infected with despair.

I had messed up somehow, gotten one of the clues wrong. She couldn't be asking me to get Roy hurt. That would teach his dad a lesson, sure, but the cost was too great. If Gaspar wanted Roy, it was to do him harm, same as what happened to Kevin Henrikson. And if that was Her plan all along, to put Roy through some kind of torture . . .

No, no that couldn't be right. She was the one I trusted, the one who saved my life time and time again, the one who made my life bearable, something worth saving. She was my friend— closer than that. She was my *Only*.

"Where are You?" I whispered. "Why is this happening? Why can't You help me?"

Nothing answered. Despair spread its wings wide over my house, and the floor seemed to creak and groan, the very building crying out under the darkness.

Oh, Roy, I thought. What have I done?

I WAITED UNTIL LATE THAT NIGHT,

when the house was quiet, when everyone was asleep. I took the car again.

I drove out of my neighborhood, down past the main strip and to the town square, the "historic" part of town, the part they advertised on the tourism pamphlets at city hall. I almost never came here. Sure, the houses were pretty, but it was a throwback to darker, sadder times, with slavery and the murder of Native Americans and everything else awful that happened in the South.

There was the clock tower, unburned in the Civil War, the city hall. An old clothing store, what used to be a blacksmith's shop. Rows and rows of new buildings, restaurants and boutique stores, bars with flashing neon. The moon was high and pale as a spotlight, the clouds river-rushing past it, the buzz of street-lights and cicadas, the night creatures out to hunt. I passed a man limping down the highway, a baseball cap pulled low on his face. Why is a man like that out in the night? Where is he going? How can you live in a place your whole life and still have everyone be a stranger?

I kept driving into the old neighborhoods, toward the old homes where the rich lived, all porch lights and rocking chairs, sweeping oaks and perfect lawns. I stopped in front of a house I actually like, a favorite of mine, with blue spires that rose from the top like a miniature fairy-tale castle. Someone had left the porch lights on, and they cast an eerie glow over the emptiness.

That's where I first saw it. A single red feather hung over the doorway. It glimmered there like a drop of blood.

I began to notice others, above other doorways. Not always a cardinal feather, sometimes a blue one, or a black one yanked from a crow. House after house after house, I saw them. Sometimes they were fake, painted on, or dyed plumes like the kind you can buy at a craft store. I passed businesses, little feathers painted on their signs, rich-lady boutiques with a bundle of feathers dangling over the CLOSED sign in the doorway. Chiseled above the gates to the county courthouse, visible from the streets, a long spiny feather. Even in the glistering stained glass of the First Baptist church, what I had always taken for a tongue of fire from Pentecost now dangled above the apostles' heads as a bloodred cardinal's feather.

I cut down a side street, passing shut businesses and quiet houses, the occasional TV flickering bluely in an upstairs window. I rode past families of raccoons and doddering armadillos scrounging in the night, stray cats stretched out over upturned garbage cans, and stopped at the old town cemetery. I parked on a neighborhood street so the cops wouldn't see Mom's car. I took my flashlight and walked through the gates, past all the fresh graves, the dirt piled high and orange, the flowers still in bloom, into the center of the graveyard, where the town founders were buried. The graves were ancient and crumbling, the tombstones jutting crookedly from the earth, so old they seemed like they were a part of the landscape, like they had sprouted roots that spread deep beneath the town. Every single one of their headstones bore the engraving of a feather. I walked to the heart of the cemetery, where a ring of cedar trees surrounded the oldest of all the graves, the Simpkins family plot. I stood in the middle of them, the trees like tall robed priests surrounding me. The air was colder here. The wind trembled the leaves just slightly.

A yellow dog peered up at me from among the headstones. It let out a howl, long and mournful. I shined my flashlight at the monument erected in the center of the grove, an obelisk etched with the Simpkins family crest. And below it, in perfect artistry, the outline of a bird, its wings spread wide in the shape of crucifixion.

Reverend Sanders was right. The Paradise Society had been here from the beginning, and now they were coming back.

"Where are You?" I said to Her. "How could You do this to me?"

The night answered with its hum, the secret buzzing like the approach of some far-off army.

I walked back to Mom's car. There was one more person I had to see.

THE SIGN ON MISS MATHIS'S DOOR

had changed. Now it said I HAVE A SECRET. I didn't like that. I didn't like that at all.

Miss Mathis sat in her chair, same as usual. The cigarette smoke was even worse, all the stamped-out butts sticking up in her coffeepot, the dog lying there like the corpse of a dog. She had a half-empty bottle of wine on the coffee table.

"Hi, Miss Mathis," I said.

There was a silence then, just the wheezing of the tiny dog, the long exhale of Miss Mathis and her cigarette. She seemed to be glaring at me through her sunglasses. I knew in some way that I was in trouble, that I had done something wrong.

"You went and saw him, didn't you?" she said. "It ain't no good to lie to me, you know that."

I nodded.

"Figured you would," she said. "Figured you were that stupid. I bet he even sent something back with you, didn't he? Bet we're being spied on right now. That's fine, that's fine. Can't say anything it don't know already. Now, sit on down, Miss Mathis has to tell you a story. Figured one day I'd have to tell somebody, but that don't make the telling any easier. You mind refilling me, dear? I don't think I can say this sober."

I poured the rest of the wine in her coffee mug.

"Is it about the Wish House?" I said.

Miss Mathis nodded.

"It's about the Wish House, and a hell of a lot of other things, too," she said. "Mostly though, it concerns this character you call the One Wish Man."

"You knew the One Wish Man?" I said.

"'Course I knew him. But to me, he was just called Gaspar. And believe me, Gaspar was powerful. I mean, he could do anything. *Anything.* We'd be at one of his soirees out in the woods and he'd be performing miracles like party tricks. Change water to wine, change it back again. Calling up ghosts from all over, the spirits of the long dead and the not yet born, have deceased husbands spill their guts to their still-living wives while all of us clanked champagne glasses and laughed. Gaspar could raise your dead fucking pet if he wanted. See the future too, in the hazy way some of us can. A lot of the money you see rumbling around these parts came from him."

"Was that the Paradise Society?" I asked.

Miss Mathis frowned at me.

"Where you go hearing a name like that?"

"I saw Luther Simpkins," I said. "He's locked in an attic. He flung blood at me."

"My, my, girl," said Miss Mathis, "you do get around."

"I know you're one of them," I said. "You're one of the Paradise Society."

"I *was* one of them," she said, lighting a cigarette. "And I'll regret that until the day I die. But you can go ahead and judge me all you want. Hell, I deserve it. Gaspar got a lot of us rich folks even richer. We're all still living off it, even kids and grandkids. Those will be your pearly-white elites of this town, you understand me? And Gaspar was our leader, more or less. The great intercessor, the one who spoke right through the veil, who talked to demons face-to-face. We always asked him about it, 'Gaspar, how'd you get your power? How did you learn so much?' He would just laugh it off. We laughed too, of course. We were living it large. What did we care where the power came from, so long as it came, so long as we were allowed to do whatever we pleased? Well, one day I found out."

Miss Mathis settled back into her chair, sunglasses dark over her eyes. Her mouth twitched. When she began to speak again it was almost a whisper.

"Jesus, I don't know if I can tell the rest of it. But I suppose I got to. Been waiting forty years to tell someone, and wouldn't you know it, that somebody turns out to be you. Cléa's spitting image. You look enough like her to be her sister, you know that?"

I remembered the picture I saw of Cléa at Uncle Mike's. I didn't feel as beautiful as her, not by a long shot.

"I'm not just talking looks, honey," said Miss Mathis, like she could read my mind. "I'm talking *spirit*, now. There's something in you that reminds me of her. And, well, Cléa was a dear, wasn't she? She was a star, like she walked into a room and we all adjusted our orbit accordingly. Cléa had power like that, a presence, a magic sparking every word she spoke."

I wanted to tell Miss Mathis that wasn't how I was at all, that I'd spent the last eight years being a kind of blank space, hiding myself from people. If anyone thought I was a star it was Her, not anybody else. Well, except for Roy. Maybe he saw me that way, too.

"I met Cléa the same way I met you," said Miss Mathis. "That mysterious way that certain like-minded folks tend to find each other. Some people call that fate. I just call it the way things are. Like begets like, after all, and me and Cléa were a pair. Her momma had known a little spellcasting, tiny magics, and she wanted to learn some herself. Well, you can't teach things like that, not really—they just sort of bubble up in a person, and the best thing you can do is help them bring it out in themselves. 'Course, Cléa didn't need my help. She was a goddamn natural. I started bringing her along to Gaspar's parties. They were getting more and more lavish. This town always had a dark element to it, an extra shadow over things, so to speak. That's why there are so many goddamn loonies running around in such a small place. It draws us like a barbecue draws the Baptists.

"Anyway, I liked showing up places with her. Cléa was about your age, maybe a little older, and she always wore these dresses that seemed to flutter around her, like how light reflects in water. I liked to walk into a room and have everybody turn and stare at us, compliment me on how beautiful my daughter was, which always made me feel old and got her laughing. Cléa could really make you feel like something special, she could. I miss that. All these years later, I miss her."

I wanted to tell Miss Mathis that I understood, that I knew what it was like to miss your person, your Only. But this wasn't my story now, it was hers. Miss Mathis took a deep breath and kept going.

"One night at the Wish House me and Cléa snuck off from the rest of the party. See, Cléa wanted to explore. Gaspar's house had many rooms. It was like a museum, dark places galore where any number of mysteries might be buried. Seemed like a bad idea to me, but I was drunk, and Cléa could convince me to do just about anything. So we crept deep into Gaspar's house, further than any of us had ever dared to.

"We had candles, you know, nothing brighter or fancier than that, and the lights were off in all the rooms and hallways we passed through. It was spooky, and if it spooks a woman like me, then you know I'm not bullshitting. But me and Cléa were drunk and were having our time, opening doors, stealing deeper and deeper into the Wish House. Until we came to this one room, bigger than all the others. We heard a noise in the corner, a sort of snicker. Cléa grabbed my hand and we both froze, and I dropped my candlestick. We were scared, both of us knowing now we had gone too far. I heard it again—laughter, like cackling, the kind that makes you feel sick to your stomach. It was coming from the back corner of the room.

"I wanted to leave, just turn tail and run, but Cléa wouldn't have it. 'Come on, Eugenia,' she said. 'We have to see.' I know she was thinking that we had found the secret to Gaspar's power, and if she found out, then maybe she could be just as powerful as him. Cléa always did have a thing for power. Hell, all of us in this walk of life do. And it's our downfall every damn time.

"I kept walking softly, trying to make as little noise as possible. For some reason Cléa's candle didn't seem to cast very much light at all, like the dark was too thick, like it was a living thing and it just kept hogging up the light. As we came closer, the snickering stopped. It turned into a sort of grumble, a murmuring to itself, not like any animal I ever heard. Soon we got close enough to see what was making that racket, and I had to slap my hand over my mouth so I wouldn't scream.

"It was a boy, not much older than you. He was naked, except for a pissed-on pair of shorts. His body was covered in what looked like tattoos, magic stuff, stars and symbols, the kind of equations real magicians use, like alchemy. His eyes were a deep black, and I knew he was possessed. Not just by one demon, mind you. By a whole legion of them. Power radiated out from him like a goddamn nuclear reactor. It tingled you down to your toes, believe me. We'd found the source of all Gaspar's power, this little boy stuffed full of demons.

"He got on his knees, the boy did. He was begging us to help him. I got scared, I tried to back away. But then he reached his hand out to Cléa. And when he did, one of the tattoos on his arm cracked a little bit, and a drop of blood spilled out. That's when I realized that those weren't tattoos. They were scabs. Gaspar had carved his magic into the boy's flesh, a spell written on human skin, the kind of thing you can't wash out.

"I told her we got to go, and now. She said no, that this boy needed our help. Cléa pointed to a place on the boy's stomach, a flap of skin half hanging off. On it was carved a feather, the symbol of the Paradise Society, followed by a bunch of slashes like some weird handwriting. The boy had just about clawed it off himself. Cléa said that was the part that was keeping him there, that little binding spell on his skin.

"And before I knew it, Cléa had slipped a knife from her garter—she always came to these parties armed, a lesson maybe you should learn—and took a step toward the boy. She was whispering to him, cooing at him, singing this soft little lullaby of a song. It was working, it was her magic, she was calming him, drawing closer to him. By the time I realized what she was doing, it was too late.

"Cléa slipped the knife over his stomach. The skin came off in one clean flap, easy as if a surgeon had done it. 'It's okay,' she said. 'I know it hurts. Let's get you bandaged up and to a doctor.' And the boy looked at her, and I swear to you he smiled.

"Then he jumped at us. Smacked Cléa right in the face, a bright-red bloody fistprint on her cheek. The boy took off running. We chased after him, but he busted through a window and ran into the woods. We followed him as best we could, called out to him, walking through the woods and moonlight. A howl came up from the Wish House, a fierce sort of wail that sent shivers over me. It was Gaspar. He had figured out the boy was gone, his power was gone. I knew he'd be searching these woods, too. By then it was nearly daylight, and I figured the boy had hightailed it right out of town. Me and Cléa joined with the other guests leaving the Wish House, everyone drunk and disturbed, laughing as if we didn't all know something important had happened, as if we didn't all know the good times had ended.

"Not too long later we heard the boy got run over, that he was dead. Found out his name was Kevin, that he was some kind of runaway. Cléa was all torn up about it. She thought it was her fault. 'Hell,' I said, 'you sprung him loose. You saved him. It was his own fault he got run over.' But she wasn't content with that. You got to understand me: Cléa was *good*. Hell of a lot better person than me, anyway. I wanted to leave the country, book it as far away from Gaspar as I could, start my life over. Cléa, she wanted to stay, she wanted to fix it. 'He'll just come back if we don't,' she said, 'same as he always has, through the ages. We have to end it, Eugenia. We have to destroy the Wish House.'

"I told her hell fucking no. There was no way we were powerful enough to destroy him, much less the House. If she wanted to commit suicide, she was on her own. I will never forget the look that she gave me when she left, when she walked out this very door. And then we didn't talk again, not for months. Until one day she showed up at my doorstep. She had that rosewood box in her hand. She said, 'Keep this, and if anything happens to me, guard it with your life.'"

Miss Mathis wiped a long wet tear from her cheek. She lit another cigarette and took a deep drag of it, breathing it out like the dregs of a lifetime spent with worry and regret. I realized the "loathsome company" that Gaspar said Kevin had fallen into wasn't the Paradise Society. No, it was Miss Mathis and Cléa, the ones who tried to free him.

"I should have gone with her," said Miss Mathis. "Cléa shouldn't have had to do something like that alone. Maybe we could have beat Gaspar. But I didn't go. I was a coward. Cléa walked into those woods and never came back. I was so scared Gaspar would come for me next that I didn't even want the rosewood box in my house. So I took it over to Miklos's and had him cuss me for an hour, did I know where his daughter was, how could I have let something happen to her? I put the box in his hands and left, and I didn't see him again for forty years.

"Gaspar vanished after that, too. Forty years gone, and now he's back. You can feel it, can't you? The change in things? The woods crying out? You can hear the birds outside weeping at night. Something big is coming, and once again I missed my chance to stop it. Always was a coward."

The smell of the room, the stink of cigarettes and dog piss, the sad and lonely woman crying in the chair in front of me. It was almost too much. I almost couldn't ask the next question.

"Miss Mathis?" I said.

"Yeah, honey?"

"Is that scroll over there Kevin's skin?"

She nodded at me.

I got up and let myself out, shutting the door quick as I could behind me.

AT HOME I COASTED THE CAR, LIGHTS

off, into the driveway, but I didn't go back into my house. Instead I walked through the woods and into the starlight, to the place where I first met Her. I sat on a tree stump next to the wrecked shack, the weeds and tall grasses scratching my knees, the moon like a sad white flag waving over me.

Hi, Clare, a voice said. *Did you miss me?*

I felt Her again. The whisper of hands through my hair, the brush across my cheeks, soft as a breeze. Her warmth, the quiet glow inside me that happened whenever She was near. How good it felt to feel Her again, to not be alone anymore. How much I had missed Her, how much I loved Her, how good She could make everything all over again . . .

But no, that wasn't Her. Something wasn't right about it. This warmth was a false warmth, a disguised darkness. I whirled around and faced it now, blacker than black, the night's own shadow. The Wish House spirit had followed me here. I could make it out finally, could see where it ended and normal night began. I stared down deep into it, and felt it glaring back at me with nothing but hate.

"Are you Nicolas?" I said, and the darkness glowered.

Maybe this demon was just like Her. I mean like She really was, not how I wanted Her to be. Maybe She was just a lying, wicked demon who wanted nothing but what was good for Herself. Maybe She just leeched onto me and sucked up my life and wouldn't let go.

God, that sounded just like what drugs had done to my dad. How they kept him hidden in our house, or else banished away from us for days and days, how we couldn't depend on him, how they controlled every move he made. How they kept him vacant and apart from us, how they put him in a place where no one, not even my mom, could reach him.

Was that what She had done to me? Hadn't She kept me alone all this time, cut off from other people, from kids my own age, from boys, from my own mother? Hadn't She paraded me around the night like a puppet, seizing full control over me whenever She wanted?

I sat down and covered my eyes with my hands, my head hot and flushed and fevery. I didn't want to believe it. More than anything, I didn't want it to be true.

The way She hurt me when She was angry. The way She made miserable anyone else I loved. The way She only wanted me for Herself, how She wouldn't dare share me with anybody else.

And now She expected me to hand Roy over to be scarred and tortured. Why? Because of who his fucking father was?

I couldn't do it. I couldn't give Roy to Gaspar just to get Her back. Not if Gaspar intended to make some sort of treasure chest out of Roy, a pouch for all his demons. Roy would be a slave, carved up and ruined, his mind and body destroyed. And it would be my fault. No, I couldn't do that. No way in hell could I ever. I turned my eyes to the darkness and I stared that demon down. I took a deep breath and spoke.

"You can't have him," I said.

The darkness glared back at me.

"You can't have him. I won't let you."

The demon seethed at me, it writhed and twisted, the blackness, the anger.

"Leave," I said. "And don't come back. You are not welcome here."

It gnashed its teeth at me. It swallowed up moonlight and howled. The edges of things dissolved and night stretched its hand out to my face. My nose filled with the scent of burning, with sulfur and charred flesh.

"No," I said. "You cannot have him. I won't let you. Now get out."

I stood up off the stump and stepped toward it, scared, but I wasn't stopping. The moon burned brighter than Heaven, and all the stars flung their light. I stared the demon down right where its eyes should have been.

"Leave!" I screamed. "Begone now and forever!"

I heard a rasping noise, a scrape of metal on metal, the sound of worlds ripping apart. I fell to my knees, covering my ears. It was loud as the tornado that touched down by our house when I was a kid, that ripped our neighbor's tractor off the ground and catapulted it down the street. The roar filled my ears, filled my nose and lungs. It was as if it was coming from inside me.

Then nothing. Silence, and the normal night noises.

I said no. I did it. I scared the Wish House spirit away.

I had also just lost Her forever.

I fell down on the ground and let myself cry. The quiet kind, my body shaking, the cool grass and the mosquitoes and lightning bugs swarming around me. I would miss Her always, even if She wasn't who I thought She was. Because She had saved me. For years and years and years, She had been the only good thing in my world. I loved Her, it was true, I loved Her more than I had ever loved anyone in my life, even Mom and Dad. But She was a liar. I felt a hole open up in me, an emptiness that I knew would be with me the rest of my life.

But I had done the right thing. There was no way I could give Roy to Gaspar, not to have him do what he did to Kevin.

"I hate You for this," I said. "And I'll miss You always."

A wind shivered the trees, and it felt like She heard me.

I walked back to the house and shut the door and turned to go upstairs, but there was Mom, sitting on the steps.

"Where you been, honey?" she said.

"Out." No, that was too harsh. I was going to be nicer to Mom, remember? "I mean, I had to take care of some things."

"I know you've been taking the car out, sneaking away at night," she said. "I have half a mind to tell Larry, except I'm scared of what he'd do." Mom put her head in her hands and sighed. "I just wish you'd tell me what was going on."

I thought about it for a second, I really did. I nearly told my mom everything, about Her, about Roy and Miss Mathis and the One Wish Man. I almost did it right there. But who would believe something like that? She probably just would've thought I was crazy or lying. It was impossible to explain.

"I'm sorry, Mom," I said. "But it's over. I won't be sneaking out anymore."

"I've heard that before."

"Yeah, but this time I mean it," I said. I sat down next to her and laid my head on her shoulder. "Things are going to get better now. I'm going to get better, I promise you that."

"We'll see, I guess," said Mom, but she was smiling. "Now, go upstairs and get you some sleep."

Mom kissed me on the cheek and I went up to my room. I looked all around, but it was empty. There was no one there but me.

I crawled into bed. I felt like a new Clare, like a new person with a new future, my own, finally, the world open for me to search my way through, alone. But it was a good alone, because I had chosen it. I was heartbroken, sure, but hopeful. I had my mom, and I had Roy. For the first time since I lost Her, I felt like a new life was possible for me.

That night I slept deep and rich and full and I did not have any dreams.

DO YOU KNOW HOW GOOD IT FELT,

after a month of listless, haunted sleep, nightmares and spying demons and a great yawning emptiness, to wake up rested? To have to be woken up by your mom, because you slept through her knocking on your door for the first time in your life? Even better, to wake up to your mom smiling at you, with a plate full of pancakes with whipped cream and strawberries piled on top of them, like you haven't been lying to her for years, like she knew it all and forgave you already, like today was the start of your brand-new, better life?

Because I can tell you right now, it felt pretty damn amazing.

"Saw you slept in today," Mom said, "so I figured I'd go back to making breakfast."

"Thanks, Mom."

I meant it, too. I wasn't trying to hide anything. It felt good to be honest for once, to say something and not mean anything else by it.

"No problem. I'm glad you're feeling better. For real, this time."

Again I wondered how much Mom really knew about me. Probably a lot more than I ever dreamed she did.

I dressed and walked downstairs. Eyeball met me right at the foot of the stairs and licked my fingers. It was good to have him love me again, for him not to be afraid anymore. The whole day seemed mine, and only mine, for the first time in ages.

"Just wanted to remind you that today is my and Larry's anniversary," said Mom, "so we'll be leaving you alone tonight. Think you can manage that?"

"Shouldn't be a problem," I said.

Larry walked in, grumpy. He coughed and whispered into my ear, "I'll bring you home some leftovers if you promise to start back cooking in the mornings. You're a damn sight better at it than your momma."

I nodded at him, and he winked at me.

I guessed today was the start of a lot of new things for me.

I spent the morning lazing around, reading in the sunshine, playing with my dog. I spun a couple of my dad's old records as loud as they would go. That felt good. The day was hot and sun-drenched and jungle-humid, the kind of Southern summer day that demands you loaf around. I was happy to oblige it, happy to soak the heat into my skin, to breathe in the sticky air, to fill myself with this world. Only twice was I sad. Looking out over the woods, seeing how the path to where me and Her met was a little bit grown over, wondering if that spot was dead to me forever. That hurt me a little, same as looking back over an old photograph.

The second time was different, a little weirder. It came later in the afternoon. I was lying on the couch, flipping channels on the TV, when suddenly this stab of loneliness hit me like an icepick to the chest. I swear to you it burned—the feeling of being stranded in this world alone, like clutching to a life preserver in the middle of a big black ocean. It stole the breath right from me. For a moment I wished She would come back and swoop me away, into the Hidden Place, where I could be safe and calm and never worry about anything again.

After a minute I began to breathe regular. All the colors of the world seeped back into place, and that fierce, fanged panic left me. I hoped it was gone for good. Still, it had been a strange moment, and it scared me a little.

But life was like that, wasn't it? You're happy, swimming along fine, and then all of a sudden terror swoops down like a hawk and yanks you up, right out of the water. That's just the way it had been all my life, even back when I was a kid watching Mom and Dad fight it out in the kitchen after Mom would flush Dad's stash down the toilet or something. My life had always been filled with panic gashing like lightning through the calm.

Yes, but She had always been there for me during the hard times, guiding me through them, holding me close until they passed. And that just made me lonesome all over again.

My phone buzzed. It was Roy. Thank the universe for Roy.

"Hi there," I said.

"Hey," he said in a quiet voice, not his usual happy way.

"What's wrong?"

"Nothing."

"Oh, come on. I can always tell when something's the matter. So why don't you just go on and tell me?"

"It's nothing," he said. "I just had this dream last night, and it's made my whole day feel weird. Like I can't shake it or something."

"Wow," I said. "Tell me about it."

"Nah," he said. "It's dumb."

"Come on, Roy," I said. "You know how I feel about dreams."

"Maybe some other time."

I waited a minute, a little scared to ask this question.

"Well, my parents are going out for the night," I said. "Want to come to my house and tell me about it?"

"Yeah." Roy laughed a little. "Yeah. I'd like that a lot. My dad will be at a deacon's meeting anyhow. They go to Outback Steakhouse once a month."

Of course they do, I thought. Bloomin' Onions for all.

"That'll work," I said. "I'll pick you up at seven."

I waited outside Roy's house in Mom's car for about ten minutes before he called me.

"I know this is going to sound weird," he said. "But my annoying neighbor Mrs. Perkins is totally standing at her window, watching your car."

"Whoa," I said. "Creepy."

"Totally. She watches everything that goes on in the neighborhood. So just drive down the street a bit and I'll wait till she goes off somewhere else and I'll meet you."

I drove the car up a ways and watched the daylight die. It was a hell of a sunset, like the sky broke open and let out all its gold.

After a while Roy came walking up to my car, hands in his pockets. He looked good, like he'd dressed up for me a little. Again he wore the shirt I picked out for him, and he had on new jeans.

"Got yourself some new britches, I see," I said.

"Yeah. Dad decided I was about due."

"He was right," I said. "Hop in and let's get to where we're going."

I cranked the music and we drove out to my house, the last blotch of sunlight vanishing in my rearview mirror.

THE HOUSE WAS STILL AND EMPTY. I'D

switched off most of the lights before I left, and it looked spooky from my driveway. I called for Eyeball, but he didn't come running. As we walked through the front door, I felt myself catching my breath.

"It's so quiet," Roy said.

"Then let's whisper!" I said. "Come with me."

I led him through the living room and toward the stairwell.

To be honest, I was a little nervous. Me and Roy had never been alone in a house before. Just the car, or in the woods. This felt different somehow, a little bit illegal even. That only made it more exciting.

"Where are we going?" he said.

"To my room."

"I haven't been there since the day I first met you," he said. "When me and Dad were here."

On came the loneliness again, deep in my heart. It staggered me. I grabbed the staircase rail and my hand tingled. The clocks in the hallway ticked louder and offbeat, like time was mashing in and out of sync with itself. A cricket was lost somewhere inside the house, its ghostly scratch and chirp too loud for something so small and invisible. I guessed it was going to be a long time before I was over losing Her. I guessed it might take me forever to get over it.

"Are you okay?" said Roy. "I'm sorry. I shouldn't have brought that up."

"It's fine, Roy. I'm all good."

I shot him a smile in the darkness. When we got to my room I put a record on, *The Moon and the Melodies*, one of my dad's favorites.

We lay on the bed together, propped up on pillows, listening to the music. The sun was gone now, leaving nothing but the first stars out my window.

"I like this music," said Roy, after a few minutes. "It's all shimmery, and the lady sounds like somebody at church who has the Holy Spirit, like she's singing in tongues."

"It's the Cocteau Twins," I said.

"Well, I like it."

I could tell Roy was feeling antsy. He kept thumbing at his cuticles, and he wouldn't scoot any closer to me than was necessary. That was okay. I was feeling pretty nervous, too.

"So, tell me about your dream," I said.

"Nah," he said. "It's pretty sad. It'll probably kill the mood and everything."

"What mood?" I said. "Go on. I'm all ears. Literally. Ears all over the place."

Roy drooped his head and sighed. This seemed like it was

really going to be tough for him. That was okay. I knew what dreams were like. I leaned in close to listen, so close I could almost feel his breath on my lips as he spoke.

"Well, it was a dream about a long time ago," he said. "I was watching something that happened to me when I was a kid. I could see myself, though, like it was on TV. I was about four years old. It was a dream of a bad day, one I hadn't thought of in ages. I guess I'd wanted to forget it, you know?"

"A memory dream," I said.

"Yeah, definitely. It was from back when my mom was real sick. Like when she was bald and weak and wore her pink bathrobe all day. It was tattered where our old dog, Nora, had chewed it. Nora died when I was six and no one had the heart to get a new one. Dad kept trying to hug Mom and she kept pushing him away. She kept asking him to heal her. You know how my dad does these healing services, where they lay hands on people and everyone shakes and stuff? Well, it was like that. And Mom kept saying, 'Heal me,' and Dad said, 'It doesn't work like that.' And Mom kept talking about how it was useless, how God must be deaf or something. How there was no reason to pray for anything, because God wasn't listening.

"You can imagine how mad that made Dad. He started yelling at her, saying how she had blasphemed and everything, how she needed to repent. And Mom just blew up. She kept screaming about Dad being a liar, saying that Dad had cheated on her, that he had a girlfriend or something. I didn't even know what that meant at the time. I only understood it later, you know? I think a lot of being a kid is like that."

So that's what Roy's dad was so upset about in his office when I asked about his wife. How he kept going on and on about regret, about guilt. Maybe that was why Reverend Sanders was so hard on Roy, why he tried so hard to keep Roy from messing up like he had.

Roy stopped talking for a minute. He covered his face with his hands, and I knew he was crying. That was okay, he could cry around me all he wanted. I waited. When Roy started talking again his voice shook and cracked, like he was barely keeping it all in.

"That's where my dream ended," he said. "But I remember a lot more of what happened that night. I remember Dad didn't say anything for a minute. He just sat there with his eyes closed, like it hurt too bad to open them. And Mom started hitting him, just slapping him in the face and he sat there and took it. I guess he felt like he deserved it. Mom was real weak then, from the chemo and everything, so after about a minute of hitting him she was tired out, she just slumped over on the floor. And my dad bent down over her and scooped her up, like she weighed nothing. I remember her robe coming open, seeing her ribs, just how skinny and sick she was. 'Roy,' said Dad. 'Can you cover your momma up?' I did. Me and Dad carried her up the stairs and lay down in bed with her while she cried and slept. I think we lay in that bed for a whole day together, me and Dad on each side of her, like we were protecting her from something, doing everything we could to keep it away. And two weeks later she was dead."

Roy began to cry again, and I kissed his lips, I kissed his eyes.

"I never told anybody that before," he said. "Never."

"Thanks for telling me," I said, and I meant it. I realized I wanted to share Roy's pain. I wanted to hurt with him, as if his hurt felt a little bit like a gift.

"I used to think it was just Her who was real," I said. "But you, Roy. You're real, too. I wouldn't have survived the past month without you."

I kissed him again.

"I love you," he said.

"Without you, I'd be dead," I said. "Without you, I wouldn't have any hope at all."

The more we kissed, the hungrier Roy became, groping and pulling and biting, like something long kenneled broke loose and set free. He had my dress off, and then everything else, and there I was, naked and moon-white.

"Do you want to?" he said.

I nodded.

"Are you sure?" he said.

"Yes," I said.

I placed my hands on his belt and undid his pants and pulled off his shirt and then it was happening, it was happening.

It didn't last too much longer after all that.

Afterward I was lying on my back, a little away from him. Both of us naked and bare, panting like Adam and Eve in their fresh new garden of moonlight.

We lay there in silence, the slowing rhythm of our breaths like time itself flowing slower, softer. The room was full with darkness and starlight. Roy had his eyes shut tight. He was whispering to himself. He was praying.

I stroked his hair.

"You okay, Roy?"

He nodded at me.

"Are you sure?"

Roy smiled and said he was. But it seemed a sad smile, like something was wrong, something he couldn't talk about.

"I thought I would feel different," he said. "But I don't. I don't feel any different at all."

"I know," I said. "I feel closer to you, that's true. But I don't feel like I've changed one bit."

"Me either."

Roy's lip quivered and I could tell he was about to bust out crying. I pulled him close to me and told him everything was okay, that it was fine, that he could cry all he wanted to, I didn't care, I wouldn't judge him. Roy cried and cried and cried. It was like I always knew this would happen, that this was my role, preordained, and I held him until the sobs softened and the sound quieted down and he was still. I brushed his cheek with my hand. I wondered if this was how She felt all those years, comforting me, taking care of me. I wondered if it was like this for Her.

I held him close to me and listened to him breathe soft and warm against my neck and felt a different kind of peace, warm and human and held tight in my arms.

The ride back to Roy's house was quiet. What could you say? There didn't even seem to be the right music for it. So we listened to the tree frogs and the night bugs and the buzz of the busted streetlights blinking. It was a nice night, not too hot, not too muggy, rare for this time of year. I dropped Roy off right in front of his house. I kissed him and he stepped out of the car, waving at me until I was out of sight.

Lightning bugs lit the whole way home.

THAT NIGHT, I LAY ON MY BED AND

listened to records, the Replacements and Kate Bush and a new one I'd bought on my own, a lady named Grimes. For the first time since She was gone life didn't seem so awful to me. I wasn't alone anymore, I had Roy. I trusted him with myself and with my body, and Roy trusted me, too. I'd never been so close to any other person before.

It had to be the same way for Roy. Sneaking out to be with me, disobeying his dad, all the things we had done together. It took real bravery for Roy to do that, to go against so many things he had grown up with his whole life. And as much as I didn't like Reverend Sanders, I had to admit he was different than I thought he'd be. It's like he really did want what was best for Roy, and for the town too, he was just kind of a dick about it. I mean, his job was to cast out demons, wasn't it? How would he have known how important She was to me? He could have asked, sure, but when did adults ever ask a teenager a question and really want to know the answer? I didn't like Reverend Sanders, not by a long shot. But I began to see that maybe things weren't quite as simple as I'd always thought them to be.

I wondered if Reverend Sanders really had cheated on his wife. The way Roy described it, his dad seemed pretty heartbroken about the whole thing. Not to mention how Reverend Sanders had acted in his study. Maybe that's why he was always preaching to Roy about sex, about being close to people. Maybe part of the reason people were so awful to each other was out of guilt, out of the fear of being hurt again, or of hurting other people the same way they'd been hurt.

Things had changed for me. I missed Her, and part of me always would. But my life was different now—*I* was different— and I was happy about it. Who knew where the future would take me? Maybe Reverend Sanders would come around to Roy and me seeing each other. It was doubtful, but why not? I could go to church with them. Maybe Roy's dad would accept me. After all, I was proof that what he did and believed in worked. Wasn't I cleaned up and all demon-free? Who could reject a story like that?

What had Roy's dad said about Jesus? *He forgives and forgives and forgives.* That sounded pretty good to me. At the very least, I liked the sentiment.

That night I had dinner at the table with Mom and Larry. Mom cooked pork chops and they weren't too greasy—even Larry liked them. For dessert we had my grandma's old recipe for banana pudding and it was wonderful. Banana pudding was probably the only thing Mom was truly great at cooking—though to be honest there isn't much cooking to it—and we all agreed it was delicious.

Larry wasn't even that drunk. It was hard to believe life with them could be so happy.

After dinner I lay back on my bed with Eyeball and shut my eyes and smiled. I knew that I had made it, that good things were coming, that I could love and be loved. My heart was free and wide now, and I waited for the world to come walking in.

My phone buzzed. It was Roy.

"Hiya, Roy," I said. "Did you miss me already?"

But Roy was crying.

"My neighbor saw me," he said. "She saw me get in the car with you. And she told my dad."

"But we waited," I said. "I drove to the end of the street."

"She saw you drop me off. She saw us kiss." Roy sucked in a deep breath. "I told my dad about you. I had to."

This was bad—this was really bad. I knew how Roy's dad could be, I knew how he could command you be still and you were still, how he could bid you leave and you would have to go. It was the same thing he did to Her. It wasn't Roy's fault. I tried to calm myself down.

"It's okay," I said. "I promise, it's okay. He had to find out sooner or later. We'll get through this."

"It's not okay. I did something that can't be taken back."

Roy was crying so hard it was tough to understand him. He kept taking these horrible gasping breaths, like he was drowning.

"Just slow down and talk to me about it," I said. "I'm here."

I could do this. Roy loved me. I could be there for him. I loved him, too.

"It's your fault," he said. "Dad explained it all to me. How you tempted me. You led me astray. You made me do things with you. I never would have done that on my own. I'm faithful. It's your fault."

My fault? But we had made a choice together.

"What are you talking about, Roy?"

"Dad made me get on my knees right in front of him. He cried, he said we had to pray for God to forgive me and make me pure again. That God would do it but I had to repent, I had to confess it all to Heaven and repent. So I did, Clarabella. I told him every-thing. I told him every word of what we did."

My heart was cracking and I could feel myself losing control. All the joy that had built up in me broke and fell. It was funny, how fragile happiness can be, how quickly it can up and die on you.

"Roy, what we did wasn't wrong. We did it because we love each other."

"He was so mad, Clarabella. My dad kept screaming and screaming. He said that I didn't understand what I had done, how bad it was."

Roy's voice broke, he was weeping so hard his breaths came in gasps. I was crying too, trying to hold myself together, trying to stop this conversation before it ruined everything forever. This wasn't Roy's fault, it was his goddamned father's. It was that ass-hole reverend bullying people, beating shame into his son. And I had almost come around to liking him. I had almost been fooled.

"Please calm down," I said. "Roy, please listen to me."

"You're a slut, Clarabella. You made me sin against God. He explained the whole thing to me. You're like Eve, you talked me into it. It's all your fault."

My heart went cold. It was like someone stole the breath from me, like the way cats do in ghost stories, sucking the air out of a baby's lungs. This wasn't right. He had no right to call me that. No one did. It was his dad's fault. Roy would never say that about me. He loved me. He told me so himself.

"But Roy," I said. "You love me, right?"

"My dad is going to call your stepdad. I just wanted to warn you."

He hung up.

I felt the world go crooked, everything at sharp right angles, my room stretched for miles, the ceiling warped into a black hole. Dark lines like spiders crawled under my eyelids. I stumbled over to the garbage can by my dresser and vomited. My whole body ached, like a tornado had wrecked through my room and slung my body against the walls. Even the blood in me hurt, the big gaping emptiness in my belly roared open and wide.

A few minutes later the downstairs phone rang. I knew good and well what that meant. I closed my eyes tight as I could until they swirled with colors, until I held a sunset under my eyelids. Soon I heard Larry huff up the stairs, stomping them two at a time. When he busted into my room he nearly yanked the door off the hinges.

"What in the hell have you been doing?" he said.

I just stared at him.

"Fucking the reverend's kid? Are you out of your goddamn mind?" Larry paced around my room tugging at what was left of his hair. "Do you understand what this does to me, profession-ally? In the church? Because the church is business, it's where my business is made. You have to be psychotic. We thought you were possessed. But it's all you. It's always been just you."

Mom peeked her head into my room.

"Let her alone," whispered Mom, like she was scared.

"Stay the fuck out of it," said Larry.

"Don't you talk to her like that," I said.

Larry slapped me. He slapped me so hard it knocked me off my feet. My lip was busted and I spit blood.

"Please," said Mom, but Larry turned a scowl on her so fierce she wilted.

"Get downstairs," he said, and I heard Mom scurry off. Larry looked back at me. "You better not set foot outside this room until I come up here and drag you out myself." He snatched my cell phone off the bed. "And you'll be fucking forty before you ever see one of these again."

Larry slammed the door shut. After a second I could hear him and Mom screaming at each other. I heard the words "institution," "mental home," and "straighten her out for good."

But they wouldn't do that to me, would they? Yeah, Larry definitely would. He would lock me up forever. And Mom would let him, because she was broken and afraid, because she didn't know what else to do.

I lay on my bed. I didn't cry, and I didn't move. I just lay there and hugged myself. Never had I felt so alone in my whole life.

Except for one other time. It was long ago, real long ago, when I was just a girl. The day my dad died.

I REMEMBERED IT SO PERFECTLY—THAT

day had happened so many times in my mind. I was eight years old and standing in the kitchen, staring at my dad sprawled out on the chair.

"Daddy?" I said.

I climbed up onto his lap and leaned back against him. I put my ear on his chest, same as I had a hundred times before when he was passed out, when I was scared and wanted to make sure. I would lay my head against his chest and feel his heart knock against my ear like it wanted me to open up and let it in.

But this time his heart was silent.

I touched his face, the skin cool, his lips already blue. I saw the needle on the table. My daddy was dead.

I sat there in his lap. I couldn't move, like it was me who had died. My breaths came in stabs, quick and shallow. Black gashes crowded my eyes. My world had died, life had died, everything was ruined and nothing would ever be good for me again.

But then I felt Her near me, just a whisper in my ear.

I can make it all better, She said. *I can make it quiet for you. I can make it safe here, all pretty and warm.*

"Please," I said. "Help me."

Oh, I want to, Clare, I want to help you so bad. But you have to let me. Can I come in?

I nodded.

Say it.

"Yes," I said. "Please come in me and live."

I felt a rush in my body, the sound of wings beating the air, a harvest of insects. The world dimmed, the colors softened, everything seemed warm and alive and moving. She was inside me, soothing me, whispering quiet into my blood, caressing my bones, healing the hurt places in my soul.

And for the first time, I found myself in the Hidden Place. The great wide grassy hill, the cliff down to the waters. The sun bright and warm, the breeze tickling my hair.

"Where are we?" I'd asked.

Home, She said.

She knew me so well, She knew me all through my bones, yes She did. *There, there, little Clare, I'm here for you, always I will be here for you, never you fear, never fear again. I'm with you now. I'm never leaving you, not ever.*

I felt so calm, so lovely and loved, like the world was made of only the softest things—the edges were blurred, everything existed to hold me and to love me. I was so happy I fell right asleep, just like that, safe with Her in the Hidden Place.

Until Mom woke me up screaming.

I was still in the kitchen. I had fallen asleep right there in my dead daddy's lap. Mom yanked me off him, she threw Dad on the floor, started banging at his chest with her fists. Mom screamed and cried and begged for me to call 911. But it was all like it was happening in another room, miles and miles away. I felt safe and happy, because She was there. Because She had draped a blanket over my face, a gauze over my eyes, She had swallowed me up in a warm haze where nothing could hurt me, where nothing could touch me again.

I missed Her so, so bad.

It was stupid to trust Roy. He was just some boy, a kid, nothing like Her. If She had lied, then She had a purpose for it. She never wanted to hurt me, She always only wanted what was best for us. I was so stupid to think I could ever trust anyone except for Her.

I needed Her here now. I needed Her with me. I needed that feeling, that safety and escape. I needed Her to save me now, I needed Her to come and make everything better for me. I needed Her to carry me out of all this pain. Why had She let Reverend Sanders take Her? Why hadn't She fought?

Why had She left me here all alone?

The room darkened, my bed began to shake. Static hissed out of my stereo, and my lamp lightbulb exploded. The door to my closet eked open, spilling shadows across the floor. My bedroom filled with despair, tangible, thick as smoke. The Wish House spirit had never left me. It was here now, just as it always had been, waiting just out of sight, biding its time.

I knew exactly what I had to do.

"Yes," I said to the demon. "You can have him. I'll bring him there tonight."

And the darkness smiled.

YEARS AGO, WE WERE AT THE HIDDEN

Place, just me and Her, gazing at the stars above the black of the water, the dazzling millions of them bright and white as ancient tiny suns. I was writing on paper and a fierce wind came and blew it out of my hands, swooping it like a crane out above the sea. She smiled at me.

It's like a wish, She said, *a prayer cast over the waters.*

"But You don't know what I wrote," I said.

I don't have to know, She said. *All writing is dreams. Writing is a prayer for something better, or for the best things to last. Even when it claims it isn't. Even when it pretends to be something else.*

"You're awful smart for an eight-year-old."

For a fourteen-year-old, you could stand to be a little wiser.

That hurt my feelings, but I didn't want to show it. But She knew. She knew right away.

Did I hurt my Clare? Did I make her feelings smart?

"Shut up," I said.

I did. She giggled. *I made dear Clare mad.*

"What are you going to do about it?"

Watch.

I put my hands over my face.

She pulled them away, staring deep in my eyes. My bones felt fluttery and hollow, my tongue tasted honey, my insides were all aglow with warmth and light.

A wind swept up from the ocean water, the salt spray stinging my eyes, even all the way up here, all the way up on our cliff. The birds cried out and the clouds gathered like wolves above us, grey and circling. I heard the far-off grumble of thunder.

"What are you doing?" I said.

Watch.

Lightning lashed the sky. It burned in purples and whites and blues, the sea erupted in light everywhere the lightning struck. The rain fell, a grey mist over the world, thick as smoke in the far-off places. I was getting scared, my hair was wet, the rain stung against my skin.

"Please, stop it," I said. "It's scary."

No, it isn't. Calm is scary. Calm is boring. But a storm. A storm is beautiful.

Then rose the water spouts, dark and twisty as octopus tentacles. They danced over the water, binding sea and sky, bending and swaying around our cliff, an elegant destroying monster bellowing up from the deep. I covered my eyes, terrified.

"Make it stop!" I screamed. "Make it stop!"

Shhh, Clare, She whispered over the roar. I don't know how, but I could hear Her, I could hear Her inside me. *Open your eyes. Don't be afraid. You have to trust me. You have to trust.*

I felt Her take my hand, pull me up to my feet. I didn't want to open my eyes. I didn't want to look. The wind screamed in my ears, the thunder burst the sky, it was too loud, I didn't want to. But onward She pulled me, the wet grass stinging my knees, my dress sopping wet, stuck to my body. We walked and I covered my eyes, I wouldn't watch, but still She drug me onward. Until finally we stopped. The rain pelted my skin, the wind yanked my hair back from my head.

Okay, She said. *Look.*

"No. I don't want to."

Clare, She cooed. *Dear, dear Clare. Be brave now. You must look.*

"Please."

Clare. I have you, silly. There's nothing to fear.

I opened my eyes. The waves rose high as battleships and dashed themselves against each other. The cliff shook with the power of the endless waters. The rain flung itself sideways, and the water spouts curled around each other, rushing tornadoes of water. A bright red rip of lightning seared the clouds, and I could somehow see the eyes of stars winking white through the chaos.

Do you see now, Clare? Do you see?

"Yes," I said.

I saw it all, I felt it all, the roar and holler of the entire world, the wild fury of life flung down from the heavens, the fathomless waters of the deep in their fiercest maelstrom, I felt it all in my heart. And I learned something that day, something I never will forget.

"The storm," I said. "It's beautiful."

I WAITED UNTIL MOM AND LARRY WENT

to sleep. It didn't take too long. I always marveled at Mom's ability to pass out no matter what the crisis. Larry probably just used sleeping pills. I put on my white dress, the one She picked out for our funeral, for the day Roy's daddy took Her from me. I also grabbed my backpack, stuffed it with the rest of Miss Mathis's thousand dollars and Kevin's notebook. Thunder growled outside, and lightning licked the far-off sky. Larry had hid all the spare car keys, and I didn't dare sneak into their bedroom, not tonight. I walked right out the front door, just because I could. Eyeball wandered up to me, eyes big and black in the nighttime.

"Are you mad at me?" I asked him.

The dog whimpered and licked my fingers. Thunder boomed and he scampered away, to the back porch, to the doggy door that let him in and out of the house. Above me the clouds drifted thick and strange and swirly, all blacks and greys like a spellcaster's smoke. Of course, Larry hadn't done a thing about my bike. It was right there, leaned against the side of the house, same as always. But if I was going to get to the Wish House, I'd need a car. Good thing I knew exactly where to find one.

I dropped my bike in Miss Mathis's driveway. The sign on her door said MADAM IS INDISPOSED, but I knocked once and went in anyway.

"Miss Mathis?" I hollered, so she wouldn't think I was a robber. "You there, Miss Mathis?"

Miss Mathis sat in her easy chair. *Designing Women* played on the TV. Prissy yipped at me from the floor.

"Who in the hell?" she said. "Christ, Clare, you scared me."

Miss Mathis tried to stand up, but she toppled right back down in the chair. Her coffee mug sloshed onto her sweatshirt, a big purple stain.

"I'll get you a towel," I said.

"Don't bother. This is my boozing shirt," she said, smiling a little, sunglasses teetering on her nose. "What can I do you for?"

"I need to borrow your car," I said.

"That so?"

"It's pretty important."

I didn't say it was an emergency because people ask questions when you say a word like that. I hoped Miss Mathis was so drunk she'd just hand the keys over to get me out of there so she could get back to doing whatever it was she was doing. Besides, if Miss Mathis found out where I was going, there's no way she would give me her car.

"It's a bit late for cruising around, ain't it? With that little boyfriend of yours, I wager." She giggled and coughed. "I remember raising hell. I remember staying out late."

"Please, Miss Mathis, where are the keys?"

"In the kitchen, I believe," she slurred. "Hanging there on a little hook."

I ran to the kitchen. It smelled awful. There were half-dirty dishes piled all over the place, cigarette butts, candy bar wrappers. But I couldn't find any little hook and I saw no keys.

"Oh, Clare," Miss Mathis hollered. "They're right here."

I went back in the living room. She was sitting in her chair, dangling the keys from her pinched fingers like a mouse by the tail.

"Silly me. Had them in my pocket the whole time."

"Toss them to me," I said.

"Not too good with the aim, Clare. Don't be rude, now. Come over here and I'll put them right in your little hand."

I walked over to her and stuck my hand out. Prissy looked up at me and wagged her tail.

"Little closer," said Miss Mathis.

I bent down toward her. I could smell her rancid breath, see the purple stains on her teeth.

"Please, Miss Mathis," I said. "Can I have the keys now?"

Her hand sprung out quick as a snakebite and grabbed me by the back of my neck. Her grip was strong, her nails dug in and it hurt. She pulled my face close to hers, like she was going to kiss me. I tried to yank my head backward but I couldn't move, and for the first time I realized that Miss Mathis was stronger than me.

"You got something on you," she said. "A mark. Let me see. I was too damn self-pitying to see it earlier, and I'm too drunk to miss it now."

Miss Mathis dropped the keys from her other hand and yanked the sunglasses off her face. One of her eyes was dead, no color to it, white as an egg. A burn scar snaked across the lid, and one brow was gone, the skin around it all mottled and warped. It was like her eye had been poisoned, like she had seen something she wasn't supposed to and it left its mark on her forever. She held my face close to it.

It was like looking into the moon.

Miss Mathis placed her palm on my forehead and shoved me backward. I stumbled. The dog yipped at me.

"What have you got in that backpack?" she said. "What have you been hiding from me?"

Miss Mathis stood up onto her feet and this time did not topple.

"I found this in Cléa's room," I said.

I held the notebook out to her. Miss Mathis snatched it from my hands. She flipped through the pages once and stopped, squinting at the drawings.

"You little bitch," she said. "You had this the whole time, didn't you?"

"I'm sorry," I said.

"These drawings are the key, you know that?" She held up the hermit page, where Kevin had drawn all those weird symbols in the shadows. "In the margins of the drawings, the goddamn Rosetta Stone to Gaspar's magic. I could have translated that flap of skin weeks ago."

"But I had to see it first," I said. "I had to see Gaspar and the Wish House for myself."

"Folks should know better," said Miss Mathis. "Some places just shouldn't exist. A field lies fallow for a reason, Clare." She tossed the notebook onto her coffee table. "I know, Clare. I gave it my pleasure. I touched that evil. Folks should know better."

Her hands outstretched toward me, fingers long and clawed, my blood under her nails.

"Don't go back there. He'll eat you, little Clare. He'll gobble you right up."

I saw the keys where Miss Mathis had dropped them on the floor. I bent down and scooped them up, scrambling for the door. Miss Mathis was still drunk, she was old, she couldn't catch me.

"Don't you go back to that house," she screamed. "Don't you let that man near you. Don't you let him touch you. Hear me, Clare? Don't you go back to that house!"

But I was already out the door, already to her driveway. The Cadillac started up on the second try, and there was gas in the tank. I pulled out of the driveway and into the pouring rain, the storm having just decided to rip the clouds open and explode. The last thing I saw in the rearview was Miss Mathis, waving her arms at me. "Please, Clare, don't you go."

THE RAIN FELL IN WIND-BORNE SLASHES,

fierce and wild. It was hard to see, hard to keep the car from skidding off into a ditch. Thunder boomed above me and the sky lit up in greens and purples as whips of lightning flung down from the clouds. It was like a warning, the sky conspiring to tell me that what I was doing was final, that there would be no going back to my old life, that nothing would ever be the same again.

I pulled over at Little John's gas station, I figured for the last time. Rain slammed against the overhang, whipping horizontal against my face, and I heard tornado sirens moaning in the distance.

I used the pay phone to call Roy's number. He answered after half a ring.

"Clarabella?" he said. "Oh, thank God. I've been trying to call you like a million times."

I think that broke my heart a little bit.

"Look, I'm so sorry," he said. "I shouldn't have talked to you like that. It's just, my dad can get real scary when he's preaching at you and you start feeling like the whole world is falling in on you, like God has a sword raised up and is about to strike you dead. I never should have called you that."

"Called me what?"

"You know."

"A slut. That's what you called me."

"Yeah," he said. "I'm sorry."

"But you still believe it, don't you?"

For one solid breath he was quiet on the phone. It was long enough.

Just do it, Clare, I told myself. Say it already.

"I called to tell you goodbye, Roy."

"What? Where are you going?"

"You know already," I said. "Thanks for the last month or so. I never thought I could be happy like that again."

I hung up the phone. I'd be lying if I told you I didn't cry about it.

The storm was raging by the time I got to the Bird Tree. I stepped out of Miss Mathis's car into the pelting hot rain. It was there, the cardinal crucified and bloody, nailed to the tree. I wondered if it was the same bird, doomed for some reason, eternally punished like Prometheus to be tortured and never die. I didn't know if it was better to lose one bird for always or a single bird each night. Who could make a decision like that? Who would ever want to?

The path was a mess, puddles and fallen limbs, trees ripped in half by the storm. But the moment I stepped into the woods it was like the wind didn't touch me, like the rain parted and the tree branches spread themselves wide and let me pass. All around me the storm roared and yet it did not lay the softest finger on my body.

The forest is making room for me, I thought. It's been waiting for me all this time.

The woods held a curious light. I was being watched, the invisible creatures hunched on tree limbs, cowering from the storm. Their eyes glowed behind each leaf, gazing down from the clouds and stars. It was like reality stretched so thin I could tear it with my fingers, like I could pull a thread and it would unravel, just like a sweater. Even the animals bowed their heads as I passed— raccoons covered their eyes, opossums hung in exclamation marks from the trees. The woods were watching. The woods wondered what I was going to do next.

Something else was with me, a whisper through the leaves, a patch of moonlight where there was no moon. The black-haired girl, the one who helped me through the forest last time, she was there too, walking a little ways behind me. I could feel her eyeless stare, grim and worried. I was starting to get an idea of who she might be.

Soon the Wish House loomed before me. Its doorway hung open and black as a well. Constant lightning cast a glow over the grounds. I knew She was here somewhere, waiting on me, watching. I took a deep breath and stepped inside.

I passed through the Wish House, trailing puddles in my wake, my dress stuck to my body, my hair matted and cold. I thought about Miss Mathis's words: *A field lies fallow for a reason.* Who knew what old dead bones poisoned the earth beneath this house? It felt as if the House was alive, as if it knew I stood there inside it.

Gaspar was waiting for me in the black curtain room, same as before. Seated in the chair, his face to the fire. This time the room smelled awful, like an army of rats had died in the walls. Flies buzzed fat and hungry around the room. I felt like I was standing in a slaughterhouse. I wanted to huddle and warm myself by the fire but I was afraid to.

Gaspar rose from the rocking chair and turned to face me. He wore a tuxedo with a black bow tie, as if he had dressed up for the occasion. His hair was slicked back, and he was clean-shaven now, his face gaunt and scarred but handsome somehow. He didn't seem so old and tired anymore. It was like he'd reverse-aged, like each minute he was growing younger. His face was flushed, his hair a fuller grey, his lips red and moist when he smiled.

"I told you I was beautiful once, didn't I? Yes, but the girl did not believe Gaspar. And why should she? When last she laid eyes on Gaspar he was old bones in a suit, was he not? Was he not?"

And he bent over laughing.

"I called Roy," I said. "He's coming."

"Well I should hope so, little one, for your sake. Lest you be forced to take the boy's place. Lonely little girls work just as well as lonely little boys, didn't you know that? You wouldn't like that, now, would you? Being the human temple for a thousand hungry demons?"

The look on my face made Gaspar laugh.

"I thought not. No, no, the girl wants just her one. Her always and *Only*, does she not?" He leaned in close to me and clicked his teeth in my face. "Don't you know that when you walk through these doors, you belong to me? And I take something from you, and I never give it back again. I take and I take again, until one day you're mine. Perhaps you saw some of them outside, in the woods? Perhaps they are even here now, stitched into the curtains, peering out from the wallpaper? Can't you feel them watching?"

"What about Luther Simpkins?" I said.

"His body escaped, but his mind did not. I offered that man the earth, and for a time he took his pleasure." Gaspar waved his hand dismissively. "Bah. He is corrupted now. May he remain so."

"What's that smell?" I said.

Gaspar giggled and twirled about the room, waltzing an invisible partner through the stink and flies.

"All the pretty flowers will grow once more in the Wish House, won't they, little girl? Yes, they will. They will grow and prosper, and so shall we all, and Gaspar will be beautiful again. The men and the women will come from miles around, from worlds apart, just to see me."

He stopped and clapped his hands.

"Oh, and we shall have the loveliest parties!"

"Is that what all this is about?" I said. "Your parties?"

He bared his teeth at me and growled.

"No, you stupid little girl. You disgusting, filthy creature." He straightened himself and stood on his tiptoes. "Power is its own reward. Or have you not learned that yet? Have you not held power yourself, felt it throb and pulse in your own little veins? Yes, I think you have. Yes, I believe you miss that."

"No," I said. "I miss Her. Not the power. Just Her."

"Then you are a bigger fool than I thought." He giggled. "A fool, yes, but a useful one. A most disgusting, lovely little fool, yes she is. The girl who shall bring Gaspar his new toy. The spirits will love him, yes, I've been assured. My helper does not lie, no it doesn't. They shall make a home in the boy's chest and I will sign the boy like a contract, yes I will. Oh, they shall all be reunited in him!

"Can you imagine the glory, the honor, to be the dwelling place of such spirits? Of such creatures beyond time, of wisdom from the creation of the world, when all was waters and darkness. They were born soon after the first stars, and they shone bright for a time, with their own light. And yet, the light was not for them. It despised them, it spat them out, wingless and alone, to wander the earth. But there is wisdom in the earth, yes there is, there is dominion and power, there are rivers of blood on which they may feast like dogs."

Gaspar turned a pirouette, he leapt nimble as a ballet dancer, he twirled himself like a dervish before the fire. When he stopped to face me he had two silk scarves in his hands, like a magician.

"Sit down," he said, "and I shall bind you."

"Do I have to?"

"The girl asks such silly questions, yes she does. The boy must come voluntarily, must he not? And he must come to save you, the sweet little girl needing saving, or else why should he come? He comes because he loves you, yes? Yes, you are a disgusting little creature, my lovely. Oh, you will be perfect for us!"

The One Wish Man led me by the wrist over to the chair and

set me down in it. Then he tied me up, binding my wrists and ankles with the long silk scarves. He did it gently, taking care with me. It scared me, how delicate he was, like my skin was made of wrapping paper, like it would tear so easily. It would have been better if he was rough. The stink of the room made me gag in my mouth and flies swarmed my face.

"I have a question," I said.

"The little darling shall ask away, will she not?"

"Did you kill Cléa?"

Gaspar lowered his face to mine, his eyes gleaming deep and black in the firelight.

"Of course I killed the little bitch," he snarled. "She tried to burn my house down."

Gaspar danced laughing to the corner of the room and drew back a bit of curtain and vanished behind it.

I sat there in the chair, bound and helpless, while the One Wish Man watched me unseen, and—it makes me feel so guilty, so horrible to say this—I prayed Roy was on his way.

I WAITED WHAT SEEMED LIKE HOURS.

My legs itched, my head hurt, the smell of the room made me sick. It was hard being tied up for so long, such a helpless feeling, like Gaspar could just walk into the room and slit my throat and there wouldn't be a thing I could do about it.

Maybe Roy wouldn't come. Maybe I'd been wrong about everything, and I'd just wind up Gaspar's plaything for the rest of my life. I'd deserve it, I guess. Trapped here forever. Flies flurried around the room. One landed on the tip of my nose. I shook it off and it came right back. More gathered on my eyelids, buzzed into my ears, crawled through my hair, until I couldn't stand it anymore, until I thought I might scream for Gaspar to come back and kill me himself.

And then a voice behind me whispered, "Clarabella!"

My heart about cracked in half when I heard that. I had to bite my lip to keep from crying. It was Roy.

"Is it safe?" he said.

"Yes," I said. "The One Wish Man's gone right now, but he'll be back any minute. We got to hurry."

Roy ran up to the chair and untied me, my hands first and then my ankles. He batted the flies from his face.

"What's that smell?" he said.

I shook my head.

"I don't know, I don't know. Roy, he wasn't like I thought he would be. He wasn't anything like She said he would be."

"Figures," he said. "I'm just glad you're okay."

"Are you alone?"

"My dad was right behind me, but he got lost on the path somewhere."

Of course he did. The Wish House didn't want him. The woods wouldn't let him pass.

I was untied now, free to run if I wanted to. Roy headed for the curtain, but I didn't move.

"What are you doing?" he said. "Come on."

I tried to smile at him but I knew it just came out sad.

"I knew you'd come," I said. "It's just like you, thinking you know what's best for me. Thinking that I always need saving."

"We have to hurry, Clarabella. Dad will be outside, waiting on us. He'll get us out of here."

I had to tell him the truth. Otherwise I wouldn't have enough strength to go through with it. I had to get angry, I had to light the mad flames of myself. I fixed my face in a scowl.

"She was mine," I said. "She stood by me through everything.

And you took Her from me. You and your horrible father. You had no right. No right to do that."

Roy backed away from me, confusion all over his face.

"I came to save you," he stammered. "And . . . and . . . he had you tied up."

But I wasn't looking at Roy anymore. I was looking at the man walking out from the curtains behind him.

Gaspar stood at his full height now, taller than anyone I had ever seen, like some wicked scarecrow stretched long in my dreams. Roy backed right into him.

"You must be Roy," said Gaspar.

Roy tried to run but Gaspar slung his arms around him and lifted him off the ground. He draped a white silk scarf over Roy's face and Roy went limp, like the scarf was drugged. Gaspar dropped him to the floor. I flinched when Roy's face smacked the hardwood.

"Don't worry, little darling, I didn't kill him," said Gaspar. "No, never would Gaspar do a thing like that. What good would the boy be to us dead? The spirits don't envy the dead, not at all. They want the living."

"She isn't like that," I said. "She's different from all your demons."

"That may be, little one," he said, "though I deeply doubt it. Now, go and wait in your corner. Gaspar shall summon you when he is ready."

Gaspar laid Roy down on the hardwood. He bound Roy's arms and legs with a scarf.

I sat down in the corner and hugged my knees to myself as Gaspar spun his magic.

Gaspar traced a circle three times around Roy with a stick of chalk. He filled the spaces around Roy with symbols and runes, the long scripts of magic like what Kevin drew in his notebook. It was amazing to watch him work, the surety of the strokes, the squint-eyed focus of a master. There was the eye and the triangle and the spiral, the stars and hooks and scepters, the lines of unpronounceable words, the strange scribbled language of the alchemists. Other figures too, things I had seen in my dreams, and elsewhere, words woven into the clouds of the Hidden Place, whispered by the wind and waters, scratched into the bark of the trees. This was an older language, one humans didn't dare to speak.

Gaspar lit a candle at five points along the circle, long white slashes connecting them into a star. He hummed while he worked, a soft strange melody, something ancient and eternal, the first song ever sung. I was in the presence of an older evil, one that has been from the beginning and would go on long after I was dead. All around Roy there danced a living cosmos of chalk, a summoning song etched on the floor.

I knew Gaspar would write all these symbols again, once more. Except he would do it with a knife, he would carve them right into Roy's flesh.

"The little wretch is learning," said Gaspar, smiling at me. I knew he could hear me thinking. I knew he understood my heart, and it shamed me.

I would have to keep my thoughts quieter in the moments to come.

Roy shuddered and coughed, he blinked his eyes open.

"The grub arises!" said Gaspar. He slapped Roy on the cheeks.

"Wake now, you stinking, naughty little boy, and take heed, for now Gaspar needs you. Wake and bear witness!"

The One Wish Man walked to the corner of the room and drew back the curtains. Finally I knew what caused that awful smell.

Behind the curtains hung the slaughtered carcasses of animals. They dangled from rope and barbed wire: cats half-skinned, strangled dogs with their tongues hanging out. An eyeless owl noosed with a chain. Cardinals and cardinals nailed like a smattering of blood drops all over the walls. Behind them, a stabbing, jotted language scrawled wild across the walls in red, gashes and spirals and eyes, eyes all around us. A wolf's head nailed over a boarded window, deer antlers poking out like thorns all over the wall, like Christ's crown unraveled. I saw animal bones in the corners, a single plucked cat eye, the smashed skull of a horse. The fire had died low now, just the hiss of embers. The sky was black beyond the windows, as if there was no outside, as if this room was the only place left in the world.

"Clarabella," whispered Roy. "Clarabella, help me."

I couldn't even look at him.

Gaspar placed an unlit purple candle on the floor. Next to it he laid a curved knife.

"Come, my darling," he said. "You sickening little creature."

I sat down across from him, the candle and knife between us. Gaspar took my hands and held them palms-up. He stared deep into my eyes—his the molten color of gold—and I could not look away.

"You have lost someone dear to you and you wish for her return, yes?" he said.

I nodded.

"Say it, little girl. You must speak the words aloud or it is useless, yes?"

"Yes," I said. "I want Her back."

"Please, don't do this," said Roy, his voice barely a croak.

"You are not to speak, you mongrel," said Gaspar. "You are merely to bear witness. We understand this, yes?"

"Clare, you don't need Her," said Roy. "You can stop this."

"I said, be silent!" roared Gaspar.

The firelight dimmed, and a wind rippled through the room. Roy cried out in pain, he writhed like a flipped beetle on the floor.

"The little boy shall learn, will he not? When he is the host for our friends, yes? When the legion makes its home in him, when he is my treasure chest of gold coins, my very own purse? Yes, the spirit chose wisely."

I watched as Roy went still and bowed his head. I realized that he was praying.

Gaspar turned to me.

"Now we shall continue, won't we, darling?"

I nodded at him.

"You seek a lost spirit, do you not? One who was bound to you, who beat inside your heart, to whom you gave meaning, to whom you gave life. Is this not true? Yes, yes. Now the spirit is lost, do you see? She wanders through the dry places, seeking rest but finding none. She has been rebuked from the child, yes, forbidden to return. The little boy shall recognize these words, yes, I believe he shall, but he cannot speak, for Gaspar forbids him. He knows the fate of the wandering spirit. The spirit can find no rest, can She not? Is She not so very lonesome? Does She not straggle through the empty space, through the starving places, looking only for Her one true love? Yes, of course She does. And shall I call Her back for you, little girl? Is it Her you truly want?"

"Yes," I said.

Roy moaned in pain. I tried to ignore him.

"Then it is Her you shall have," said Gaspar.

Gaspar leaned in close to me and whispered. His breath stank of sulfur, of lit matches and fire and the dust of a thousand years.

"A person is a kingdom, a mansion, and inside each soul there are rooms and rooms. Does the girl know that? Of course she does. Inside her there is a kingdom of rooms, and she must go inside herself, the girl must enter into the locked door and pass down the great hallway and she must find the spirit's room, the one that she has given to Her. The girl must light a lamp in that room for Her to see by, that the spirit may find Her way home from whence She wanders. Does the darling little wretch not see?"

"Yes," I said. "Yes, I can see it."

It was true. I saw the vast insides of myself, like a Heaven of rooms, a whole city of me. Of possibilities, of desires, of who I could become. I saw my mom ancient and grey and dying in one room. I saw my stepdad Larry asleep on the sofa in another, each memory and person assigned a place and an order. Some doors I was scared to open, rooms that I knew held my dad, that held Luther Simpkins and Richard Holbrook, that held myself fanged and bloodied and wild, the old-lady me, my own death waiting for me tucked away in some secret room like a bride at the altar.

And another room, the most important room, one that wasn't

a room at all. It was the wide-open air of a mountaintop, surrounded by cliffs, with green grasses and bluebells and white
taffy clouds whisking above. The Hidden Place. This was Her
room, I knew it, this was where I kept Her. But how? I thought it
was a place She had made for me, and not the other way around.
Had I carried it inside me this whole time? I set a lantern on a
rock overlooking the ocean and I willed it night there, I watched
the sun darken and the moon rise and my lamp glow like a lighthouse over the churning waters.

I was breathing heavy now, panting, my chest heaving up and
down. I felt as if I was running, like something was chasing me
on the inside of myself.

"The boy and his father placed a mark on you, did they not? A
protection," said Gaspar. "Yes, yes, they did, the fools. And now
we shall break it."

He giggled, and the fire shot sparks from the hearth.

"I needn't tell you that this will hurt."

My body shook, and I was sweating. I couldn't get any air, like
something was sucking the breath out of my throat before I could
breathe it. I felt white-hot spiders crawl inside my veins. I heard
a great rushing of wind, as if the moon and the sky and the stars
all reared back and howled.

Gaspar was quick. He grabbed my hand and slid the knife
across my palm.

Blood came out like a secret. It whispered onto the floor.

The purple candle lit itself, a flame rising like a small tongue
of fire.

I could hear myself screaming.

Then . . . then, I don't know exactly.

It became like a dream.

The colors shifted and brightened, the world focused. I could see the cracks in the grains of the wood, see the blue flecks on the backs of a horsefly, every tiny miracle of everything. Time flooded through me, thousands of years in an instant, forgotten things, horses and camels, drowned islands, a broken statue in front of an altar, a column of fire, a great wind on a mountain. I saw a ball of entwined rats scuttling over the bloated bodies of children, I saw a one-eyed witch drinking blood from a snake, I saw two men in suits shaking hands in a barren field in the snow. I saw the stars and the cosmos, the swirling bright order of things, the fire of the beginning and the end. I saw all of it, felt it all, time eternal and every moment fire-hot and burning in my veins, all of it inside me, roaring in my blood.

I felt Her with me again, Her warm and flooding light, all the goodness and hope of Her, the love, the love, the deep and knowing love.

"I missed you," I whispered.

I missed you too, Clare.

Gaspar laughed.

"I brought Her back to you, did I not? Yes, Gaspar did, he did just what you asked. Oh, it has been so long. It has been so long for Gaspar to work his magic, to have the fire dance in his bones again."

I felt Her take my hand, I felt Her petting me, Her fingers on my skin, stroking my arms and my face and my hair, whispering, *I am yours, I am yours, I am yours.*

"*Thank you*," I said to him, and it came out in Her little girl's voice.

"Now it is time for Gaspar to take his boon, is it not?" he said.

Roy's head perked up and he stopped praying.

"His boon?" said Roy. "Clarabella, what is he talking about?"

"*Clare is sorry*," She said through me, in Her high, lisping little girl's voice. "*Clare is very, very sorry. But you're the boon, Roy. You're his present.*"

Gaspar rose to his feet. He took the tuxedo jacket off, loosened the tie, unbuttoned the shirt, let it drop to the floor. I saw his tattoos, hundreds, his whole body a mystic scroll, scars that lifted like caterpillars off his flesh. He carried the curved knife. In the fireglow it gleamed gold.

"You do me honor, little boy, you filthy disgusting creature," said Gaspar. "You pay tribute to me with your flesh, with the fresh parchment of your skin. I shall do wonders with you, boy. I shall carve your name upon the stars."

Roy prayed out loud now. He begged God for mercy.

"*We had no choice*," She said through me. "*When you cast me out, I was lost. I wandered and I wandered, but I could not find her. I could not find my Clare. Only he could call me back, and he would only do it for a price.*"

Gaspar crouched before Roy. He smoothed Roy's hair back, laid his hand softly on Roy's cheek. Roy went still, his voice silent.

"Shhh," he said. "Quiet now, little boy. It picked you, yes, it did. It chose you itself."

"Who?" Roy whispered.

"*Clare's very sorry for you*," She said, giggling, petting me. "*But I'm not.*"

Gaspar stood tall and began to sing, his voice loud and rich and full, a reverend's singing voice. I realized the whole room—the animal carcasses, the writing on the floor, the symbols, all of it—was part of a spell prepared just for Roy, a putrid cage to bind him inside. I backed into the corner of the room, into the darkness. I listened to Her whisper to me, cooing softly, like a little girl does to a new pet.

The room grew hotter. The darkness thickened, it became an ocean surrounding us, a swirling, gasping creature. The bloody symbols on the wall began to glow. Something was coming, I heard the vast beating of a multitude of wings. The Wish House shook, the floors trembled, the walls throbbed, a living heartbeat. Demons circled the room in a murky spiral like vultures over a carcass—picking, preening things, the fetid fanged demons that spent decades wandering—summoned down to a feast of blood.

Roy screamed for someone to help him, for his dad to burst into the room alive, for his mom to come back from the dead. He screamed for me to rise up and save him.

Gaspar had his back to me. He was bent over Roy, holding the knife. Demons filled the room thick as smoke, shrieking in their ancient voices. I could hear them, I had Her ears now, I had Her mind. I heard their stories of torment and woe, the clacking of their chains, the groaning and pain they endured on their horrible trek through this earth. But most of all I felt their power, a ravening mob desperate to find a home in Roy, the first human friend I ever loved, the boy who broke my heart.

Gaspar flipped Roy onto his stomach. He would doom Roy now, spill a little blood and let the demons feast. They would fill him, a treasure chest of magic for the One Wish Man to plunder at his whim. The Paradise Society would gather round him, the parties would begin again, the lust of the flesh, the money and power, Gaspar's world restored. Roy would be chained in this room, his skin hacked to pieces, rippled with magic to keep him still, to keep the demons sated. Roy would spend the rest of his life here, unless he got lucky like Kevin and someone cut him loose, or else chewed through his own skin and got run over quick on the highway. That was Roy's fate, and it would be forever.

Gaspar took Roy's hand and raised the knife.

I saw in the corner of the room a girl. I recognized her from a photograph—thin and pretty, with long hair and a white billowing dress, black holes where her eyes once were. It was Cléa, and she smiled at me.

Roy screamed.

I could tell you this was the story of the fourth time She took control over my body, but that would be a lie. I did this. Me and Her did it together.

With all Her power I leapt onto Gaspar's back and dug my teeth into his throat. I thrashed and shook my head, wrenching the tissue from his neck, slicing the veins, ripping through his esophagus. Gaspar swung the knife at me but missed. I knocked the knife away and clamped on tighter to his throat. I wrapped my legs around Gaspar's waist and sunk my teeth deeper into his flesh. I tasted bone. I gnawed and ripped and tore, like a sick wild dog. I swallowed Gaspar's blood, and it didn't taste bad, it didn't turn sick in my stomach.

I didn't let go of Gaspar until he fell to the floor.

All around me I heard the shrieking of betrayed demons howling in the void. I heard the thousand-year agony of doomed spirits denied their feast of flesh. I heard the gears of the world groaning with all that pain and time.

Roy was crying. I took the knife and cut the scarves from his wrists and ankles. He stood up, gazing at me in horror. I could see myself reflected in his eyes, my torn and blood-splattered dress, the gore slathered on my teeth.

"Clarabella . . ." he said. "Clare?"

I dropped the knife on the floor.

"*Go*," I said.

Roy turned and fled. I watched him vanish into the darkness of the house, his terrified footfalls fading toward the front door. He would make it out. Roy would be free.

Gaspar's body twitched. He crawled himself toward the knife.

It didn't make any sense. How could he still be alive?

But She knew the answer to that. She told me that no one could kill Gaspar, or at least not the spirit that drove him. That Gaspar was from forever and he was a part of mankind, same as goodness was. I kicked the knife away, watching it clatter across the floor. I took the candle and set flames to the curtains, let them billow up in sickness and black smoke. I watched the animal hides catch, the poor slaughtered beastflesh. I watched the room blaze in a hot fury.

I walked through the doorway, into the darkness of the rest of the Wish House. I could see it now as it truly was. Critter bones scattered across the floor, the shredded curtains, the busted windows, the carpet gone fetid and rank. The ruined chandelier dangling above me like an eye plucked from its socket. The warped hardwood of the floor, the long red carpet like a mildewed tongue stretched down the hallway. The paintings cracked and broken on the walls, the portraits ghastly and torn. The knick-knacks replaced with rotten fingers, teeth, and bones. Rats skittered around my feet. Doors hung from their hinges, the furniture was cobwebbed and splintered, melted candles were frozen in puddles of wax red as blood. Flies buzzed in swarms around my face. I didn't dare use the front door, I didn't dare risk someone coming for me. I found a busted window and crawled out it. I realized my hand was cut. But it didn't hurt, it didn't matter. The fire had caught, it was spreading. I could smell the stink of the Wish House burning.

The night was clear now, the Milky Way slathered across the sky. I saw through Her eyes, my soul rose a great distance and I could see everything.

Roy's father, stumbling through the woods behind Miss Mathis, his eyes bright with fear and love for his son, mumbling a silent prayer that She let me hear, a prayer begging forgiveness from God and from Roy and even from me. Tears muddying the dirt on his face, the limbs scratching his forehead, drawing blood. I watched his eyes widen as the Wish House came into view, as he saw his son running through the darkness of the forest, away from the flames and into his arms.

Miss Mathis marching ahead of them, holding aloft the skin of Kevin Henrikson, singing in her scratchy strange voice the secret words inscribed on his flesh as they began to glow, lighting the pathway. She would finish what Cléa had started. She would destroy the magic surrounding the Wish House, let the fire I started consume it forever.

Farther She let me drift, higher and away.

I saw the Simpkins mansion, rich folks filing out in a rush, stumbling in high heels, rushing to cars parked out front, the gates wide open for once, while from upstairs came a horrible cackling laughter.

Mom wrapped up in a blanket on the couch, Larry off snoring in the bedroom. Mom crying, curling and uncurling her fists, a new toughness growing inside her, all that pain finally becoming something like power.

Uncle Mike asleep in his bed, his eyelids fluttering, his lips mumbling in the night. He was dreaming, and I could see his dream: Uncle Mike on a beach in Patmos, his wife and Cléa at his side, all of them smiling and happy, a family forever. I wished the best for Uncle Mike.

I saw other things too, nearby visions, I heard every drip of rainwater fall from each leaf, I saw the air bend the starlight as it fell to earth. I saw the creatures of the forest gather around me like saints, a crowd of witnesses assembled. It was the reckoning of a grave injustice, punishment meted out for centuries of pain. The wind carrying the news, the night birds like angels gazing down from on high. Above them the galaxies spiraled in the blackness, the teeming world hidden far and away, the silky light stretched across the vast universe, the burning heart of everything that gave our world its life.

The forest dirt cold beneath my bare feet, the moon just a half wink in the sky. I felt Her inside me, warm and good.

Don't be sad, Clare, She said. *Gaspar was an awful man, and he deserved what he got.*

"I know," I said.

We have money now. We have the old lady's car. We can leave. We can leave and go wherever we want.

I found a knocked-over tree and sat down on it. My jaw hurt from chewing, my stomach swirled. I plucked a hunk of Gaspar's throat out of my teeth, and I thought I'd be sick.

What's the matter? She said.

I felt the moon like a single squinted eye gazing down on me, wondering at what I was going to say.

"This was Your plan all along, right?" I said. "You wouldn't have let Gaspar take Roy, would you?"

Of course it was, silly. I'd never let anything happen to that boy. He helped you, didn't he? He helped us.

But the thing was, I knew She was lying. I knew it in my heart.

"Why are You lying to me?"

I'm not.

"You are too. You're lying like I don't even know You." I was getting mad now, my feelings hurt, all the months of pain writhing in my belly along with the blood and gore of Gaspar. "This isn't the first time either, is it? You've lied to me before."

It's my nature, She said. *I never lied to hurt you. Hasn't it always been for our good? Didn't I bring us back together, just like I said I would?*

"Will you please just tell me the truth?"

She was silent a moment. I could feel the forest pressing in, all the lost souls from outside the Wish House, those Gaspar had tortured and murdered, the spirits he held captive. All of them watched and listened.

Are you sure you want to know, Clare?

"Yes."

Okay, then. If you must know.

"Tell me."

Gaspar sent me back into the world when you were just a little girl. I was supposed to bring a child here to him. You were to be his next.

My hands shook, and I could feel the old panic coming on. That had been Her plan from the beginning. To take me to Gaspar, to have me locked in a room and tortured. That's what She chose me for.

"Were you Kevin Henrikson's demon?" I said. "Were you Nicolas?"

I have been called by many names.

She was Nicolas, not that nasty Wish House spirit. It was Her—it had always been Her. She lied to me from the very beginning. I began to cry. I was sobbing in big gasps, tears streaking the blood down my face.

Shhh, Clare, don't cry. You don't understand, not one bit. This is an old story, and a very long and sad one. I don't think you will want to hear it.

"Tell me everything," I said. "All of it."

That I can't do, silly. There are some things that are not for humans to understand, not even you, my Only. But this much I can tell you.

When Gaspar first summoned me, my job was to trick the children. I was to draw them close to me and then guide them to him. I was the lure, do you understand? Gaspar sent me into the world to find him a child, one who would come willingly, who would submit himself to be united with me. And then Gaspar would invite other demons inside, and they would bring him power. Do you know what this world is like for us, for my kind?

"No."

Shall I show you?

I nodded.

My eyes went foggy, the night dissolving into a haze, and I knew this was a vision. I saw before me the earth stretched out cruel and empty, all blackened ground and not a tree in sight, nothing but the dark shadows of vultures circling miles above. The light was unbearable. The demons straggling in the burning sunlight, dragging limp legs and slumped shoulders, faces eaten away by maggots, searching for even a drip of water to wet their tongues in. The horrible thirst, veins gone dry as dust, the gouging emptiness inside. It was Hell for Her, the earth was, an endless doom. The misery of knowing it was impossible to die, and that She would wander the earth like this forever.

Then I heard a whispering in the darkness, what began as a hiss and became the boom of thunder: Gaspar's voice summoning Her. I felt the burn of Gaspar's binding words, how they snatched Her like a hook in the flesh, seared lightning-hot, and dragged Her back to him, how powerful that bond was, a blood covenant stronger than family. How Gaspar sent Her to ensnare the first kid, how She crawled inside the child, the simple relief of a hiding place from that hideous sun. I felt Her like it, the adoration of the children, the weak and simple and easy, how She fed on the lonely and brought them to Gaspar. It wasn't just Kevin Henrikson, and it wasn't just in this town. No, there were others. Maybe the Wish House could be anywhere.

I was very good at it, and Gaspar would reward me. It was safe inside the children. I wouldn't have to roam the dark world thirsting and alone.

But even that respite became a burden, a pain. The slavery to Gaspar, to his wickedness. I felt what he made Her do, the guilt of it. Yes, She felt guilt, every creature does. She knew the horror of what She did, and it shivered Her down to Her core. There was a Bible verse about that, right? One Roy told me: "The demons also believe, and tremble." That's how it was for Her, that's how it became, that's how it would be forever.

Yes, that's what it was like. That's exactly it. I knew you would understand me, I knew you could feel what it was like. That's why I had to get away. When I was with the last boy—Kevin—a girl set us free, and we ran. I was blind with freedom, I wanted to escape, I would have run him so far from here, I would have kept him safe, I would have, Clare, it's true. But we were struck down. And I roamed for a time, I did, years I escaped, but Gaspar found me, same as he always did. Gaspar called me back, chained me again, sent me out to seek someone new for him.

"To find me."

To find someone, yes, She said. *But I found you.*

"Because I was lonely and strange and afraid, just like Kevin. You chose me because I was so easy to fool, because I would believe anything."

But you weren't easy, Clare. You were extraordinary. You were unlike anyone else in the world. Don't you understand? It was you. You were good, and you loved me. I didn't know what that was like, how that could feel. Don't you remember, silly? Don't you remember how happy we were?

"Yes, I remember."

I loved you, Clare, with all of my being. I never had a friend before, not a real one. I loved you, and I made a deal with Gaspar, to save you. I promised that I would bring him someone else.

"And you picked Roy?"

Yes, She said. *I picked Roy. But I did it for you, Clare. I did it so we could be together. You're my friend, silly, the only one I ever had. You are my Only.*

I thought of Roy, tied down, Gaspar bent over him with the knife. No, more than that. I thought of me, tied up in a chair, my back to Gaspar, vulnerable to all the world, with no one there to protect me but myself.

No one who loved me would put me in a position like that. No one who loved me would ever leave me in the hands of someone like Gaspar. I guess that meant I didn't love Roy either, since I did the exact same thing to him. Even if he wronged me, he didn't deserve that. No one deserved that.

Maybe I didn't know how to love someone. Not yet, anyhow. Maybe love's not something you're born knowing, it's something you have to learn. It's something I wanted to learn. I didn't want to keep hurting people like I had, to keep being hurt all the time. It was too much. Something had to change, something permanent. There was no other choice. Not if all this evil was going to end. Not if life would ever get to be better for any of us.

"No," I said. "I don't think I want to go with You."

But this is what we wanted. This is everything we ever dreamed of.

"It used to be what I wanted," I said. The words hurt me, they stumbled out dumb and useless and irrevocably true. "But I've changed. I'm a different person now. When You left I had to change."

You want to go back to the boy, don't you?

"No."

You weren't supposed to like him so much. I never thought you would, not like that.

"Listen to me," I said. "I don't want him either. I want to be alone. I want to figure out life by myself for once."

I could feel Her hurt, I could feel Her heart shattering inside mine. I didn't know if the tears on my face were Hers or my own.

"I want You to leave me now," I said. "I mean it."

Please, Clare. I'm your Only, you said so yourself. You did all this to be with me. We were going to be together forever.

"I need You to leave." I was crying, I could hardly speak the words. "I love You. I *do*. Even if You are a liar. You saved me, and I will never not love You."

Then let me stay.

"No," I said. "I'm my own now. I don't belong to You anymore. I don't belong to anyone but myself."

When She stepped out of my body it was like lightning ripping the sky in half. My eyes blinded and my ears screamed, it was like my bones splitting from inside the marrow. Nothing has ever hurt me so much, and I pray nothing ever will hurt like that again. It was the separation of something final, the death of a dream.

And She stood before me, hazy but real. She was a little girl with long black hair and a white dress down to Her ankles. Her face was blurry almost, like when something's moving too fast in a picture. But I could see Her eyes, and I knew it was Her.

She growled at me, her mouth twisted into a black hole with fangs jutting from her gums. She could rip me to shreds if She wanted. She could pick me up and bash me into a tree until my skull broke open. I could smell Her breath, a stink of burning, of sulfur and decay. Her fingers twisted into claws, Her fingernails sharp as razors.

I could slit you open, She said. *I could spell words with your guts.*

I was crying, I was crying so hard.

"But You won't," I said. "Because You love me, too. You love me, and You would never do anything like that to me. You would never hurt me."

She seemed to shrink then, to dissolve a little. The moonlight shone through Her clear now, as if She weren't more than smoke.

I only ever did what you wanted, She said. *Everything I did was just for you.*

"I know," I said. "I'm sorry."

Who will take care of me now? I'll be all alone.

"No, you won't."

Because behind Her stood someone else now. Cléa, eyeless and lovely, with a sad, smiling face. I knew Cléa had been with me, helping me from far off—she had been in the Wish House with me and Roy. A brave girl, and a powerful one, even in death.

"Will you help Her?" I said to Cléa.

Cléa nodded.

I don't want to go with her, She said. *I want to stay with you.*

"Cléa will take good care of You," I said. "Cléa will take You somewhere nice, won't you, Cléa?"

Cléa nodded.

"Come along, little one," said Cléa, her voice like someone humming a song. Cléa took Her hand and She didn't fight, She didn't scream or pout or holler. She held Cléa's hand and was brave. Oh, I would miss Her so much. I would miss Her so much I thought it would kill me. They began to walk away from me now, hand in hand.

"I love You," I said again, but She didn't look back at me. Together She and Cléa walked toward the woods and vanished into the black.

The smoke from the burning Wish House floated high above the trees, and in the far-off distance I heard the sound of sirens coming. I had done it. She was gone and She was never coming back. Blood dribbled from my fingers, dripping softly on the leaves. I had never felt more alone in my whole life.

I hadn't realized how bad my hand was cut. It had bled all over my dress, mixing with Gaspar's blood. There, too, on my leg—a deeper cut, one I wasn't even sure how I got. In the Wish House, I guess. When I—when we—leapt on Gaspar, during all that. Or maybe when I crawled out the window. But there it was, my leg gushing up blood, my hands torn. It was funny how quick and easy flesh tore, how you could wound yourself so deeply and not even know it. I felt sick, woozy, tired all of a sudden.

I lay down in the cool leaves and let the moonlight cover me like a blanket. I couldn't stop crying, the rain falling again, soft on me, the warmth of my own blood sticky on my arms, on my thighs. I curled up in the leaves and earth and shut my eyes—it felt good to shut my eyes, it felt good not to think, it felt good to lie there on the earth all alone.

I don't remember much after that.

Just little snippets of things, moments.

The sound of tires on a narrow road, brush and small branches snapping, voices hollering, "There she is."

Two sets of hands on me, lifting me up, sitting me down somewhere soft.

The soft murmured prayers of voices, a man's and a boy's, the wind through the open truck window cold on my bare skin, my blood caked thick and fat all over my legs and spilling down the car seat.

They came back for me, I thought. They didn't leave me to die.

The blood hot and sticky on my hands, the pain in my leg.

The moon and the stars. Black streaks of thunderclouds off in the distance.

I WOKE UP IN THE HOSPITAL. MOM WAS

there holding my hand. She looked like she hadn't slept at all, like she'd spent the whole night crying. The IV hurt, my head hurt, my legs hurt, and my whole body felt beaten and mangled.

"How you doing, sweetheart?" said Mom.

"Been better."

"I'm just glad you're alive."

I felt that way, a little bit. I was alive. But so empty too, vacant, like an unused wing of a house. It was hard to feel alone in your own body. It's hard to feel safe in your own bones.

I looked around for Roy and his dad, but they were gone.

"Where'd they go?" I said. "Roy and the reverend, I mean."

"They didn't stay, honey. The boy wanted to, but his dad wouldn't let him."

"Figures."

Mom put her hand on my head, brushed my hair aside. It's the kind of loving gesture moms are so good at, the kind that comes less and less the older you get.

"They aren't bad people, honey," she said. "They're just too severe sometimes. They try so hard to do the right thing they wind up hurting about as much as they help."

Maybe so. My head throbbed. I hate breathing that fake, clean stench of hospitals, how they just smell like chemicals, all the dirt and sickness scoured and burned away. The white color of everything, the beeping noises, the blank TV screens that exist for no other reason but to kill time. Hospitals scare me. They always have.

There was no one here, not a doctor or a nurse, just my mom. No one but my mom . . .

I shot up in the bed, afraid.

"Where's Larry?" I said. "Is he going to take me to the mental home? Are you going to lock me away?"

Any minute I expected Larry to come barging in the door, police officers at his side, for them to handcuff me for arson and straightjacket me and throw me where no one would ever come see me again.

I tried to climb out of the hospital bed and run, but Mom held me, she grabbed my face in her hands and stared at me, her eyes red-rimmed and sad, my own mother heartbroken.

"Larry's gone, sweetie," she said. "I told him he had to leave. I told him he had to leave and he could never come back."

I stared at her in wonder. Had she done it, really? Was this still my mom, always so small and terrified? Had she finally changed, become brave? Or had she just done what she had to do, to keep me?

"I'm sorry, Mom," I said.

"Me too," she said.

Mom began to cry, and I did too. In the hospital room, amid the antiseptic stink and beep and thrum of hospital machinery, Mom reached for me, and we held each other and we wept and we clung together. And we were not alone.

ACKNOWLEDGMENTS

Thanks to Mary Marge Locker, for reading this a million times. Your faith and love keep me going every day.

Mom, Dad, and Chris. Your love and support means everything.

The brilliant Jess Regel, my agent, my guide, my confidant. Thanks for sticking with me.

Maggie Lehrman, for her faith in this book and for editing it with so much love, compassion, and understanding.

Emily Daluga, for her patience, kindness, and skill.

Will Stephenson, my genius Terror Tuesday buddy.

Megan Abbott, the world's actual living greatest.

William Boyle, the brave and strong.

True hero Jack Pendarvis.

Liam Baranauskas, the realest heart on earth.

P.S. Dean, who I trust the most.

Len Clark, for the faith and friendship.

Suzanna Best, who loves scary movies as much as I do.

Tom Franklin, for giving me hell about the original short story, pushing me, and challenging me until I wrote it better (and then I still had to start over twice).

Thanks be to God, always.

To all my friends. I wouldn't be anything without y'all.

ABOUT THE AUTHOR

Jimmy Cajoleas grew up in Jackson, Mississippi. He earned his MFA from the University of Mississippi and now lives in New York.

Read on for a sneak peak at
Jimmy Cajoleas's latest novel,
Minor Prophets

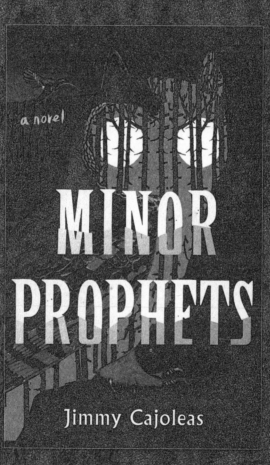

THE NIGHT MOM DIED I HAD A VISION.

I was half-drowsing in my bed, my headphones cranked, watching the ceiling fan swirl. It was probably four in the morning, and I couldn't sleep. I could never sleep. I'd read until two-thirty, when my eyes started burning, and I shut all the lights out, turned the music up, and prayed for a sleep miracle, but that miracle just wasn't coming. I was in the middle of that kind of gray state between waking and dreaming, and I got this strange feeling, like I was being watched, like I wasn't alone in the room anymore.

I looked toward my window.

A man's face was there, grizzled and wild-eyed, staring into my bedroom. It was like I was paralyzed, like I couldn't move at all, not even scream. Because I knew this man, and I knew he wasn't real, that he only came in my visions. I called him the Hobo, and when I saw him he was always watching me, his eyes bloodshot and raving, his beard ragged, his face pressed against the glass, like any moment he would smash his face through and come for me. He was a bad omen, a promise of horrible things to come.

I felt the terror grip my chest, the horrible tingling in my arms and legs and face that meant the rest of the vision was coming, that meant the world was about to split in half and reveal itself to me.

In a flash I saw it all.

Mom's car swerving through the night. The right front tire rattling weirdly, shaking itself free, rolling off towards the highway median. The car jerk and spark, yanking itself from the road, slamming into a tree. The car crumpling, now half a car, the hood smashed skyward, limbs gouging the windshield. The stillness after the collision. Smoke and the smell of burnt tires.

Mom's bare bloody arm, limp, dangling out the window.

I saw other things too.

A sunset glimmering over a lightning-split tree, two gray clouds that looked like eyes watchful in the distant sky.

A blank gravestone, lightning bugs floating around it glowing holy in the nighttime.

A cloud of hummingbirds red flitting wild over a field, a whirlwind of color and fire.

A woman who looked like Mom, but older, gray-haired with eyes that sparkled like the stars.

An owl, wings spread wide like a crucifix, perched on top of a barn.

Horace's Trans Am in the garage, Murphy sad in a black dress searching the trunk, as if inside hid some kind of secret.

When I came to, I was screaming.

I flicked my lamp on and the room was empty. No man was at my window, no hummingbirds anywhere.

I know what you're thinking. I'd just finally fallen asleep and had some kind of a nightmare. But I told you already. It wasn't a dream, not some random assemblage of the day's events thrown together haphazard in the back of my mind, not a weird brain film collage that means absolutely fucking zilch.

It was a vision.

A warning, a premonition.

I had to hurry. I scrambled out of my bedroom and onto the stairwell to find my stepdad Horace screaming at Mom in the foyer below.

I saw Mom look back at him, her eyes fierce and burning. She wore jeans and a plaid button-up and combat boots, and her long hair was wild and blonde and tangled, like she'd been fighting in her sleep.

"Just you goddamn wait a minute," he hollered.

I hated Horace. I hated Horace more than I'd ever hated anyone in my life.

"This ends now, Horace," said Mom. "I'm going, and don't you fucking try and stop me."

Mom left, slamming the door shut. I ran down the stairs and outside, but she was already in her car, swerving out of the driveway. I chased her down the street in the hot starlit summer night, waving at her, screaming, begging her not to leave, until her headlights disappeared around a corner.

My sister Murphy came walking outside, half-awake and worried.

"What's wrong?" she said.

I yanked her out of the way as Horace's Trans Am came roaring past us, cutting over the neighbor's lawn, laying black tire tread all over our street.

Please, I prayed, please let this one be a false vision. A lie, like so many of the others. Even though I knew it wasn't. I could feel in my bones that this one was real.

"They're just fighting, Lee," said Murphy. "It's okay. She'll come home in a few hours, same as usual. Right?"

But I couldn't answer her. Because I knew that wasn't true. I knew exactly what was going to happen.

I knew Mom was never coming back.

THINGS HAD BEEN WEIRD WITH MOM
the last few months. She just hadn't been herself.

Like the time two weeks before when I went downstairs for a midnight snack and found Mom peeking out the windows, snapping the blinds shut, like she was watching for someone, like someone was out there waiting on her. Before I could ask what she was doing, Horace swooped in and threw his arm around her, trying to coax her back into bed, them whisper-fighting the whole way.

Or the time when Mom opened our front door one afternoon and screamed. Murphy and I came running up behind her.

"What is it?" I said. Mom only pointed, her hand trembling, her eyes all bleary with tears.

It was a hummingbird, its throat ripped open, its guts splayed across our welcome mat.

"A stray cat probably did it, Mom," said Murphy. "It's just nature."

But Mom turned and ran to her bedroom, slamming the door

behind her. I knew hummingbirds were Mom's favorites, but this wasn't like her, not at all. I mean, Mom was the toughest woman I'd ever known. I'd seen her take a machete and chop the head off a cottonmouth that wandered up the gutters to our home with no second thoughts. She was never one to be mortified by gore.

Or the strangest of all, the morning when I woke up early and found Mom staring up at the living room wall, the furniture moved away and all the pictures taken down. A picture was painted on the prim white, a kind of mural, wild slashes of colors like blossoms blooming, all light and energy. It covered the whole wall, maybe six feet tall and four across–a painting of a tree, little flames hovering all around it like birds, a giant gash down the middle of it, like a cave you could crawl into. It wasn't exactly a realistic painting, but it felt real, if that makes any sense. It felt real in the way my visions feel real, how you could crawl into them and live forever. Realer than real, that's how mom would describe her dreams, and that's what this painting felt like too.

"Mom," I said. "Who did this?"

She seemed startled by me, and even more so by the mural sprung up on our living room wall. Mom looked at her fingers, her clothes, all speckled with paint

"Why," she said, "I suppose I did."

That tree loomed down at us. There was something so familiar and strange about it, like maybe it had fallen out of an old memory that I didn't remember having. I realized Mom was shaking.

"We have to cover it up," she said. "Quick, before Horace and Murphy wake up."

"But this is amazing, Mom," I said. "I didn't know you could paint."

"I can't paint," she said. "Not anymore. Now help me."

We took what was left of the white and covered over everything as best we could.

I told Murphy about it later and she could hardly believe me.

"That's insane," she said. "I've never seen her so much as doodle on a napkin before."

"I know," I said. "And Murphy, it was good. I mean really good."

"Why does all this worry me so much?" she said.

"I don't know," I said, "but it does me too."

See, none of this made any sense if you knew our mother.

Mom was a badass, a chain-smoker who had never attended school a day in her life but could fix a flat and clean a gun with equal precision. She was gruff, and rude, and a total genius. Mom had homeschooled us since we were kids. She taught us basic self-defense as toddlers, and she trained Murphy herself in Brazilian Jiu-jitsu until Murphy accidentally broke Mom's arm in the sixth grade while performing a particularly vicious reversal. I have never seen our mother prouder. She even had Murphy sign the cast first, in Murphy's shaky looping scrawl.

I guess maybe all the weirdness started when Mom married our stepdad, Horace, about a year back. Yeah, definitely marrying Horace was the first time I started to worry about her.

Because Horace was a hard man. Six-foot-seven, two hundred and fifty pounds of unsmiling cruelty. I would watch him smoke cigarettes while he did dumbbell lifts in his garage, his mostly-bald head shimmering except for one wet lock dangling down in front. We called it the "unicorn" when he wasn't around. That is because if we mocked his desperate hairstyle in front of him, he would have thrown us down the stairs. Not that Horace ever actually laid a hand on us. He never needed to.

For example. One night three months before, Murphy stayed out well into the night, doing God knows what with God knows who, and she did not return until three a.m., exactly six hours after her curfew.

Did Horace scream at her? No.

Did Horace whip her? No.

Did Horace ground her? No.

Did Horace take Murphy's 1967 Fender Telecaster and hurl it through her window, shattering glass onto the driveway, the second-story drop snapping the neck of the twelve-hundred-dollar vintage instrument into pieces?

Yes, that's exactly what Horace did. As our mother watched on, curiously silent.

As if in awe.

So marrying Horace was Mom's first out-of-character act. We never thought she would get married, never even considered it. At first–maybe for six months or so–she was happier than I'd ever seen her before. I mean, Mom positively giggled, walking around arm in arm with the asshole, and that was a welcomed sight. I don't know if you can understand this, but when you've seen your mom bounce from guy to guy your whole life, always disappointed, always somehow let down that yet another fellow couldn't measure up, it was a real joy to see her with someone she actually liked, someone she seemed to respect. And he was good to her, he really was, at first. They seemed happier than I ever thought Mom could be. We even sold our janky old bungalow and bought a newer, nicer (but way more boring) two-story borderline-McMansion, because that's what Horace wanted, and we all moved in together. But each day, as Mom became less and less recognizable as the strong, brilliant, estimable single mother who raised us, Murphy and I became more and more worried. Mom blew us off, saying she hadn't been feeling well and she had a headache and could we please leave her alone. We plead our case to Horace, who told us to–and I quote–"mind your own fucking goddamn business." If you can believe that.

"She's our mother," said Murphy once. "So it is our own fucking goddamn business."

At which point Horace merely pointed his finger at her and held it there, one inch from Murphy's face.

I waited for her to bite it. I hoped she would snap it clean off at the knuckle.

But such was Horace's power–the fierce, unblinking stare, and the menace of his outstretched pointer finger, the lit cigarette smoking (indoors, a thing which had been inconceivable in our house before)–that it cowed even Murphy. She shrank from him, trembling.

For the life of me, I could not understand what Mom saw in the guy. And I guessed now I'd never know.

THE DAY OF THE FUNERAL WAS GRAY, threatening rain, the sky all rumbles and groans. No one came to the service except a few kind-hearted busybodies and some old lady named Shondra that nobody knew. None of Murphy's cool friends showed, and I didn't have any friends anyway. I figured at least a few of Mom's exes would be there–Mom had more than enough to pack the place–but turns out jilted ex-boyfriends don't show up to funerals. Not even our grandmother came, our mother's own mother. It would have been nice to meet her for the first time. After all, this was the woman who had paid for everything in my and Murphy's and Mom's life–even down to our old house, the one we had before we moved in with Horace–through this bank trust she set up for us. I had always wondered about her, begging Mom to let us know her, to go and see her some time. But Mom would just go grim and refuse, same as always. I wondered if Grandma even knew that Mom had died.

Horace kept his distance from us. He hadn't said a word to us all day, not when we ate breakfast together (cold Cheerios in skim milk), not when he drove us to the funeral, not even at the visitation, standing next to our mother's mannequin-looking body in the casket. I mean, what they had done to her was shameful. She looked fake, like some kind of human Barbie doll, her face caked with the kind of makeup she wouldn't be caught dead in, a contented smile on her lips, the sort of placid look I never saw on Mom's face in her life. I couldn't look at her.

At the service nobody spoke except the preacher, and he didn't have a clue who Mom was. It was insulting, him droning on about being in a better place, about God forgiving, about all of us meeting again in the hereafter. What fucking hereafter? Mom didn't believe in God or the afterlife or anything except the moment, the right now of everything. And right now, Mom was dead—a corpse, emptied-out and embalmed, a husk. There was nothing left of my mom in that casket, or maybe anywhere else. The whole thing felt like a mockery.

I was so grateful for Murphy, that I didn't have to do all this alone. I sat there, bawling my eyes out, watching Murphy try not to cry, her back unnaturally straight in that black dress of hers, gripping the pews all white-knuckled, holding everything in. I wish I could get her to just let go a minute, but that's not the kind of thing Murphy did. I was the weepy one of the siblings, something Murphy managed to never give me any hell about. Murphy's good like that.

I couldn't figure out why Horace was acting so weird. I mean, he wasn't ever a warm person, but you could at least expect fury or anger from him, some bit of wild, frothing rage under the surface. But that day he just seemed preoccupied, like something else was on his mind. It was strange, you know?

At the gravesite, which was unbearable, by the way–a gray-grassed plot of nothing, little tombstones with their humped backs slouching around us, Mom's coffin up on this mechanical lowering device, a little blue tarp slung up to keep out the rain–Horace kept looking over his shoulder, scanning the trees for somebody, like he was afraid of being watched. I couldn't figure out what he was doing, or what he was looking for.

The time came for us to sprinkle soil on the casket. Horace was supposed to go first, but he didn't notice. It was like he wasn't paying attention at all. He just walked up to the casket, tossed some dirt on it, and stormed off, like he had something better to do.

We found him sitting in the Trans Am, honking at us. Our mother was dead and the asshole was honking at us. He rolled the window down and stuck his head out of the car.

"Move your asses," he said.

It was the first words he had spoken to us all day.

After the funeral, Murphy and I hung out in the garage, still in our nice black clothes, while Murphy smoked. I was shell-shocked and numb, all cried out. I kept trying to write a funeral poem for Mom, the way Auden wrote one for Yeats. "Mad Ireland hurt you into poetry," and all that, but nothing was coming, nothing seemed right. I couldn't stop thinking about my vision, Mom's car sliding wheel-less over the pavement at a hundred miles an hour. They'd told us she didn't feel anything, that she'd died instantly. I sure hoped so. And what an awful thing to hope, you know? It made no sense about life, that the best thing you could ask for was an instant, painless death. I mean, what did that say about the world, about living in it? How easily, how quickly an entire life–the whole universe of a person–could just vanish forever. What was to become of us, the ones left behind? Who was going to take care of us? Horace? Are you kidding me?

Murphy stomped out her cigarette, walked inside the house for a minute, and came back with a pair of keys.

"What are those for?" I said.

"It's time we check out this trunk situation," she said.

"What are you talking about?"

"Well, you saw a bunch of weird shit in your vision, right?" she said. "One of those things was me in this goddamn dress opening Horace's trunk. Since it's going to happen anyway, I figure we might as well get to it."

"You really want to do that?" I said. "I mean, it wasn't a happy vision. And besides, my visions don't always come true. You remember all the times I've been wrong."

Murphy was the only person I still told my visions to, the only person who ever listened and gave a shit. But Murphy knew as well as I did that for each one of these visions that came true–each one that happened more or less how I'd foreseen it–I'd have another that fell way off the mark, or else flat didn't make sense at all. That was just the way with visions, and it was tricky business to count on them.

Murphy smiled at me, a little sadly.

"Well, you've been right so far this time," she said. "I might as well check."

Murphy walked over to Horace's car. She stuck in the keys in the trunk and popped it.

"Please don't," I said. "It's not worth it. Horace will kill us."

"There's something in here," she said. "Look."

I peeked over her shoulder as Murphy rummaged around the lining of the trunk, moving around a bunch of clutter and a particularly heavy-looking tire iron, until she lifted the covering off of a secret compartment. Inside were a bunch of manila file folders and a Ziploc bag full of handwritten letters.

"I knew it," she said.

Murphy went for the folders and I snatched up the Ziploc bag. I pulled one out of the bag and read.

Please just let me see them, Jenny. Please bring them to me, just once. You know I can't bear to leave the Farm, I can't travel. I just want to see my grandchildren once, before it's too late.

Holy shit. These were from Grandma, and there must have been hundreds of them. Why didn't Mom ever tell us about them? More importantly, why were they in Horace's trunk? Was it because he was afraid we'd go snooping through Mom's things after the funeral and find them? Was he trying to keep us from contacting our grandmother for some reason? I mean, I understood that she and Mom didn't get along, but why Horace?

"Uhh, Lee?" said Murphy. "Look at this."

She held a stack of pages and I read over her shoulder. It was a bunch of legal documents, all signed and notarized. Murphy flipped through them. They seemed to be adoption papers.

Our adoption papers.

"What the hell is this?" I said.

They didn't have anything to do with Mom, or our birth. They were newer than that, dated not more than a month ago. Murphy flipped to two typed, identical statements, one for each of us, that read "I hereby consent to my formal, legal adoption by Horace Dunluth Powell the III," complete with our signatures. Forged, of course. There's no way in hell either one of us would ever consent to be adopted by that asshole.

"Oh my god," she said. "Horace adopted us."

"Why would he do that?" I said. "He hates us."

"The trust from our grandmother," she said.

The garage seemed silent then, eerie. I wondered about all the bugs and spiders hidden in the corner of this place, tucked away in boxes, lingering there, silent and listening, waiting for what we would do next. It felt like the moment before one of my visions came, when the world got soft and foggy, when I felt the electricity of the whole earth in my fingertips, when it was like all of reality would get torn open and the guts of the world would be revealed.

"In your vision, you said Mom's wheel fell off, right?" said Murphy. "Like it had been loosened or something?"

"Yes."

I looked back and forth between the tire iron and the adoption papers. We were both thinking it, but only Murphy was brave enough to ask.

"Does that mean Horace killed our mom?" said Murphy. "So he could have all the money to himself?"

That's when I realized Horace was standing right behind us.

"The fuck do you kids think you're doing?" he snarled.

Murphy whipped Horace's tire iron from the trunk and whacked him across the skull with it. There he lay, face-down on the floor, a red swelling dripping welt on the back of his bald head.

"What do we do now?" I said.

Murphy looked up at me, eyes all sad and scared and full of wonder. "Run, I guess."

I know what you're thinking. If you find a folder full of forged adoption documents in your shitty stepfather's trunk, not to mention the tire iron he probably used to sabotage your mom's car, why don't you go straight to the sheriff with it?

Well, I'll tell you: it's hard to report your stepfather to the county sheriff when the county sheriff is your stepfather.

We had no choice. We ran.

We took Horace's Trans Am, the only non-government-issue vehicle on the premises. We made it about thirty miles outside of town before Murphy finally spoke up.

"Shit," said Murphy. "I forgot my phone. I must have left it back in the garage. And goddammit, I got blood on me."

It was true. It looked thick and scabby on the black of her dress. I handed her a tissue out of my left pocket and she dabbed at it, but the stain was there for good.

"I hate this dress," she said, her eyes watering. "I hate funerals."

"Me too," I said.

I kept the car steady on the highway, trying not to cry, the sunset like a gaping wound up in the sky.

"Oh god," she said. "What did I do?"

"You were smart, that's what you did," I said. "You saved both of our hides."

"But what happens now? You have another vision or something? The cosmos telling us where to go next?"

"Maybe," I said. "You remember I saw Mom in my vision that night, but an older version of her? I think maybe that was Grandma. I think we're supposed to go and find her."

"Are you kidding me? She didn't even come to the funeral."

"But you saw all the letters she wrote, right? Grandma's been trying to talk to us forever. She has to take us in now. We need her."

We'd never been to Grandma's before, of course, but Mom sometimes talked about the house where she grew up, in Benign, Louisiana, this placed called "The Farm." None of the letters I saw had a return address on them, but I was pretty sure Grandma still lived there.

"I know it isn't the best plan," I said, "but do you have a better one?"

"Will Grandma even want to see us?" said Murphy.

"Judging from those letters, definitely," I said. "Besides, she set up that trust for us, didn't she? We're her family, Murphy, and that means something in this world. At least, it should. We'll hole up with her until we figure something out. And we need an adult to protect us from Horace, since for all legal purposes he's our father now."

"Fuck that," said Murphy.

"That's what I was thinking," I said.

"Aight," said Murphy. "To Grandmother's house we go."

The story continues in

MINOR PROPHETS